A STRANGER STILL

ANNA KAVAN

A
STRANGER
STILL

PETER OWEN
London & Chester Springs

PETER OWEN LIMITED
73 Kenway Road London SW5 0RE
Peter Owen books are distributed in the USA by
Dufour Editions Inc. Chester Springs PA 19425–0007

First published in Great Britain 1935
Published in this edition 1995
© The Estate of Anna Kavan 1935, 1995

ISBN 0–7206–0955–0

A catalogue record for this book is available
from the British Library

Printed and made in Great Britain
by Biddles of Guildford and King's Lynn

CONTENTS

PART I

		PAGE

PART II

CONTENTS

PART I

In a Quiet Street

THE superior suburb of Hornchurch contains
many roads of small, neat houses, each separated from the pavement by a small patch of
garden. And these front gardens contain lilac, may
and laburnum-trees which in the flowering season give
the roads the effect of popular dance halls festooned
with garlands of coloured paper.

The buses that go lurching and grinding along the
great main thoroughfares haughtily ignore these quiet
turnings. The people jolting uneasily on their seats do
not look, or else gaze out with apathetic and unseeing
eyes, lost in the harassing preoccupations of the day.
Vainly for them the little gardens are bright with flowers.
Vainly for them the lilac builds up its scented pyramids,
opens a thousand florets, and pours out, in unsought
generosity of offering, all the sweetness that is hidden
in its white or purple beauty. The passengers scramble
out at the stopping-places, encumbered with worries,
parcels, newspapers, umbrellas and attaché-cases, finding no solace in the peaceful, flower-bordered street,
hurrying home as though the light spring air held some
dangerous quality from which they were not safe until
they had shut their doors upon it and closed themselves
in with their familiar cares.

The crowds who morning and evening pack the trains to overflowing scarcely spare a glance from their papers for the too familiar vista which presents itself, slightly foreshortened, at the foot of the embankment. Vainly for them the gardens spread out their gay mosaic, splashed with the exotic yellow of laburnum, while the roads between run like still, tropical rivers, gleaming purplishly.

The travellers in the trains and trams and buses hurry heedlessly along, hurrying to earn, in the breathless city, the right to return at evening, preoccupied and weary-eyed, to the modest beauty of which they have never become aware.

Worcester Road was one of these quiet streets of sober little houses, detached or semi-detached, and Number Seven was as unpretentious as the rest. A small brick house, whose front windows were somewhat darkened by the shade of a mountain-ash growing at the garden gate. A gravel path in need of rolling, a bush of white lilac, a grass patch and three rose-trees sprawling against the house composed the rest of the garden which was divided from the road by a wooden fence about four feet high.

The garden gate creaked on its rusty hinges, and would not latch properly. Every time there was a strong wind it blew to and fro, emitting disconsolate sounds like some large bird in distress : and the neighbours, hearing these plaintive noises, would exclaim in an exasperated way, " Why can't those people next door get their gate put right ? " And soon somebody was sure to remark that they were queer people at

Number Seven and that their garden was disgracefully neglected.

And yet, neglected as it was, there was something about Number Seven which distinguished it as a habitation of beings of a slightly different social order, though it was difficult to say what contributed to this effect. Perhaps it was the colour and quality of the window curtains, perhaps the cars that often stood outside the shabby gate, perhaps nothing more tangible than an air of dissociation from the rest of the street, which originated in the untidy little garden.

2

Suburban Train No. 16

EXACTLY at midday, Germaine Lewison, born Germaine Deligny, a native of Switzerland, finished packing her trunk in the front bedroom of Number Seven, Worcester Road. As she moved about the room with her quick, firm step, her solid, well-shaped figure shown off by a dark green dress of excellent cut, her round, smooth, rather high-coloured face was remarkable for its expression of pleased excitement and expectancy. Into the tray of the trunk, which was half empty to allow for the three new frocks she intended to buy in Paris, she folded some sheets of fresh tissue-paper before she shut down the lid. Her strong fingers with their brightly tinted nails manipulated the lock without effort and placed the key in the inner compartment of her crocodile handbag. The label, clearly addressed in her flowing handwriting, was already attached to the

trunk ; and the trunk itself, a neat, business-like, expensive piece of luggage, was competently packed with
fashionable and becoming garments which she knew
would emerge uncreased at the end of their journey.
Beside the trunk was a hat-box, and on the top of the
hat-box was a dressing-case in a cover of dark green
cloth.

Germaine Lewison stood regarding this luggage with
complacency but also with a slight frown between her
narrow, plucked eyebrows. As luggage, it was credit-
able and quite satisfactory ; but it seemed rather a lot to
take for a week's visit to her father at Suresnes on the
outskirts of Paris. Especially as her father happened
to be the owner of a modest little café on the river bank.
Martin might think it strange if he should notice it.
But then she gave her shoulders a little twitch, her large,
capable hands made a slight outward movement, with
fingers extended, and on her face there appeared a fleet-
ing expression that was very typical of her : a contemptuous, irritable, dissatisfied look.

Why on earth should she worry about Martin ? She
had been deceiving her husband for so long that she no
longer felt any need for caution. It was only a habit of
prudence which led her still to consider him. Of course
Martin would not think it strange that she should take
so much luggage. Even if he were to see the three new
dresses specially chosen to suit Gerald's somewhat
eccentric taste he would not suspect anything. If she
had taken a dozen trunks for her week's visit he would
have thought it quite normal. Or, more probably, he
would not have thought about it at all. He accepted
everything she did so unquestioningly. It really seemed

almost humiliating that he should be so completely unsuspicious. Naturally, it was convenient, and flattering too in a way, but all the same Germaine found it irritating. Once more the contemptuous look came on her face, followed this time by a half-pitying smile. Really, deceiving Martin was too easy, like taking sweets from a child. It was almost indecent. But no one had the right to be so unsuspecting. And, moreover, it was insulting to her. Given neither to self-criticism nor to introspection she felt it both natural and justifiable to be aggrieved because her husband's trustful nature allowed her to visit her lover with impunity.

She moved, dismissing the subject, and her calculating eyes, set rather close together in her round face, glanced about to see that nothing that should have been packed had been forgotten.

The bedroom, cleared of most of her belongings, looked larger than usual. For the bedroom of a small suburban house it was an unexpectedly luxurious room. The deep blue carpet had a rich pile, the walnut furniture, a little too large for the room, was elegant and well-made, the window curtains were patterned with a clever modernistic design. An oblong of bright spring sunshine rested like a decoration on the Queen Anne bureau and on the two leather-framed photographs which stood there. Drawn by the brightness, Germaine's eyes rested for a moment with the casual detachment of familiarity on the photograph of herself. Taken two years before by a fashionable photographer, the picture still pleased her, though she had since changed her style of hairdressing to a more up-to-date and becoming mode. It was time she had a new photograph, she decided ; she would have one taken as a surprise present for Gerald. The thought of her lover brought a momentary softness to her face during the tiny period of time in which her eyes travelled on to the photograph of her husband. Martin had been photographed during the war in his uniform as a lieutenant in the artillery. Above the badges, his large, good-looking face stared out with a dominance it did not possess in reality, the weakness of the mouth disguised by the small military moustache.

Germaine glanced at her husband's photograph, and immediately, in a second, a complex series of reactions was set up in her somewhat limited brain. Instantaneously she was aware of resentment, irritation, pity, contempt and a vague retrospective sentimentality. Prudence also made its powerful appeal. Martin Lewison was perhaps an irritating man, perhaps an ineffectual man : in any case he was an easy-going, generous husband. She could not afford to run any risk of losing him. She knew perfectly well that in Martin she had got a good thing and a safe thing. She must not endanger her valuable possession through over-confidence. But there was nothing to worry about. It would take a revelation from heaven to open Martin's eyes to what was going on.

Sharply and arrogantly she turned away from the pleasant pictured face of Martin, her husband.

Her own face reflected in the large mirror next claimed her attention. She would be cautious, but she could not disguise a rush of joyful anticipation that made her bright cheeks still brighter. At last, at last she was going to escape from all this tedious suburban existence, the boredom, the perpetual irritation, for a week of love and

6

excitement. If Martin could have seen her then with her flushed face softened almost to girlishness by her excitement, he might have wondered.

Germaine powdered carefully, and in this order: her forehead, her cheeks, her nose and her chin, drew a moistened forefinger along the narrow black arch of her eyebrows and put on her hat and coat. In her hat she at once looked older, harder, more sophisticated and less intelligent, handsomer and less attractive; in fact, more her true self. The putting on of the hat defined her personality more sharply. She was one of those women who are never seen bareheaded in public and with whom the removal of the hat seems to constitute an act of intimacy.

Downstairs, the maid told her that Martin Lewison had not returned from his studio. The frown lines appeared again under the short black veil which now covered Germaine's forehead. When had he left the house? At ten o'clock as usual. Had he said anything about coming back early? No. Had he left any message at all? No. The girl answered these questions in a quiet, respectful voice but with a closed, sulky face which showed that she hated her mistress. Germaine too looked at the servant with covert dislike. The expressions of the two women were oddly similar.

As soon as Germaine knew that her husband was not in the house, that apparently he had no intention of returning to say good-bye to her, a cloud came over her pleasurable excitement. It was really too bad the way he had neglected her lately. Why, she scarcely set eyes on him for days together. Out of the house in the

7

morning before she was dressed, he was hardly ever back till dinner-time, and then as likely as not he would wander out again after dinner to spend the rest of the evening in his studio. Not that she wanted him to be always hanging round her. It suited her much better to have him safely out of the way. But there were certain standards of decent behaviour which must be maintained ; appearances to be kept up. Germaine felt that she had been slighted, and her face, which still became in anger the face of a little Swiss bourgeoise, was sullen as she watched the taxi-driver staggering across the front garden with her trunk on his shoulder.

But then, as she herself crossed the garden, her mood changed again. In the few steps between the door of the house and the wooden garden gate her mind threw off its cares and became buoyant and gay. Her high heels crunched on the gravel path, then clicked with a clean-cut sound over the pavement to the waiting car. She got in and sat down feeling as if she had escaped from prison. The maid put her dressing-case beside her on the seat, said good-bye and closed the door of the taxi. The car started forward with a jerk. Out of the tail of her eye Germaine caught a glimpse of the mountain-ash stirring tremulous leaves in the light breeze. Then it was gone, the house was gone—she was off.

A tremendous sense of relief came over her as she left Worcester Road behind her. " Hateful place, hateful road, hateful houses ! " she said to herself with intense feeling. The taxi bowled merrily along streets of front gardens and peaceful little villas, turned into a busier street of shops and drew up to the station.

8

Germaine strolled on the platform with easy elegance in the sunshine, waiting for her train. She felt young and full of self-confidence. The mean, grimy station with its vulgar advertisements, its hideous roof and its long, empty, dismal platforms had no power to depress her. When the train came she stepped into the carriage without looking back and sat without looking out of the window. There were very few passengers at that time of day, and in a minute or two the train moved quietly and unobtrusively out of the station. The solitary porter lounging on the platform with his hands behind him stared idly after the receding guard's van on which were written in dingy letters the words: Suburban Train No. 16. For a few moments the tail end of the train was visible as a rapidly diminishing cube which seemed to contract upon itself in the hazy distance. When there was nothing to be seen but the polished rails shining vacantly in the sun, the porter began to walk off in the opposite direction, whistling through his teeth as he went.

3

Martin and a Jig-Saw Puzzle

At three o'clock that afternoon in another part of Hornchurch, Martin Lewison was preparing to leave his studio. The large still-life upon which he had been working was fixed to the easel whose long wooden arm reached almost to the skylight above. There was not a great deal of room in the studio, and as he passed behind the easel with a handful of dirty brushes, his

9

thigh grazed the edge of the table on which the group
of fruit was arranged in a beautiful old china dish.   One
of the apples rolled a little out of place, and he stooped
over the table while his thick, sensitive, rather ugly
fingers carefully re-balanced the apple on the chalk
smudge which marked its correct position.

The little room was uncomfortably warm, for the
May sunshine had been beating down all day long on its
flimsy roof, and Martin would not open a window because to do so would alter the light.   He had taken off
his jacket, and wore a dull red woollen pullover which,
fitting tightly over his chest and broad shoulders, made
him appear more massive than usual.   His torso was a
trifle too heavy for the lower part of his body.   If the
line between knee and pelvis had been an inch longer he
would have been a finely proportioned man.   As it was,
his legs in their good grey flannel trousers looked just a
little too short.

He took down his tweed jacket from a hook behind
the door.   While his arms fumbled their way into the
sleeves his face was turned with a concentrated expression
towards the canvas on the easel.   Yet he was not, as he
usually was, absorbed in his work.   It was only his
superficial attention that was fixed on the canvas, and
that only as it were from the force of habit.   All day
long some extraneous worry had kept burrowing into
his consciousness and distracting his attention so that
he could not enter into that state of calm, oblivious,
almost mindless absorption in which he generally
worked.

He sighed, and the three deep horizontal lines on his
forehead contracted till three whitened ridges of flesh

appeared there. It was no good trying to work to-day : he might just as well go home.

Martin Lewison opened the door of his studio and stepped out into the open air. Pausing to lock the door after him, he glanced at the building with a sort of humorous toleration. It was one of those standard portable buildings which are bought in sections and put together on the site where they are to stand. This one had been set up on a narrow strip of land between the railway embankment and the playing-field of some commercial firm. The smoke from countless engines had blackened it, alternate rain and heat had tortured the cheap roofing material into unsightly corrugations, the once green paint was a dirty grey, blistered all over by the sun, and the whole erection, owing to the continual vibration of passing trains, had subsided several inches at one end so that it had a permanently lopsided appearance.

Everyone laughed at Martin and teased him about his shabby studio. Why didn't he have a decent studio in town—he could easily afford it—instead of hiding away in this wretched suburb ? But really there were perfectly good reasons for his conduct. His wife hated the country and wanted to live in town, whereas he loathed London—the reek and noise of the city really made him feel ill. Hornchurch seemed to him a reasonable compromise. And then, the little house in Worcester Road was part of some property belonging to his father : he had no rent to pay while he lived there. Oh yes, it was all perfectly sensible and sound. Sometimes he had played with the idea of moving into a better studio. It would certainly be pleasant to have a more roomy place where the lighting was better and where it would be easy to get a model occasionally. But then it was also convenient to have one's studio within walking distance of one's home. That walk at the beginning and end of the day had become important to him as the time when his thoughts flowed most freely, when he schemed most easily for his future work. In time he had even come to feel a kind of laughing affection for the dilapidated little shack by the railway. It represented freedom to him and his escape from the world. It was the one place where he was inviolable, absolutely secure from outside interference. No one ever came there except by his invitation. His wife had never set foot in the place.

He was walking now along an asphalted footpath fenced with wire on both sides. To the left rose the steep grassy slope of the railway embankment, spangled with coarse yellow dandelions; on the right was a huge board advertising the bicycles manufactured by the firm owning the playing-field.

Hatless, in his well-cut clothes which needed brushing and pressing, Martin walked quickly along the path. After the stuffy warmth of the studio the light, sunshiny air felt fresh and exhilarating. A freight train rumbled heavily above, filling the atmosphere with smoke, vibration and noise. Accustomed to the endless passing of trains, Martin's brain did no more than register automatic awareness of the clattering wagons.

He began to think how he had once tried to explain to his friend Gerald Gill the motives which led him to live in Hornchurch. Gill had been full of one of his own wild theories at the time and had barely listened. Martin had shut up pretty quickly. It seemed to him that his friends never listened to what he was saying. They heard his opening sentences, jumped to some entirely erroneous conclusion, and afterwards put words which he had never uttered into his mouth. How annoying this might be if one let it become so, he thought. People on the whole were incredibly obtuse and self-centred.

He had come now to the end of the open ground and was walking away from the railway up a street of semi-detached houses. Fifteen minutes of walking through similar garden-bordered streets still separated him from Worcester Road. He walked fast, with that slightly stooping gait which sensitive children sometimes assume and never succeed in losing in after life. It was as if he wished to pass through the streets as inconspicuously as possible, while at the same time he drew attention to himself by going without a hat.

To-day, in spite of the pleasant spring afternoon, he was not enjoying the walk as much as usual. He turned into St. Peter's Road with its avenue of young plane-trees, stepping through the delicate, lace-like shadow-mesh of the new leaves. A group of laughing children ran by. From habit he noticed the decorative grouping of their unconscious poses, the patterning of their bright coloured clothes. He looked about him with his usual appreciative artist's attention, to-day rather mechanical. Only women and children were in the streets at this hour, the wage-earners had not yet returned from their toil. The women glanced at him, most with approval, some perhaps with envy. He was a good-looking man, was Martin Lewison. He looked well-off, too ; one of the lucky ones. No office desk for him. Certainly he was more fortunate than most. Working towards success in the profession to which he was devoted with a profound interest; relieved by his wealthy father of all financial responsibility; above the average in health and intelligence, younger looking than his thirty-five years, kind-hearted, amusing, an amiable fellow, with a knack of quickly getting on good terms with people.

The gardens of Worcester Road were looking their best that afternoon; the crimson and pink may-trees particularly thick with bloom, the laburnum trails dazzlingly yellow, the lilac at its sweetest, the tall soldierly rows of tulips scarlet and glossy. Yet he took no pleasure in his walk. He came to the wooden gate of Number Seven and looked up at the front of the little house, lightly screened from him by the boughs of the mountain-ash. His observant greenish eyes travelled from the house to the bush of white lilac, whose fragile, delicious perfume failed to give him the accustomed pleasure. He paused with his hand on the gate in an attitude of peculiar unwillingness, and his usually cheerful face looked uneasy and grave.

Well, now he would have to confront the worry that had been pestering him ever since he got out of bed that morning. No longer could it be pushed away, out of sight, in the convenient recesses of his subconsciousness. It was very much to the fore now, threatening to occupy the whole stage of his conscious mind. It absolutely refused to be put off for another minute.

It was, of course, this business about Germaine that was worrying him. Perhaps it would have been better if he had followed his original impulse and shut himself off from the whole matter—simply declined to know anything about it. But of late it had become impossible for him to ignore the hints of his friends, his sister Gwenda's spiteful insinuations, the more or less tactfully phrased warnings of his brother Cedric and the much more outspoken comments of his father. Besides, Germaine herself had become almost unbearable in her attitude towards him during the last few months. She was for ever complaining: about his absences, his behaviour, his painting, his friends; about the house, about the neighbourhood; about the boredom of her existence; about anything and everything. She was beginning to get on his nerves with that perpetual and senseless complaining. Her rather high, rather harsh voice with its pronounced foreign accent followed him relentlessly from room to room, penetrating the insubstantial walls of the house, and when he went out to escape from it, he knew it would break over him again, like a wave, in the first moment of his return. She blamed him for leaving her so much alone, yet when they were together she did nothing but gird at him, alternately jeering and complaining. It almost seemed as if she were goading him into taking some action against her; or trying to see how far she could go.

Nevertheless, he would have let things go on as they were had not outside influence, and particularly the influence of his father, been brought to bear on him. He did not want Germaine as his wife, but still less did he want the trouble, the unpleasantness and general dislocation of his existence attendant on getting rid of her. His whole nature was profoundly opposed to any form of strife. He was a peaceable man, even, perhaps, in some ways a cowardly man; and the thought of the emotional and domestic upheaval which probably lay just ahead of him filled him with a sense of angry, rather petulant disgust. Why was he being forced to take this disagreeable action against his wife? Far better go on with the present circumstances, abominable as they were. What people failed to realise was his capacity for insulating himself, by means of absorption in his work, from the unsatisfactory state of things at home. Anything would have been better than the interruption of his work which now threatened.

He opened the gate, and for the first time the squeal of the hinges set his teeth on edge. The crunch of his footsteps on the gravel sounded heavy and despondent. He opened the door with his latch-key, went inside, and slowly and reluctantly closed it behind him. He was in for the distasteful business now.

He entered the small drawing-room, which was agreeably furnished in the modern style. This was a room for which he himself had designed the colour scheme and which always received him with a friendly impression; it was generally rather comforting. But now Martin looked about him with unusually hostile criticism. His observant eyes became colder as they noted the small details of deterioration and neglect. There was a nasty little tear in the zebra-striped upholstery of the low armchair, the black and cream hearthrug had been singed in several places by flying sparks, and a forgotten cigarette end had burned the edge of a table upon which a glass had also left a circular stain: an unwatered azalea near the window drooped its petals in the melancholy resignation of martyrdom. It was quite true, as his sister had said, that Germaine was neglecting the house

16

atrociously. Cedric's wife, Jean, had said the same
thing. He had shut his eyes to it, but now he had to
admit that everything was starting to look shabby and
uncared-for after only eighteen months' wear. Strange
that a woman as fastidious as Germaine was about her
personal appearance should be so careless of her surroundings. She had been proud enough of the furniture when it was new. Only lately she seemed to have
lost interest completely in everything that concerned
her home.

He rang the bell for the two maids and sent them both
out for the rest of the afternoon. The girls looked more
startled than pleased, he observed with remote amusement.

As soon as he was alone in the house Martin went
upstairs. There was no longer any sun in the front
bedroom from which the traces of Germaine's packing
had not yet been removed. A sheet of tissue-paper lay
on the floor, there was the forlorn, disorientated effect
of a room suddenly forsaken by its usual occupant.

It was absolutely silent in the bedroom. Martin
Lewison, standing motionless, stared as if for the first
time at the bed in which his wife had slept, studied the
shot-silk bedspread and noted its colour, meticulously,
as though he were required to give evidence about it.
His thoughts flew to the last time he had got into that
bed. It seemed a long time ago. Incredible that Germaine had once roused him to a state of violent erotic
excitement. Undeniably she was physically attractive
with her fine, strong limbs and her round, smooth, rosy
face, like a ripe nectarine. But long ago her exacting
sensuality had become wearisome to him. Perhaps it

was just that insatiable quality of her passion that had
made him turn cold and witholding. He had felt only
relief when she had ceased her demands upon him.
At this moment he simply could not understand how
he had come to marry that unintelligent, ill-tempered,
complaining woman.

He moved his head uneasily and looked with dislike at the photographs of Germaine and himself which
stood on the bureau. The two pictures seemed to be
shaming him with their silent testimony to the incomprehensible foolishness of his past behaviour. After a
few seconds he crossed the room, folded up the leather
frames and put the photographs away in a drawer.

He began to roam up and down, opening a drawer
occasionally or peering into a cupboard, as though pro-
secuting a half-hearted search. Presently he glanced into
the wastepaper-basket. In the bottom of the basket
was a layer of paper scraps, torn up fine and covered
with handwriting. He took out some of these shreds
and began to examine them. The shapes of the letters
were eccentric and unmistakable, written in very black
ink with a broad nib in a hand that was well-known to
him. He recognized the idiosyncrasies of the writing
at once, and his face lost its customary veil of amiability.

Had he found his clue already? Really, this was
too easy. The scraps of paper might have been left
there on purpose for him. And that familiar handwriting? The lines on his forehead deepened till the
three ridges of flesh appeared there. He was not particularly squeamish, but the idea of spying on the correspondence between his wife and one of his best friends
was simply revolting. His forehead creased itself more

18

and more deeply, his breathing became loud and troubled in the quiet room, so that anyone watching might have thought that he contemplated some guilty action.   Finally he picked up the wastepaper-basket and walked slowly downstairs with it.

In the gay, peaceful drawing-room at the back of the house, Martin sat fitting together the scraps of the letter. The torn fragments of paper surrounded him like the parts of an intricate jig-saw puzzle which he picked up delicately, one after another, and tried to fit into place. His face, now calm and phlegmatic, his eyes, his whole body seemed absorbed in the sensitive, tentative movements of his coarse, clever fingers which he watched with rapt attention.   The sense of the disagreeable nature of the proceeding was swallowed up in a naïve interest in the task before him.   For a long time he worked on, like a schoolboy busy with some piece of ingenious apparatus which he has constructed.   The chromium-plated hands of the clock built into the white pine panelling over the fireplace steadily travelled round their circle.

4

A Father and his Sons

WILLIAM LEWISON, a widower, grandson of the Jew, Joseph Lewisohn, chairman of the Cray River Development Trust (Canada), managing director and owner of a well-known group of stores, a slight, elegant man, rather bald, and very young for his age, which was sixty-three, liked to think that he resembled a certain film actor of the period named Adolphe Menjou.   This

Menjou, a thin, elegant, not-very-young man with a carefully tended moustache, invariably played the part of a sophisticated man of the world, a not-so-young Don Juan, who, often in adverse circumstances, displayed a quiet wit and an imperturbability which made the other characters appear clumsy and crude. He was at the same time whimsical and debonair, dignified and distinguished. William Lewison liked to think that he also moved about the world with a graceful, accomplished distinction, conducting his life with humour, dignity, cleverness and style. Rich and successful, this skilful business man considered himself the possessor of a subtle intelligence, a foresight and a psychological intuition rendering him infallible in all his undertakings. As a lady's man he had, up to ten years before, also considered himself infallible, and even now he claimed a large measure of success with women. His business ability was beyond question ; he had secured by his own efforts a considerable fortune ; intellectually he felt himself impregnable, and capable, by means of his adroit quickness in grasping and manipulating the psychology of his opponents and by his verbal fluency, of getting the best of any bargain in which he took a hand. There was every reason why he should feel justified in comparing himself with his favourite film star.

With his almost theatrical feeling for effect, William Lewison had planned for himself a background of solid, quiet, comfortable good taste. His house at Starling Hill radiated an atmosphere of reliable stability and unostentatious opulence that was most reassuring to the silk-hatted gentlemen whom from time to time he invited there in the course of business. Nine miles

out of town, Starling Hill was within easy reach of
his office, his Greater London stores, his son at Hornchurch and his elder son who was managing the large
Hendon branch of the firm. It also happened to be in
a singularly unspoilt district, and the big garden on the
top of the hill overlooked a sweep of fields and trees
which in summer, when the heavily massed foliage of
the elms blocked out the encroaching houses, had quite
a rural appearance. This too was part of his carefully
studied effect. A touch of the country gentleman
inspired confidence in people, and at week-ends William
was often to be seen working among the rare, micro-
scopic alpine plants in his rock garden, or setting out
with the full paraphernalia of rods, flies, and landing-
nets for the fishing he rented in a trout stream at Latimer.
His daughter kept house for him.

The library, with its predominant air of old-fashioned
taste and comfort, its shelves of handsomely bound
books, its massive yet elegant fireplace, its low, sub-
stantial arm-chairs with brown velvet cushions, was an
excellent setting for William Lewison. A large, colour-
ful painting of his daughter by the artist Meninsky
counteracted with its bold modern treatment the note
of old-world formality which might otherwise have
been over-insistent. The titles of the books indicated
the enlightened broadmindedness, the advanced opinions,
the wide intellectual interests of their owner.

There were two people in the library this evening.
A tall man, standing at the window, had his back to the
room. He was smoking a cigarette, and something
about his attitude seemed to suggest that he was not
quite at ease.

The master of the house sat in an arm-chair, his legs lightly crossed. A wide dark blue cravat with an inconspicuous silver design was fastened in a large, loose bow that concealed most of his shirt and gave a slight picturesque relief to his formal dark clothes. His thin, white, effeminate fingers twisted the stem of a half-empty glass on a table beside him. Resting against the back of the chair, his bald head ended behind the ears in a fringe of grey curly hair, worn rather long. This gave a touch of interest and charm, and prevented the skull of William Lewison from ever assuming the outline of commonplace baldness. And then, a final distinction, balancing the delicately curved nose and the careful moustache, a pair of finely shaped, nearly black eyes, whose abstruse gaze was masked by the shade of vigorous, greying eyebrows.

It was the lurking scrutiny of these impenetrable eyes that generated a sense of uneasiness in the figure at the window.

The latter, turning to extinguish his cigarette, revealed the somewhat harassed face of a well-looking man in the later thirties, and continuing a conversation which had lapsed remarked:

" Father, I really think you should have a little more confidence in me."

The nervous, repressed irritability of the voice in which these words were spoken was matched by the expression of the dark eyes, so like those of the father, yet lacking the old man's characteristic assurance, which now emitted a glance charged with indignation and reproach.

From the chair, in a pleasant, conversational tone, came the reply.

22

"My dear Cedric, I have perfect confidence in your ability to carry out my instructions."

In reality, William was paying little attention to the talk. His thoughts were concentrated upon his other son whom he expected and with whom he wished to speak privately. Yet his last words fell like so many calculated insults on the ears of Cedric who stepped forward with barely suppressed indignation.

"You must allow me a certain amount of authority," he exclaimed. "I must be allowed to act as I think best, at least in minor decisions. It's impossible to submit every detail to you. A dozen points may come up in the course of the day. Do you want me to spend the whole of my time driving backwards and forwards to consult you?"

"You could telephone, I suppose," the amiable voice returned.

Cedric's indignant, fascinated stare rested upon the old man. He placed himself directly in his father's line of vision and seemed to be trying to force from him a more serious consideration. But just as he opened his mouth to speak there was a movement in the arm-chair, the smooth, placable voice started again.

"And now, if you really won't have another cocktail, I think you'd better be off," William was saying. "I've got some papers here to look through before dinner, and time's getting on, you know."

The pleasing, soft voice was quite friendly and casual; but Cedric recognized the definite dismissal as well as the note of half malicious, half playful mockery. His father had risen ceremoniously to his feet, ironic politeness in every line of his pose. The son stood still in

his resentful posture. But now William took him by
the arm, cordial and urbane. Reluctantly, not having
achieved the object he had come for, Cedric was drawn
to the door.

"Are you sure you and Jean won't join us at the
restaurant to-night ? " he was being asked.

Declining abruptly, he took leave of his father,
dumbly and morosely accepted his hat from the butler,
and went out of the house. Yes, he might have known
it by this time ; he would never get any liberty of
action, any scope for his own business ability, as long
as the old man was at the head of affairs. He felt
humiliated and embittered, but all the same he could not
prevent a reluctant admiration for his father from creep-
ing into his thoughts. The old chap really had a fine
head on his shoulders, no doubt about that. But it was
no joke to work under him.

William sat down again in the library. He did not
attempt to look at the papers he had brought from his
office, but instead sat thinking about his two sons ;
Cedric whom he liked, understood and despised slightly,
Martin whom he did not understand at all, frequently
disliked, sometimes loved and always rather admired.
He also thought of his daughter Gwenda who meant
more to him that either of the others. But it was
Martin who was uppermost in his mind.

The room was full of a faint, agreeable odour com-
pounded of the smoke of good tobacco and the leather
of expensively bound books. Through the open window came the more ethereal scents of the spring evening,
blended equivocally of purity and sensuousness.

William sat thoughtfully in his arm-chair, only one

small part of his brain remaining detached from his thoughts, attentive and expectant. Before long there were muffled sounds in the house. Flood, the butler, walked past the library on his way to the hall. The front door opened and closed. There was a distant murmur of voices ; a certain voice. This was the sound for which the small alert portion of William's mind had been waiting. Uncrossing his legs, he moved in his chair to face the door of the library more squarely.

The door opened. His son Martin appeared, smiling and easy, but with something slightly strained in his expression. His easiness did not seem quite natural, the smile was a trifle forced. William saw at once that something important had happened. " He's found out something about that wife of his," flashed through his mind. It had come. It was the moment he had worked for for so long. The candid words of advice, the sub-terranean suggestions artfully implanted here and there, all the long crafty campaign which for the last year he had waged, deviously and openly, with ceaseless cunning and immovable patience against Germaine was approaching a victorious end. He suddenly felt his heart give a violent, undisciplined beat behind his imperturbable breast. At the same time he noticed with annoyance the crumpled flannel trousers Martin was wearing, the smear of green paint on the sleeve of his well-cut jacket. " He might at least have changed into a dark suit," thought the old man. But it was Germaine he blamed for his son's untidiness. " She lets him go about look-ing as if he'd been to bed in his clothes."

" Sit down for a minute," he was saying. " You're rather late, but there's just time for a drink before we

25

start." He glanced at his narrow gold wrist-watch and added : " We ought to leave here in ten minutes at the latest. I don't want Gwenda to be waiting about for us."

Flood took away Cedric's glass and brought a cocktail for Martin. The young man lighted a cigarette and sat down, crossing his legs. With the cigarette in his mouth and his glass in his hand he looked quite a man of the world. Nevertheless there was a naïve distress and perplexity in his eyes, rather pathetic, that was not concealed from his father.

" I won't dine with you to-night, if you'll excuse me," he said. " I don't feel like it. Besides, I'm not dressed for dinner in town." He gave a rapid glance, not at all apologetic, at his grey trousered legs, before going on. " As a matter of fact I was busy. I didn't have time to change." He stopped speaking abruptly. It was as if he had suddenly dried up, or did not know how to go on.

William Lewison waited a moment, while his son sat there, a heavily built young man in expensive, uncared-for clothes, with a free-and-easy expression and eyes that revealed a childlike bewilderment.

" Has Germaine left for Paris ? " asked William, giving him a lead.

" Yes." Martin seemed again about to fall into an abyss of silence : then, forcing himself to continue, he began speaking quickly and indistinctly. " After she had gone I took your advice and had a look round the house. I found some scraps of paper—a letter—and put them together. I made a rough copy. Here it is."

He took a folded sheet of paper out of his pocket. His father leaned forward to take it from him, then switched on a light.   The May dusk was already thickening in the quiet room.   The reading lamp, softly luminous, flung a circle of yellow light over the bald skull with its distinctive fringe of curls.   The old man dominated his son by the vigorous poise of his head.

" Is it incriminating ? "

" It is . . . fairly conclusive," replied Martin's unwilling voice ; his eyes remained fixed on the paper. He seemed to be on the point of snatching it away, when William put on his glasses and began to read.

" If only he doesn't read it aloud," thought the son despairingly.   But in a sort of panic he heard his father's pleasant, impartial voice starting to read out the sentences he himself had pieced together so laboriously, without at first having realised their meaning.

From the paper in his hand William found himself reading a letter from a man to a woman, describing in particularly vivid and profane language the pleasure which he had experienced in her embraces, the empty dreariness of his life without her, the rapture with which he looked forward to their approaching reunion.   All this was described with a wealth of physiological and erotic detail, a completely unrestrained licentiousness that was as remarkable as it was shameless.   William's black eyes followed the written phrases, his lips moved precisely as he enunciated the unaccustomed words in a perfectly cool and expressionless voice, but a hardly perceptible flush crept once or twice over his impassive features.   In spite of the broad-mindedness on which he prided himself, he could not help feeling that here was something shocking and indecent, a depth of corruption to which his generation could never have sunk.

Neither could he help feeling a thrill at what he was reading, and from time to time a faint, self-conscious smirk appeared on his face.

It was this smirking expression that was particularly intolerable to Martin, and stirred in him so much disgust that he found difficulty in composing his face to its usual protective indifference. A feeling of the deepest shame overcame him, though whether he felt ashamed on his own or his father's account or on account of Germaine and her lover, he could not have explained. He sat there, sunk in shame as in a morass of black mud, wishing dumbly for the reading to come to an end.

The old man's voice, however, flowed on remorselessly to the very last word of the letter.

At last there was silence in the library. Considerably more than ten minutes had passed since Martin's arrival. William sat motionless under the lamp, the letter still in his hand, his glasses, attached to their black ribbon, still surmounting the confident curve of his nose which now seemed slightly diminished. For once in his life the astute man felt at a loss. This was the moment of his triumph. He had often thought of the things he would say on this occasion—clever, penetrating things, some of them caustic and witty, some of them consoling and full of a father's heartfelt masculine sympathy—but the infernal letter had put them all out of his head. His aplomb had deserted him. In the face of so much modern depravity, he felt for the first time elderly, impotent and out-of-touch. Had the situation concerned outsiders he would have known how to deal with it, he thought helplessly. But because his son was involved, together with the woman Germaine, he could

28

not think of anything to say. He looked, almost appealingly, at Martin, who sat speechless, uncompromising and withdrawn. The old man felt the hostility which emanated from his son without understanding the cause. It was, therefore, with relief and a novel sense of flight from an unmanageable situation that William suddenly looked at his watch and stood up, saying:

"But we really must go at once. We can discuss all this in the car on the way up to town. I'm afraid Gwenda will be waiting as it is. I must tell Flood to ring up and leave a message to say that we will be a few minutes late."

There was a suggestion of artificiality about the effect of stir and bustle with which he managed to accompany the words. He was, in fact, acting the part of a gentleman suddenly finding himself in a hurry, in order to cover his temporary embarrassment.

"You'll come along, won't you?" he said to Martin, returning the letter to him with a certain reluctance. He would have liked to keep even this copy of the evidence against Germaine safe in his own possession.

The younger man had also got to his feet and was moving towards the door. Now he paused, took the letter, folded it carefully and pocketed it, saying at the same time in his casual voice:

"No thanks, father. I'm not in the right mood or the right clothes for dining out."

William Lewison was accustomed to reading faces, and he knew very well that Martin's indifference was only a protective shell. The father glanced at his son's trousers, jacket and tie. The tie was a Swiss affair made of different brightly coloured wools plaited together.

29

It was characteristic that Martin, who always seemed to wish to avoid attention, should wear these flamboyant ties. The father noted this while he was deciding on the best method of persuading his son to dine with him. When he finally spoke, it was in what he called to himself his " simple, heartfelt manner."

" It doesn't matter a bit how you're dressed : we're only going to Ruggieri's. Do come, Mart; just to please me."

For an instant his hand rested on Martin's arm, his black eyes looked into his son's face, soft and imploring. Martin felt a spasm of contemptuous affection. He knew perfectly well what his father was doing, he saw through the old man's methods perfectly clearly. Yet for some reason he was a little moved.

" All right, then. I'll come," he said, with a special smile, slow and rather secretive, that only appeared on his face occasionally. He wondered as he spoke why he was giving in. Was it simply to please the old man, or did he really want to avoid an evening alone ? Not that it mattered at all, either way.

William was delighted. He was not in a position to know that this was no victory for his winning guile. On the contrary, charmed by the apparent success of his own charm, his heart expanded in real warmth towards Martin. It was one of the moments when he loved his younger son. Through a mist of emotion he saw this large, handsome man, this complex individual for whom in some inscrutable way he was responsible, smiling at him amicably, and, as it seemed, intimately, and his heart bounded with satisfaction. Now at last he was beginning to achieve his object, to win back his son from

that detestable woman. But all he said, as he went out
of the room, was :

" While I'm fetching my hat, do get Flood to give
you a brush down, there's a good fellow."

5

A Chauffeur and his Passengers

THE chauffeur, George West, drove the powerful dark
blue Sunbeam as though it were an extension of his own
personality. He knew, as intimately as he knew his
own body, the little idiosyncrasies of the engine, the
individual peculiarities of the car as regards noise, speed,
consumption of petrol and oil, hill climbing, braking,
skidding, acceleration and behaviour in traffic. The
faintest of new noises immediately caught his attention,
and his sharp ears could distinguish at once between
engine sounds and the more innocuous body rattles.
He could even hear an infinitesimal clicking if a nail
became embedded in one of the tyres. He had been
driving ever since the age of twelve, when, as a ragged,
damp-nosed boy, he had stolen surreptitious joy-rides
on dark war-time nights in the cars from his uncle's
garage.

So now George West drove without thinking of what
he was doing, as if the big Sunbeam were an outlying
portion of his own frame, responding mechanically to
the control of his will. Even in appearance he was not
unlike a part of the car, for his lean young body was completely encased in dark, severe, hard-looking substances ;
shiny, metal-like leather leggings, neat, austere, navy

blue uniform, and dull black leather gloves. Only
between the hard, highly polished peak of his cap and
the high militaristic collar of his uniform was the flesh
of George West visible to the exterior world. And his
face too was lean, brown and hard-looking as if it were
made of leather.

Yet the mind of George West was troubled as he
drove efficiently along at a steady speed on the wide
arterial road between London and Starling Hill. It was
perhaps a pity that his driving was too automatic to
distract him from his worries, but this did not occur to
him, for he could not remember a time when he had not
driven automatically. His chief worry was concerned
with Winny his wife, who was nearly certain that she
was pregnant again. The Wests had been married four
years and already they had three children. George's
wages as chauffeur to Mr. Lewison were generous and
on the highest scale of such wages. But a wife and
three children are very expensive. His mouth took a
bitter and sardonic twist when he thought of his adoles-
cent dreams of saving enough money to start a garage
of his own. All his money went on living expenses,
there was nothing left over for the savings bank, or for
a bit of fun either. Why, it was all they could do to
manage cheap seats at the pictures occasionally, or a
common little hat for Winny, or a toy for one of the
kids. George tried desperately to push Winny out of
his mind, for the thought of her nowadays was apt to
bring on a queer sort of boring pain just over the corner
of his right eyebrow. She had been such a fresh, smart
girl when he married her, with her bright brown, permanently waved hair kept as neat as a pin, and her pert

snatches of laughter. It was that cocky laugh of hers that had got him in the first place, impudent and devil-may-care, throwing out a challenge to fate. The cheek of it ! The pathetic, sublime cheekiness of that scrap of a girl ! He scarcely ever heard the laugh now : Winny was getting tired and sick-looking and a bit down-at-heel. She didn't complain. She had plenty of pluck, had Winny. She was proud, too, and would stick to her bargain and keep a brave front as well. But her gay defiance was hardening into bitterness, something was being killed in her by this everlasting toiling and moiling over the kids. Of course, they were jolly little blighters in a way, but they weren't to be compared with Winny—Winny as she had been in the early days of their marriage, running out into the road to kiss him in front of everybody when he came home, walking up the street arm-in-arm with him, giving a skip every now and then out of sheer high spirits, and laughing that cocky laugh of hers. No, damn the kids : they had killed that Winny ; the kids and he himself, between them.

It seemed to George West in his depression that he had done Winny nothing but harm by loving her. He loved her and wanted to protect her from every evil, and all he did was to bring this toil and sickness and misery down upon her. It was not as if he hadn't tried to prevent it, either. But because they were warm-blooded young people who really loved one another, things always seemed to go wrong. George knew, naturally, that there were safe, reliable methods, methods that people like his employers used. But he had no idea what these methods were, and with his boyish sensitive-

ness, his fierce proletarian modesty, he had never tried
to find out. He had a vague general idea that such
things cost a lot of money. Anyhow, it was too late
now if Winny was really pregnant. The only thing left
now was an abortion; and abortion was a tricky business, against the law, possibly dangerous, and certainly
very expensive. He did not even know if Winny would
agree to it. And if she did, how was he to find out who
would do the job? Where was he to get the money to
pay for an abortion? Frowning under his peaked cap,
George West accelerated up a long incline, passed a
covey of light cars, and steadied the Sunbeam down into
its effortless cruising speed of fifty-two miles per hour.

The bodies of the two men in the back of the car
swayed gently in unison, swung one way or another at
curves in accordance with the laws of centrifugal force,
righted themselves and settled into a peaceful rocking
as the Sunbeam recovered its touring stride. At fifty
miles an hour the car developed a slight rolling
motion that was not disagreeable but rather pleasantly
soothing.

Sitting directly behind George West, Martin studied
the chauffeur's back view with half-abstracted attention.
That expressionless head and shoulders might have stood
as a symbol of impersonal efficiency. But Martin, because he was in the habit of looking at people and things
with discernment, had noticed the blue eyes which
looked out with appealing directness under the anonymous, visor-like peak of the chauffeur's cap. " He
looks a decent sort of chap," Martin reflected. " I
wonder what he's thinking about all the time." And
the vague, only partially formulated thought passed

34

through his mind that some time or other he must try and have a talk with his father's chauffeur.

The chauffeur, George West, was, curiously enough, at that very moment thinking about Martin who always had a smile and a joking word for him when he held open the door of the car, instead of brushing past him as if he were invisible, as the others did. " He's the best of the bunch," George was thinking. " He doesn't seem hardly like one of them." By *one of them* George West meant one of the employer class. He was no communist, but for him the world was divided rigidly into two classes : his own class, which comprised all the workers, the men of whom one made friends or enemies, with whom one played cards, watched football matches and occasionally got tight, as well as the women whom one loved, quarrelled with, married and got with child ; and the employers, the beings who gave orders, whom one simply did not regard as human at all and with whom any description of intimacy or communication was quite unthinkable.

But Martin Lewison almost seemed to come into George's own division. George did not feel separated from Martin by that unbridgeable gulf of orders given and orders carried out. Martin's face smiling at him in passing, smiled as a fellow-man, not with the conventional brevity with which *they* sometimes smiled as he held open the door. It almost seemed to George that Martin was human and approachable. His gloved hands gripped the wheel tighter in the excitement of a new and bold idea. Suppose he should ask Martin for advice about Winny ? Martin would be certain to know about abortions and about those other mysterious methods that made abortions unnecessary. He would not refuse his advice ; he would speak to George frankly, as man to man. That pleasantly human smile of his could not be a lie. It only remained to await a suitable opportunity for a talk. George made up his mind to try and catch Martin's eye as often as possible, thus quickly establishing a connexion between them. Then they would talk in some quiet place—perhaps even over a pint of beer —and all his troubles would be over. These, briefly, were the naïve workings of the mind of George West as he drove into Maida Vale. The traffic thickened here, and the Sunbeam's progress dropped to a series of spurts and delays. Approaching Marble Arch, George noticed that the boring pain over his right eye had quite disappeared.

For the first five minutes of the drive William Lewison waited impatiently for his son to continue the conversation. The old man had quite recovered from the temporary embarrassment which the unprecedented nature of the letter had caused him. He admitted to himself that he had been thrown off his balance by the first shock, but now he saw that the letter was really a godsend. It gave the case at once and unquestionably into their hands. Of course, such obscenities could not be read out in open court : but imagine the flutter they would produce in the dovecot of a respectable English jury ! If he knew anything about jurymen, that letter was good for £1,000 damages at least. A flicker of satisfaction crossed his face as he thought how conclusively he would at last rid himself and his family of Germaine. Now he wanted to discuss the matter, to hear more details and to scheme out a plan of campaign. But it was Martin's place to start the discussion. Why didn't the boy say something?

Out of those keen black eyes of his William glanced at his son who sat slouching in the corner of the seat, his arms folded nonchalantly, his eyes fixed, apparently absent-mindedly, on the back view of the chauffeur's head and shoulders. He looked as though he had forgotten all about the letter which was now reposing in his breast-pocket. But he could not really have forgotten. It was simply incredible that he should have forgotten. That indifferent, abstracted face was only a mask. Theoretically, William admired the perfect disguise, but practically he found it very annoying.

Finally he asked without any preliminaries:

" Was it Gill who wrote the letter to Germaine ? "

" Yes," said Martin, in a stiff, uninterested tone.

The father glanced at him again. He was shrewd enough to see that the treachery of his friend Gill was troubling Martin far more than his wife's infidelity. William felt sorry for the boy. It was a hard knock for him. He was devoted to Gerald Gill, the one human being he appeared to admire, and now it came as a severe shock to him to see what everyone else had seen months ago. Well, he couldn't expect to go through life without taking a few knocks on the way. He must just face up to the business and see it through. Most likely it would do him good. There was something a little soft and incapable in Martin's character of which William disapproved. This affair might well be the making of him.

" You had better make an appointment with Quested first thing to-morrow morning," he said.

" Why ? " At the mention of the solicitor, Martin's attitude changed so suddenly that William was surprised. At last he had really caught his son's attention. He saw the three ridges appear on the young man's forehead like signals of distress or disapproval.

" To show him the letter, naturally. We want to get the case going as soon as possible. There's no sense in delaying things."

" But I'm not sure that I want a divorce," Martin said slowly.

The father stared at him. Quite definitely now he felt a stab of dislike. He crossed one leg over the other and drummed the fingers of one hand on his knee where the cloth was pulled taut. He coughed, drummed his fingers, and stared antagonistically at his son.

" You must divorce Germaine," he said at last, in a quiet voice of controlled impatience, as if stating a self-evident truth to someone foolishly obstinate.

Sitting there, drumming his fingers, he began to frown. His eyes under the greying brows became introspective. He was not really troubled by this ridiculous attitude his son was displaying. Rather he was wondering whether Martin knew of his own association with the woman Germaine, the woman Martin had married. He thought of Germaine Deligny as she had been when he first met her on a business expedition to Paris. She had been quite young then, with a particularly fine skin, and a fresh, responsive, rather pouting face. It had always been a mystery to him why she, an insignificant little work-girl, had failed to surrender to his sophisticated charm. Intrigued and more than a little provoked by

38

her inaccessibility, his interest in her had lasted some time. Then, tiring of the pursuit, but still friendly and interested, he had established her in a little hat shop of her own where she had managed to do very well. She certainly had business ability. Gratified to see his investment turning out a success, William continued on friendly terms with her, visited her when he was in France, and on one occasion, he could not remember why, introduced Martin to her. Then, the year after the war ended, to this day he did not know how it had happened, he suddenly heard that Martin had married her in Paris. Helpless and angry, he had been obliged to accept as a daughter-in-law this woman who had rejected his own advances. Neither he nor Germaine ever spoke of their old relationship. He had no idea whether Martin knew of it. Should he mention it now as an added reason why there should be a divorce? But supposing his son really did *not* know, what effect would the information have on him? Did he know? Did he not know? The words fitted themselves to the rhythm of the smoothly-running car. That mask-like amiability of Martin's gave no hint of information.

While he was still occupied with these thoughts the Sunbeam pulled up at Ruggieri's. At the same time Martin was saying in a voice full of resentment and not without a trace of peevishness:

"I don't want all the fuss and bother of a divorce. It doesn't matter to me who Germaine gets into bed with. I simply want to go on with my painting in peace."

They were already crossing the pavement as his father replied softly:

39

" You will never have any real peace till you've got back your freedom."

The son did not answer; but William felt he had scored a point as they went into the restaurant.

Gwenda Lewison had waited a long time for her father and brother. Her small, mobile, provocative face with its pronounced features was tense with impatience. Nevertheless, the sight of their faces immediately conveyed to her the sense of something interesting and unusual which caused her impatience to be overcome by curiosity. Talking on indifferent subjects, they sat down at the table. When Martin looked away, Gwenda raised her eyebrows at William.

" Martin has made an unpleasant discovery." The smooth voice was at its smoothest as it added the words : " You had better tell your sister what has happened, Mart."

The father saw his son's face twist into a hard, disgusted grimace as he got up from the table. All at once, Martin felt he could not sit there through the evening with his father and sister who would discuss the affair of the letter and gloat over it. He did not want to discuss it. He did not want to think about it. Suddenly, for no reason at all, he remembered that he had not looked at the chauffeur, George West, as he got out of the car, but had walked past him as he stood holding open the door as if he did not exist, and this increased his sense of disgust. He was disgusted with himself and with the whole world.

" I'm not fit for polite society to-night. You must excuse me. I'll go along to the Café Royal for a bit," he said, speaking quickly and turning away.

His sister's face became almost comical with surprise and curiosity, but William's urbane expression did not change by a single line.

" The gentleman is not coming back. You can clear away his place," he said calmly to the astonished waiter.

6

Night Life

THE reputation of Ruggieri's restaurant at the corner of Leicester Square was founded entirely upon its cooking, which was the best in London. The restaurant was quite small, plainly and almost frugally arranged, with simple decorations and the tables set a good distance apart. It was not in the least fashionable in the sense that the Berkeley, Claridge's and the Ritz are fashionable. But a good many people who frequented those places were also occasionally to be seen at Ruggieri's. People who were interested in food, people who considered themselves connoisseurs of cookery, members of the aristocracy as well as of the intelligentsia, went to Ruggieri's restaurant from time to time. The people in evening dress generally slightly outnumbered those who were not in evening dress. It was expensive. The head-waiter, Luigi, was a quiet, serious, knowledgeable man who entered into long, muttered confabulations with his clients. There was, of course, no orchestra.

The ex-Indian judge, Sir Edward Wilbur, was something of a gourmet. He was fond of saying that the pleasure derived from good food was the only sensual enjoyment which did not diminish with advancing years.

Sitting there at his special table, savouring the carefully chosen dishes and their appropriate wines, hale, well-preserved and well-dressed, his florid face set off by his whitish hair and moustache, smiling in placid good humour at the charming young woman who sat facing him, Sir Edward might have posed for the portrait of a typical *bon viveur*.   Only two things lay at that moment between the ex-judge and complete contentment : his eternal grievance against the rules of the Indian Civil Service which had compelled him to retire while he was still, he maintained, in the prime of life, and his uncertainty as to whether Anna Kavan would consent to become his mistress.

Neither of these worries was sufficiently acute to disturb his enjoyment of the dinner which he had thought out beforehand and planned with particular care.   He was in a specially good humour because the head-waiter, Luigi, whose opinion he esteemed very highly and with whom he had consulted about a certain vintage Chambertin, had confirmed his choice and congratulated him upon the discriminating good taste with which he had chosen.   Sir Edward ate moderately and critically of the cunningly prepared dishes, drank moderately and critically of the wines which the waiters changed with each course.   He was thoroughly enjoying the evening, and without unduly exerting himself did his best to entertain his guest with leisurely conversation.   In his slow, cultivated, serious voice he was relating an anecdote of his life in India.   He had a curiously circumstantial way of talking, his reminiscences were made remarkable by a wealth of detail.   The story he was telling was interesting to him : he did not doubt that

it was of equal interest to his companion. She smiled
at him when he looked across at her; she made adequate
remarks whenever the story demanded comment. She
seemed intent and amused.

As he drew towards the end of the anecdote, a little of
Sir Edward's attention detached itself from what he was
saying and engaged in speculation about Anna Kavan.
There she sat with her elbows resting on the table and
her chin resting on her hands, gazing dreamily into his
face. She looked absurdly young, almost childish, in
spite of the fact that this was her twenty-fifth birthday
they were celebrating. Didn't she look a little too
young for an old fellow like him? Everyone would
think she was his daughter: perhaps even his grand-
daughter. One of those stupid jokes about May and
December came into his mind, but he dismissed it at
once. After all, he was young looking himself for his
age. Anna would make him a charming mistress. She
was just what he wanted. He needed contact with
somebody really young to keep him fresh and elastic.
At his age there was a great danger of becoming set
and sinking into a rut. He thought scornfully of
certain acquaintances, contemporaries of his, who were
little better than doddering. Well, thank God, he had
managed to keep himself fairly spry so far, and with
Anna's youthful influence . . . But then, for the
hundredth time, the teasing question arose: would
Anna become his mistress or would she not?

It was a week now since he had put the question to
her direct, though he had been hinting at it for a long
while before. Anna had asked for a few days in which
to think things over; there was that obscure husband

of hers out East to consider. Since then she had never
referred to the subject again. Sir Edward was not an
impatient man, he was not in a hurry, he did not want
to pester her for her decision; but he felt that it was
now time for her to make up her mind one way or the
other. He determined to get a definite answer in the
course of the evening: would it be yes or no?

He glanced across the table again under drooping
eyelids. Anna's face looked soft, childlike and dreamy;
only her eyes were a trifle disconcerting, a trifle contra-
dictory. There was something about her eyes that was
out of keeping with the rest of her face. Sometimes
they were almost olive colour, sometimes they were blue,
and sometimes they were a peculiarly limpid, cold grey.
It was when they were grey that they became most disconcerting. They were apt then to assume a remoteness,
a look of detached, impersonal observation that was disturbing and might easily become insulting. They did
not then seem any longer to belong to the face of a
very young and charming woman, but rather to a
mind grown ruthless in penetration and criticism of
masculine foolishness. Sir Edward expressed a general
realisation of all this by telling himself that her eyes
sometimes became unaccountably hard. He thought
of the different occasions on which he had made tentative advances, and of the docile, apparently amenable,
but unresponsive way in which those advances had
been received. A doubt stealthily assailed him: was
Anna naturally frigid? There was an oddly persistent
virginal quality about her, the obscure husband notwithstanding.

Acquiring an indefinably adverse bias, his thoughts

meandered after the regrettable husband. It would be extremely awkward if he were to turn up at any time and start making trouble. He was well out of the way at the moment, but one could never be sure when these undesirable characters were going to appear on the scene. Sir Edward's doubts became sharper; he had no intention of being involved in a scandal. Perhaps it would really be better if Anna said " no."

But now she was smiling at him delightfully, saying something, and calling him Teddy, the name he had asked her to use when they were alone together. He loved to hear her pronouncing the childish name; she had a way of bringing out the word with an engaging emphasis on the first syllable that enchanted the serious old man and dissolved all his doubts. She was beautiful to-night in the dress he had given her as a birthday present. How well that ice-blue colour suited her fair skin. Everyone had turned to look at her as she came into the restaurant. The heart of the ex-judge swelled with tenderness, desire and prospective proprietary pride. He now hoped most sincerely that Anna's final decision would be " yes."

Anna Kavan was growing more and more bored. Everything was intended to give her pleasure; but everything about the evening was boring. The lengthy dinner with its gastronomical finesses, Sir Edward's over-detailed anecdotes, his red face with the sagging eyelids, his slow, solemn voice, his laborious pleasantries. She forced herself to conceal her boredom, to smile and to behave politely. She even called him Teddy several times, though she could never bring herself to speak the ridiculous name without feeling embarrassed. After

all, he was a nice old thing, he had given her an expensive
dress with which she was very pleased, he was doing
his best to amuse her. She owed it to him to make the
birthday dinner a success. Nevertheless, her attention
kept wandering away. Her eyes circled the room a
little despairingly. What a dull place Ruggieri's was.

Suddenly, just when nearly everyone seemed ready to
leave, three new people entered the restaurant: a girl
in red, with a sharp, inquisitive face and dark eyes
flitting anxiously about the room; a complacent, distinguished looking elderly man, immaculately dressed;
and a heavily built young man whose crumpled clothes
looked somewhat out of keeping with the elegance of
his companions. Anna watched them sit down at the
next table. In the general boredom of the evening she
was glad of even this trivial distraction. The waiter,
Luigi, who had not expected any more clients that evening, now re-assumed his gravely attentive professional
manner and came to consult with the new-comers.
" Just like a successful bedside manner," she thought,
watching him bend over his customers solicitously
with tactful, low-voiced suggestions. The distinguished
old gentleman gave the orders, Luigi hurried off, and
the party fell into quiet conversation. Anna looked
away: apparently there was no more interest to be
gleaned at that table. But all at once the massive young
man got to his feet. Without waiting for even the
first course to be served, he said something, turned
round and walked across to the door. Anna watched
him crossing the restaurant; his wide shoulders stooped
as if in dejection, his clothes looked tight on his powerful
body, his rather long hair stood out grotesquely at the

46

back where his coat collar had disarranged it. She noticed the worried, gloomy expression on his good-looking face, the three deep lines on his forehead. Then he was gone. The old gentleman at the next table spoke to the waiter and then went on talking to the girl in red as if nothing had happened.

Sir Edward Wilbur, though not particularly sensitive to atmosphere, became aware that Anna's attention was wandering. He at once began to apologise for sitting so long over the meal. Young people could not be expected to take much interest in food : they were active and restless and preferred dancing to lingering over a glass of Napoleon 1811. He called the waiter, paid the bill and followed Anna with his short, brisk old man's steps as she made for the door.

In the taxi he put his arm round her at once. She expected this and made no movement. The taxi rattled noisily and fairly rapidly through the emptying streets, the cool air that came in at the window was refreshing after the food-scented closeness of Ruggieri's. Sir Edward sat silent, wondering if this were an auspicious moment to ask for her decision. Yearningly he looked at her out of heavily lidded eyes. Presently he slipped his hand under her cloak and began to caress her arm. He could feel her breast under the slippery, cool stuff of the dress he had given her. His breath came more quickly, he began to feel a little dizzy. Anna sat still, without resistance, but perfectly passive, inert. " Why do I put up with this ? " she thought. " Why do I allow this old man to make love to me ? " She had a sensation of unreality, her thoughts seemed to be ebbing away from her. She felt dreamy, bored, dissociated. The

taxi pulled up with a jerk and roused her. Sir Edward
had not asked his question.

They went into the Carolina Club. The big room
with its mirrors and star-spangled ceiling was brilliantly
lighted but almost empty. At midnight, when the
cabaret show began, the room would be packed with
people, but that was still a good hour ahead. There
was something almost uncanny about the empty, glittering room, flooded with stark white light. The few
people sprinkled about looked exposed and unhappy,
like goldfish swimming in a too brightly lighted bowl.
Sir Edward and Anna sat down at a corner table.
Whichever way she looked Anna could see, reflected
again and again in the sparkling mirrors, an old red-
faced man with drooping eyelids, whose shirt-front was
bulging a little out of his black coat and who leaned
amorously towards a girl in an ice-blue satin frock, who
sat beside him smiling with a strange absence of animation, as if she were not quite real.

With a startling effect of noise and abruptness the
orchestra suddenly burst into a popular tune. As
though in sheer devilment, the musicians seemed determined to fill the empty room with as much volume and
variety of sound as they were capable of producing.
The instruments blared, moaned, whined and thundered; imitated the howling of wolves, the laughter of
demons and the squealing of innumerable pigs. To this
grotesque symphony Sir Edward and Anna got up to
dance. The judge always danced twice in the course of
the evening, and he liked to have his first dance early,
before the floor became crowded. Carefully he placed
his arm round his partner and steered her into the middle

of the room, counting time with the music under his breath, and remembering the instructions he had received from the expensive Bond Street dancing school which he attended every Thursday afternoon. His feet in their neat, old-fashioned patent leather pumps moved cautiously and correctly through the steps which they had been taught. He set down each foot carefully and with forethought, breathing in through the nose easily but deeply as he had been instructed to do, and concentrating upon the rhythm. He did not speak while he was dancing.

Meanwhile the orchestra was working itself into a perfect frenzy of noise. The saxophones ululated into a crescendo of fiendish mirth, the violins wailed excruciatingly, a huge negro, running amok among his instruments, battered drums, clashed cymbals, blew whistles and rang bells in a frantic orgy of dissonance, finally breaking out in a ludicrous falsetto voice : " Who's afraid of the big, bad wolf—the big, bad wolf—the big, bad wolf ? Who's afraid of the big, bad wolf ? Ha, ha, ha, ha, ha ! "

In the midst of this infernal racket six couples gyrated painstakingly and without merriment. More than ever the dancers now resembled goldfish circling uneasily in an over-illuminated tank. Anna Kavan, automatically and unobtrusively directing her partner's steps, hummed the tune to herself, and watched in the huge mirrors Sir Edward placing his feet with an old man's precision and care, always a fraction behind the beat of the music. Why was she dancing with him, with him of all people ? She would rather have been with almost anyone else. She felt utterly bored with Sir Edward. Her boredom was so acute that she yawned over his shoulder into the brilliant room. Clear as a vision she saw the rest of the evening before her. When the dance was over there would be champagne of which she would drink one glass. She would sit with the ex-judge, alone at the corner table, and listen to more anecdotes. Perhaps they would talk a little about the events of the day, and his heavy, serious voice would enunciate heavy, serious opinions from a serious Conservative newspaper. When Anna spoke he would listen politely, and agree with a vague, mechanical conciliatoriness with whatever she chose to say. Shortly before twelve o'clock the room would begin to fill up and she would watch the people arriving. One or two of them would probably bow and smile to Sir Edward, but they would not come over to speak to him. Did they keep away tactfully because he was with a strange female, or did they avoid him because he was an old bore ? Probably the latter, she thought, stifling another yawn. The cabaret show would provide a brief respite, then there would be more tedious conversation, another dance, and it would be time to go. In the taxi he would put his arm round her again and probably kiss her several times ; he was unlikely to go further than that. The prospect suddenly became unbearable. Why should she go through all this ? No one compelled her to endure these things ; she endured them of her own free will. She seemed to realise her freedom for the first time.

The music came to an end in a final torrent of noise, howling wolves, squealing pigs, cacophonous devils. The dancers trailed back to their tables. On Sir Edward's table the bottle of Veuve Cliquot was already reposing in its silver bucket of ice. The waiter came up, opened the bottle and poured out two glasses.

Sir Edward Wilbur was glad to sit down after the exertion of the dance. Though he would not admit it to himself, the last few minutes had been about as much as he could manage. In spite of the fact that he had tried to breathe easily and deeply through his nose according to instructions, he now felt breathless and a trifle giddy. His hand trembled as he took up his glass of champagne. He drank nearly half what was in the glass and hoped Anna would not notice the unsteadiness with which he returned it to the table. He felt exhausted, his clothes constricted him, his breathing was painful, the champagne tasted flat as he swallowed it. Yet in this unhappy condition, sitting on a hard chair in the glaring, slightly sinister vacancy of the Carolina Club, Sir Edward, though he was already an old man, felt the eager longing of a youth for the woman beside him. The sensation of Anna's body in his arms, even in the impersonal proximity of the dance, had roused him to a pitch of excitement in which he felt willing to do anything, even to risk a scandal, for the sake of this girl with the soft, childlike face and the changing, cool, abstracted eyes.

"When are you going to give me your answer, Anna?" he asked her with real agitation, drawing his chair nearer to hers and touching the back of her hand.

She took her hand away, not rudely, but as though he had touched it accidentally, and her eyes went cold and evasive.

"My answer? About what?" she said vaguely. Even to herself the words sounded stupidly inept. She was ashamed of her ineptitude, but how was she to stave off this old man who looked at her with senile hunger in his flaccid smile ? What was her obligation to attend to him, after all ? She had a curious feeling that some new thought was slowly and with difficulty coming to birth in her brain.

" About the flat, of course ; the little flat in Grafton Street that I told you about. Will you let me take it for you ? Shall I sign a lease to-morrow ? " he asked urgently.

She did not want to attend to him ; she did not want to be bothered. Vaguely, abstractedly, she watched the foolish trembling of his mouth which seemed to have nothing to do with the solemn, rather portentous sounds that issued from it.

" I'm sure I could make you happy," went on Sir Edward.

Anna started, feeling suddenly awakened, and forced out an abrupt :

" No."

The judge, his lips trembling, gasped back at her :

" Is that your final decision ? Do you really mean that ? "

There was a peculiar pause. Anna said nothing more but sat passive, holding the stem of her glass and staring across the room. The " no " had been jerked out of her involuntarily ; she did not know where she had found the necessary determination to utter it. The strange sense of unreality persisted in her, making her feel irresponsible. She did not want to be forced to answer questions or to think about extraneous subjects. She needed to be alone, to hold and analyse the obscure change of thought that was working up in her. Sir Edward watched her anxiously, making odd, jerky motions with his hands. A film of perspiration had broken out on his forehead, he was extraordinarily perturbed.

"Don't say that's your final answer. You must change your mind," he implored, darting quick glances at her, and speaking in an anxious, even humble tone. "Take a little longer to think it over, if you like."

"I have thought it over," said the girl obstinately, still staring ahead.

She suddenly got up from the table. There she stood in her beautiful, supple dress, remote and implacable, looking down on him, as if from far away.

"I want to go home now," she said, adding, as he started to push back his chair: "No, don't come with me. I must be alone."

"You're going . . . Before the cabaret?" he stammered, with shaking lips, quite absurdly distressed.

She felt sorry for him, almost touched. Yet he was small and unimportant. She could not really stop to consider him. The need to understand her own mood was upon her too strongly.

"But you will think things over again?" The serious voice had lost its impressive tone and become timid, quavering.

Anna nodded vaguely, without replying, said good night, and walked quickly away before he could speak again to detain her. The orchestra, as if applauding her exit, burst into a new torrent of syncopation as she went.

Sir Edward sat in pathetic deflation at the table with the bottle of champagne and the two half-empty glasses. He could not understand at all what had happened. He only knew that he was an old fogey to whom the ways of youth were mysterious. He had not known how to deal with the girl, and now she had got up and left him. He had bungled the whole affair.

He sighed, and finished the wine that was in his glass. The waiter re-filled it at once. Long after the cabaret was finished he was still sitting there. He was tired and uncomfortable and his eyes were bloodshot under their drooping lids. He looked old and discouraged, but his thoughts still continued to dwell hopefully on the girl Anna Kavan and the possibility of making her his mistress.

7

Anna is Introspective

SHORTLY before twelve on the night of her twenty-fifth birthday, Anna Kavan entered the sitting-room of the Chelsea flat she shared with Catherine Howard. Moving quietly so as not to disturb her friend in the next room, she went to the window and opened it as wide as it would go. Outside, the Embankment lay broad and deserted with its string of lights, the dark river murmured secretively, the chimneys of the power station on the right thrust like gigantic fingers into the starry sky. She breathed in the cool air which even here smelt faintly of spring. She stood still at the open window, her mind slowly composing itself, glad to be somewhere quiet at last. The air slid cool as silk over her hot cheeks ; the darkly flowing river was soothing with its primeval indifference to humanity ; the silence restored her after the maddening orchestral hubbub of the Carolina Club.

Wearing the beautiful ice-blue dress that looked out of place in the shabby little room, Anna stood alone in the midnight silence, examining her soul. It was as if on this night of her twenty-fifth birthday someone had suddenly called her to account for herself. The sense of unreality had left her, she felt clear-headed as never before. She stood there in absolute honesty, looking into herself. She was suddenly, objectively, aware of the girl Anna Kavan, an individual human being, alive in the world, alone, without support, without obligations, capable of intelligent thought and responsible for her own destiny. For twenty-five years she had existed fortuitously. Her life had unrolled itself haphazard, without definite aim, direction or method. From laziness, from good nature, from thoughtlessness, from indifference, she had drifted into one meaningless situation after another. She had allowed chance external circumstances to control her life. She had relied vaguely for support on something indefinable and non-existent, on something outside herself. There were, she knew, elaborate systems of thought, philosophies and religions, specially designed to provide external support. But as far as she was concerned she knew they were useless, void. She was completely reliant upon herself, completely independent. She shuddered as she realised her utter freedom and the responsibility it implied. With perfect clearness she saw the futility of her past life ; saw that it must be changed. She must change everything. Now, at once, she must assume control of her existence.

She thought of Sir Edward Wilbur and of his suggestion that she should become his mistress. For the first time she thought of the proposal seriously and maturely as of a choice that she might reasonably make. Up to now she had always shelved the question, she had not seemed to appreciate the fact that a decision would actually have to be made. Now she considered the matter rationally and in cold blood. She thought of the flat in Grafton Street which she had never seen but which Sir Edward had described minutely to her. It would be amusing to furnish and decorate that flat. It would be pleasant to be petted and looked after and given plenty of money. She thought of Sir Edward himself, of his red face with the sagging, tired-looking eyelids, of his old man's body, of his slow, circumstantial speech. She thought also of his kindness and of the affection he really displayed towards her. Calmly and judicially she weighed one thing with another and made her decision against him. When she had decided she felt a sense of relief. She had taken the first step in her new manner of life. Henceforward her life was to be her own affair and not the sport of casual chance. It had been her affair whether she should become the mistress of Sir Edward Wilbur : she had decided against him. That was the end of the matter.

There and then she sat down at the table and wrote him a well-expressed, friendly letter, firmly and politely declining his offer. The ice-blue satin dress flowed about the plain wooden chair incongruously in gleaming folds as she wrote. When she had finished, she went out as she was, cloakless, into the empty streets and posted the letter. She was quite alone in the moonless London night : alone, too, in the immense solitude of existence. Yet she was unafraid ; rather, the revelation of her intrinsic isolation was a cause for satisfaction. She returned to the flat, composed and clear-headed, with a settled determination to control her future, and a conviction that the present circumstances of her life must all be altered. She must leave Catherine now, their life together should really have ended some time ago. She must consider the matter of Matthew Kavan, her husband, and decide what was to be done with regard to him. She went to bed feeling that the past was gone and that she had entered upon a new phase of living.

8

Legal Advice

THE offices of Mr. Anthony Quested, the lawyer, in Laurence Poulteney Hill were on the second floor. To reach them one was obliged to climb two flights of a dark and echoing stone staircase, passing on the ground floor a door bearing the name of a wholesale silk merchant, and on the first floor the door of a commissioner for oaths. On the second floor was a door with ground glass pannels and a neat brass plate on which was inscribed : Mr. Anthony Quested ; and below, in clearer letters which had been engraved afterwards : Mr. Anthony Quested jun. For there were two Mr. Anthony Questeds in the firm, father and son.

The door opened directly into a medium-sized room full of papers and deed-boxes. This room contained also the three old-fashioned desks belonging to the clerks, and an obsolete type of fireplace where all the winter a coal fire heavily banked with slack smouldered sullenly, and all the summer odds and ends of miscellaneous rubbish accumulated. There was a window with opaque panes which, if opened, revealed a view of a yellowish brick wall about four feet away. On the left of the outer door were two other doors, one of which usually stood open and displayed a very small room just capable of containing a desk, an arm-chair and some photographs of college football teams. This was the office of Mr. Anthony Quested junior, and was generally empty. The remaining door led into a sort of cubicle, about twelve feet by six, separated from the main office by a partition of wood and ground glass, and containing a wooden bench such as are to be seen in schools, drill halls and other institutions, as well as a shelf bearing a pile of old copies of financial papers. This was known as the waiting-room and was for the convenience of clients whom Mr. Quested could not receive immediately.

By contrast with the rest of the place, the private office of Mr. Quested senior was a cheerful room. Its door was on the right of the outer door of the main office, and its window overlooked a little courtyard or recess which formed a sort of backwater off Laurence Poulteney Hill. From Mr. Quested's window one could see on the extreme left the interminable, slow-moving stream, consisting mainly of heavy vans, that was Laurence Poulteney Hill's traffic problem : but straight in front of the window was the peaceful little courtyard with the plane-tree in the middle whose branches almost brushed the walls of the surrounding buildings.

Mr. Quested sat at his large, methodically untidy desk, confronting the telephone, the orderly disarray of papers, the calendar, the blotter, the enormous ink-stand, the baskets and files of docketed letters. He sat in a cramped, uncomfortable attitude, his fountain-pen in his hand, his thin, cachectic face with its prominent frontal bone and its waxy, nearly transparent nose bent over the papers before him. From time to time he looked up, and his pale eyes, short-sighted behind the rimless pince-nez, peered out at the courtyard below. For twelve years Mr. Quested had sat in that room from ten in the morning till lunch-time, from two-fifteen till five in the evening, overlooking the courtyard, the plane-tree, the paving stones, the walls, doors and windows of the adjoining houses, and he felt a pro-prietary interest in these things. When a dog ran in from the street, sniffed at the trunk of the plane-tree, and impudently lifted its leg before running out again, Mr. Quested felt indignant. If a messenger boy loitered in the shade over a comic paper, whistling and scuffing his feet, it irritated Mr. Quested. He would have liked to put up a gate or a barrier of some kind excluding the general public from the courtyard. When once a ragged old man had appeared with a newspaper parcel full of broken chalks and, squatting down at the entrance of the recess, had begun to make a crudely coloured drawing on the paving stones of a cottage loaf with underneath it the words " Easy to draw but hard to get," the lawyer had been seriously annoyed. It was a relief to him that a policeman soon came along and sent the old pavement artist away.

To-day the inviolacy of the place was challenged by two dingy figures. One of them, his head hanging so that no face was visible, his hunched-up body an amorphous huddle of shabby, neutral coloured clothing, had managed to fall asleep in the sun, supporting himself somehow or other on a narrow stone ledge which projected from the front of the house opposite. The thought : " One would have to be horribly tired before one could sleep in such an uncomfortable position " passed uneasily through the mind of Mr. Quested, before his eyes moved on to the other figure, a young man in a faded seaman's jersey, who leaned against the mottled tree trunk in an attitude symbolic of the eternal, joyless leisure of the unemployed. Something in the lean, cynical, empty face of this young man seemed to disturb the lawyer. It did, in fact, ridiculous as it seemed, actually remind him of Tony. Yes, actually of Tony. Mr. Quested did not want to be reminded of his son in this disagreeable fashion. He did not really want to think of him at all. Tony was nothing but an anxiety and a disappointment to him, no good in the firm, no good anywhere else. The lawyer tried to harden his heart against him. Yet he knew that the boy had only to come into the room, to stand beside him and to speak to him, for his heart to become again like water in his breast.

He sat with his fountain-pen in his hand, the nib suspended over the document to which he was just going to sign his name. He sat staring out of the

window, at the face of the young idler which reminded
him of his son's mocking and mischievous face. Then
with a jerk he turned back to the signature, forcing out
of his mind the thought of Tony and of Tony's behaviour. He signed his name in his usual small, firm,
legible hand, without flourishes.

The head clerk came in with some newspaper cut-
tings, law reports and reports of cases in which Mr.
Quested was interested. Those in which his name
appeared were marked in blue pencil. He glanced
quickly through them. No doubt about it, he had
become a prominent man in his profession. On the
face of it, his success was the result of his own ability
and effort. Only he himself knew how much he owed
to his old school friend William Lewison who had
entrusted him with all his legal business and drawn the
lawyer after him in his upward progress.

Mr. Quested had an appointment with William
Lewison that morning at half-past eleven. He took out
his watch, a valuable old half-hunter that had belonged
to his grandfather. The time was just twenty-five
minutes past eleven. In five minutes William would
walk into the office; he was never late for an appointment. Mr. Quested took off his pince-nez, and polished
the lenses carefully on his large cambric handkerchief.
Before replacing the glasses on his nose, he rapidly
passed his hand over his eyes and over his bulgy forehead. He realised that he was not feeling his best: it
was necessary that he should pull himself together for
the interview with William Lewison.

He had nothing but admiration for William's success. If he had been asked to describe his feelings for

the other man he would have said, quite sincerely, that William was his oldest friend towards whom he felt both gratitude and affection. All the same, William's domineering and self-confident character annoyed him profoundly. Unconsciously, he was jealous of William. The fact that he was under an obligation to him naturally increased his repressed annoyance.

He had not wanted to undertake this business relating to Martin's wife. It was not the sort of case with which he was accustomed to deal. Matters connected with leases and partnerships, wills and agreements, intricate and obscure questions of company law—with all these things he felt at home and qualified to give as good advice as any solicitor in London. But divorce ; that was quite a different affair. He had always avoided such things, saying, half squeamish and half puritanical, that he preferred to keep his hands at least moderately clean. Yet when William Lewison had begged him, no, ordered him, to take up the case it had been impossible to refuse. Mr. Quested could only advise him to consult someone else, some firm specialising in divorce, and this William would not hear of. " Anthony Quested is the firm that has transacted all my legal business so far, and I don't intend to make any change," he had said, smiling that charming, simple smile of his that was really so tyrannical. Of course the lawyer had given in. Angry at first, he now began to feel almost glad that he was to conduct the case. Hypersensitive on account of his own son, he had always fancied a self-congratulatory smugness in William's manner when he referred to his three children. Well, one of them at least had got himself into a mess, marrying this loose foreign woman who had run away with his best friend. He remembered a phrase which that rascal Tony had applied to the elder Lewison: " Ghastly, infallible, efficient, soulless brute." At any rate, the son wasn't so infallible, it appeared.

Before he was really prepared, William Lewison came in. William always walked straight into the private office, ignoring the so-called waiting-room. This time Martin Lewison accompanied him. As William walked into the room with his soft, almost mincing step, his slim and elegant figure set off by his perfectly cut suit, and as the lawyer looked at his serene, assured, worldly-wise expression, he was aware of the annoyance he did not want to acknowledge. He felt surprised, as he always did when he saw them together, that the slight, urbane, polished William should be the father of such a massive and unconventional-looking man as Martin with his slouching gait and generally casual appearance.

The two Lewisons sat down. Through the brain of Mr. Quested, forcing itself to concentrate upon the business in hand, flashed the unformulated thought that they occupied too much space in his small office.

Martin, his greenish eyes fixed on the boughs of the plane-tree outside the window, lounged on the hard, stiff-backed chair that was too small for his bulk, and listened with apparent indifference while the lawyer recounted the preliminaries of the case. William was sitting in the more comfortable leather chair. His elbows resting on the arms, his finger-tips pressed lightly together, he kept his dark eyes on the speaker and listened attentively and judicially to every word. Mr. Quested looked up only occasionally, arranging his

63

papers and settling them in order, as he explained that the torn-up letter which Martin had put together had as good as given them the case from the beginning. The guilty parties had now been traced to an address in Paris, and all that was necessary to complete the evidence was that someone should go and identify them, taking them, if possible, *in flagrante delicto*. As he said the Latin words, the lawyer looked at Martin with his short-sighted, inquisitive glance.

" Claydon has all the requisite particulars," he finished up, in his dry, professional tones.

" Shall we call him in ? " asked William, after a short pause.

The lawyer once again glanced at Martin, who lounged immovably on the hard chair, his legs projecting into the middle of the room. He said nothing, and it was impossible to tell whether he was attending or not. Quested picked up the telephone.

" Send Mr. Claydon in," he ordered shortly.

A middle-aged man with respectable, nondescript clothes was ushered into the room. He looked like a clerk or a small shopkeeper. His drooping moustache gave him an unsuccessful, rather effete appearance. One felt that here was a mild, incompetent man who was nevertheless a kind father and a good citizen, and who had been engaged all his life in a losing battle against taxation and rising prices. He saluted the gentlemen politely, and with respectful composure seated himself in the chair indicated by the solicitor. Then he took out a note-book and began to read.

" On the morning of May 15th I caught the eleven o'clock boat train from Victoria and proceeded to Paris, where I arrived at 5 p.m. I next proceeded to the address given me in Suresnes . . ."

Martin, who had looked up as soon as the detective entered, here interrupted :

" There's no need to read all that out to us. Just give us your information in as few words as possible."

The young man was frowning, the three furrows ploughed deeply across his brow. His nerves were rasped by the mechanical, colourless, uneducated voice and the repetition of the word " proceeded." Mr. Quested eyed him with disapproval behind his pince-nez.

" It would be better to hear the full statement," he remarked.

" I think so, too," said William, looking at his son. " We ought to be in possession of all the details."

" I don't want to hear any details," said Martin impatiently. He looked sullen and worried ; even a little boorish. His full, somewhat slack lips were set in a stubborn line.

The detective waited politely and indifferently for instructions, glancing from one to the other. Mr. Quested's disapproval of Martin increased, and he too glanced at the elder Lewison as if for instructions.

" Very well," said William, with a display of the famous imperturbability ; " we will dispense with the written statement. Let us just have the gist of your information." He smiled at Claydon : usually when he looked at anybody he smiled.

Still speaking in the same mechanical voice that sounded like a bad gramophone record, the detective related how he had gone to Suresnes and hung about the café owned by Germaine's father ; how for several days nothing had happened; but how, on the fourth day, a lady whom he had been able to identify from a photograph had appeared; how he had followed her back to Paris and traced her to a certain hotel where she was living with a gentleman whom he had also recognised from a photograph. He extracted from his pocket-book a card upon which the name and address of a hotel were printed, and laid it on the desk.

For a few moments no one spoke.

"I think that is all we shall require," said William. His smooth voice was extremely complacent. He pressed the tips of his fingers together and smiled benignly over his neat moustache in a way that irritated the lawyer.

"It only remains for someone personally acquainted with Mrs. Martin Lewison to go and identify her," said Quested, when the detective had left the room. "I suggest that you should go," he shot at Martin in a matter-of-fact tone.

"No," said the young man, with a sullen scowl. "I certainly won't go."

"All the same, I suggest that you are the best person to identify her," persisted the lawyer calmly. "It will expedite matters if you go yourself. Particularly as the gentleman in the case is also well known to you."

Young Anthony Quested suddenly opened the door, cool and smartly dressed, with rope-coloured hair and an impertinent, knowing, yet rather stupid face; his vacuous eyes examined the visitors with curiosity as he apologised with affected politeness for his intrusion and made a pretence of withdrawing. Martin at once got up, went over to him, and began a conversation. The

two young men stood talking together in the doorway,
leaving the elders curiously isolated.   William Lewison
smiled a slow, intimate and significant smile at his old
school-fellow.   " That's what it is to be a father,"
the smile seemed to say.   " The young rascals go off
and amuse themselves, leaving us to do all their dirty
work and get them out of their scrapes."   His confi-
dential smile almost became a wink.   The lawyer
smiled back unwillingly.   He did not believe that there
was no superiority in William's attitude.   William
might possibly think of his son Martin as a young rascal,
but that was a very different thing from calling him a
waster and a ne'er-do-well.   Tony was certainly a young
waster in William's opinion, a degenerate, a thoroughly
bad lot.   He had always discouraged any sign of friendship between Tony and his own children, as if he feared
some contamination.

" You don't want me any more for anything, do
you ? " Martin asked from the doorway.   He sounded
quite cheerful now, and had regained his amiable, off-
hand manner.

Mr. Quested felt deeply indignant : did the fellow
think the whole world was being run for his special
benefit ?   He behaved like a spoilt leading lady with
his whims and temperamental caprices.   First of all he
was sulky and obstructive, and then he got tired of the
whole business and wanted to clear off without settling
anything at all.

" You haven't decided definitely against going to
Paris, I hope," he said, stiff with displeasure.

" All right.   I'll go," said Martin carelessly, as if it
were a matter of no importance.   He came back, picked

up the card upon which the name of the hotel was printed, took the lawyer's frail, bloodless hand in his somewhat coarse fingers, nodded to his father, and departed with Tony Quested.

" Things aren't too easy for him just now," William said. " His nerves are all on edge."

The high-and-mighty Lewison actually seemed to be apologising for his son's behaviour. Mr. Quested was mollified.

" And now about those leases of yours," he began, turning with relief to a fresh file of papers before him.

William Lewison drew his chair nearer the desk. The two old friends were soon in the thick of what was perhaps their five-hundredth discussion of legal technicalities. Their voices droned on with a placid sound in the dull little office. The air smelt of soot, papers and stale tobacco. The hazy London sunshine came in at the window, the shadow of the plane-tree flung an indistinct filigree over the littered desk with its film of dust and tobacco ash. In the middle of the discussion Mr. Quested suddenly sighed as he happened to look out of the window. The young man in the seaman's jersey was still loafing in the courtyard below.

9

Anna Smiles in a Superior Way

CATHERINE HOWARD was tired of her friend Anna with whom she had been living for nearly two years. For months she had been growing more and more dissatisfied, more and more impatient with Anna. Now, suddenly, in the warm spring weather, the whole relationship seemed unbearable to her. She felt furious with Anna. She felt the oppression of the other girl's personality so strongly that she had a sensation of actual physical constriction in her company. Anna infuriated her, her charm, her intelligence no less than her egocentricity and her lack of animation.

The two of them had taken the shop together, meaning to make a success of it. At least, Catherine had felt sure that they would be successful, starting the fashion for a new sort of woollen work, making coats and jumpers on a new plan, and catching the attention of fashionable women. Everything in the Beauchamp Place shop was hand-made and exclusive and very expensive. It was Anna's money which had started the business, for Catherine had nothing to speak of. Anna's aunt, who was quite a wealthy woman, had been persuaded to finance the undertaking, although she disapproved of her niece's independent, rather *declassé* existence. Catherine, however, had been the moving spirit in the affair. The shop had been her idea in the first place. Anna had really done nothing but acquiesce, partly because she wanted to please her friend of whom at that time she was very fond, and partly because, perhaps, she was a bit carried away by Catherine's enthusiasm.

The two girls were about the same age ; and they had the same slight modern build. Catherine was the more striking, her small, intense, determined face almost heart-shaped, with the deep point of hair growing down in the middle of her low forehead, and her immense, brown, liquescent eyes. Anna looked vague and childlike

69

beside her vivid, resolute friend. Yet it was Anna who really dominated the relationship. Catherine felt her influence like something soft, deadening, intangible and inescapable wrapping her round and impeding all her activities.

Catherine did most of the real work. She really kept the shop going. From ten till one and from two till six she sat in the poky, stuffy little workroom, supervising the half-dozen work-girls, stretching the loose meshed nets on the rickety wooden frames, plaiting the long, thick skeins of wool that lay about everywhere like brilliantly dyed, severed horses tails, always on the watch for mistakes in the intricate patterns. It was rather a complicated business altogether : a process of darning elaborately fantastic, complex coloured design upon the foundation of the different coloured nets. The work-girls needed constant watching if they were not to go wrong.

It was all a trifle too complicated to be really successful, in spite of Catherine's efforts. The work went too slowly to keep pace with the orders, they needed a larger workroom, more employees. In the endless winter afternoons when the workroom stifled in the fumes of the gas-fire, the girls were dozy and glum, bending sleepily over their frames. And in summer it was even worse, with the sunshine seeping implacably through the cheap yellow blind. Catherine was beginning to feel that she would go mad with irritable exhaustion in the interminable afternoons, shut up there in the stuffy back room with the stupid work-girls. Surely she was born to better things than this ?

And yet it had been she who wanted the shop. She acknowledged that it had been her enthusiasm that had launched the enterprise. Even now, at times, she felt flickers of the same enthusiastic excitement. She told herself that it was only Anna's influence that hampered and depressed her and kept her back.

For the shop was so nearly being a success. They had plenty of customers, thanks to their advertisements in the most exclusive fashion papers. The original, somewhat startling garments had caught on, particularly in certain theatrical circles. And the queer showroom in Beauchamp Place with the sombre velvet curtains, the elaborate pelmets, and the wild, rather sinister designs painted on the tall double doors was effective, to say the least of it. A sort of Russian Ballet effect, off stage. As it was, they were making their expenses and a few pounds over each week. But every shilling of profit was swallowed up in improvements of various kinds. They needed to expand, to put fresh capital into the business. No fresh capital was forthcoming.

It drove Catherine into a frenzy to see success so near and yet so inaccessible : and it seemed to her to be all Anna's fault that they could not achieve it. Anna as a working partner really enraged her ; she was such an incalculable, elusive creature. Not that she was idle or irresponsible in the ordinary sense : but she simply refused to become entangled in practical matters, with obscure elusiveness she slipped out of every responsibility. When she saw Anna standing about in the showroom, standing languidly with polite, indifferent, abstracted gaze, while a customer fussed over patterns, a madness of irritation invaded Catherine, she wanted to rush in and strike her friend in the face. It was so infuriating to her to see Anna existing always a little apart, as it were ; refusing to become embroiled with reality. If only she could get hold of someone more enterprising, more practical and enthusiastic, she felt sure that things would go ahead. But then, Anna's money was in the business ; and every now and then she would turn out an unexpected asset. It was she who had painted the strange, sweeping figures on the big doors.

On the day after Anna's twenty-fifth birthday, Catherine was in a particularly bad temper. A series of small annoyances in the workroom had increased the sense of aggrieved resentment which she felt against the other girl. She sensed, too, a slight alteration in Anna's conduct which she could not account for or define. Perhaps it was that Anna seemed more self-contained, more impervious than ever to the claims of actuality. She still seemed passive, dreamy, detached ; she still moved about the shop in that curious negative, unanimated way that Catherine found so exasperating. But there was a change in her. Catherine resented the change without knowing what it was.

At four o'clock in the afternoon the routine of the shop relaxed for a few minutes. The kettle was boiled in the workroom and tea was made. The work-girls lounged over their thick white cups, some of them produced cheap pastries from greasy paper bags. The stuffy back room smelt of sweat, of insufficiently washed female bodies, of strong tea, of wool, and of the huge tailor's iron that was heating on the gas-ring. Snatching up the two cups of tea which she had poured out for

Anna and herself, Catherine fled from the intolerable atmosphere.

In the showroom things were decidedly better. The light, oblong room with its weird decorations felt airy and cool. There had been no customers for the last half-hour and everything was neat and in order, a white woollen coat with an exotic Chinese design carefully arranged on the stand. Anna sat at a desk on which red stags were painted, a sheet of the headed notepaper in front of her. Catherine put down the cup beside her with a little crash. Why should she wait on the other girl? While she had loved her friend she had always protected and looked after her, feeling herself so much the more practical and efficient of the two. Now the habit of service still lingered. A fretful expression came on Catherine's face, her large eyes looked strained at the corners as she sat down a little apart with her own cup of tea. She looked across at Anna with rage in her heart. To think how she had strained and strained herself for the benefit of that unresponsive, ungrateful creature! She recalled the way Anna seemed just to wait to be helped, accepting service as though it were her right, relaxing into a sort of sleep of acceptance, always taking, taking, and never giving even so much as her real attention in exchange : seeming not to notice how Catherine wore herself out, straining to protect her from the business of life.

Catherine drank her tea in angry gulps, her heart hot with a sense of injury. When was this unbearable situation going to end? How much longer was she to be tied to this Anna, this burden, this spectre from the past who had outstayed her time? When was she

73

going to be able to live her own life without this incubus ?
She was not born to live under the shadow of someone
else ; it was this perpetual denial of herself that made her
a failure and brought the drawn, aggrieved look to the
ends of her eyes.

" It can't go on," she blurted out suddenly, from the
midst of her thoughts.

" What can't go on ? " asked Anna, opening grey
eyes wide beyond her abstraction.

To Catherine she looked only half present, half conscious, her face seemed a blank. It was this entranced
condition that Catherine hated so much. Anna seemed
to attend to what was going on, to listen and observe
and to speak when it became necessary : but all the time
the other girl doubted whether she were really aware,
whether she realised what was happening.

" Our lives can't go on like this. I can't go on
looking after you, and running the shop all by myself
and taking the whole responsibility for everything.
You've got to come down to earth and do your fair
share of the work." Her voice sounded nervy and
overwrought, trembling on the verge of hysteria.

Anna looked at her with dreamy attention from the
desk.

" It's rather odd you should say that to-day of all
days," she remarked.

" Why odd ? " Catherine stared with large, angry
eyes, surprised and suspecting some trap.

" Because I came to the same decision last
night," Anna said, a soft, distant amusement in her
voice.

" Oh ! " said Catherine, staring. " What decision

74

are you talking about?" She sounded hostile and indignant, suspicious.

"I decided that it was time for us to stop living together," Anna said.

Catherine's eyes went glazed, astounded, under the shock of the cool announcement.

"Oh, really! Do you propose that we should separate, then?" It was what she had really wanted, hoped for, but now she felt outraged all the same. Anna, as usual, had contrived to do the unexpectd thing and had taken all the wind out of her sails in doing so. The callousness of it, too, springing it on her suddenly in that casual voice as though she were talking about the weather: such ingratitude after all her straining and protective affection!

"You'll want to take your money out of the business and spoil my chance of success, I suppose," she said, with a sharp catch in her voice, like a sob. "All the work I've done will just be wasted . . . it'll count for nothing at all."

Anna looked across at her as if unconcerned, indifferent.

"No, it doesn't matter about the money," she said.

She drew a sheet of paper towards her and started to write. Mechanically her hand set down the words in answer to a customer's letter, but she was not thinking of what she wrote. She was thinking about her decision to take control of her own life. How many absurd, unpleasant and inappropriate situations she had allowed herself to drift into in the past. There was her marriage to Matthew Kavan. There was this shop with all its senseless elaboration of complicated labour. There was the affair of Catherine Howard who had once loved her, who supervised work-girls, had business ambitions, wanted to get rid of her and was now staring at her with hostile resentment because she had decided to go. There was old Sir Edward who had taken her out for expensive, boring evenings at the Carolina Club and had almost succeeded in making her his mistress. All these things had happened to her because she had not realised that her life was her own affair. Now she was wiser. No more such inept incidents should occur.

With fury and amazement the other girl suddenly saw that Anna was smiling. It was neither a mocking, a callous nor a cynical smile, but it was a superior smile. Catherine felt her blood boil with indignation.

10

Concerning a Gesture

GERALD GILL was growing discontented. The life of sensual enjoyment which he had been living with Germaine for the last few days was beginning to leave a nasty taste in his mouth. For nearly a week now he had existed in a sort of trance of physical sensation, a state of complete absorption in sensuality. At first it had been perfectly satisfactory, he had felt exalted, almost rapt, going about in a condition almost of ecstasy. It had seemed to be just what he wanted for the complete fulfilment of his being, this preoccupation with passionate love that was like a secret knowledge he carried about with him, a dark and powerful secret of his own blood. When he walked along the streets he felt

76

forceful and strong like a giant among the flimsy, wispy Parisians who seemed to disperse before him as the waves part before the bow of a destroyer. It was as though a magic potency enveloped him and emanated from him, making him formidable.

> " And all should cry, Beware ! Beware !
> His flashing eyes, his floating hair !
> Weave a circle round him thrice,
>   And close your eyes with holy dread,
>   For he on honey-dew hath fed,
> And drunk the milk of Paradise."

But by imperceptible degrees this feeling of exaltation waned, vanished and gave place to an undefined malaise. The erotic prepossession which had enveloped and uplifted him like an ecstatic dream now began to assume the characteristics, half exciting, half oppressive, wholly obsessional, of a delirium. Like a man in a fever he felt uneasy, over-stimulated, abnormal. He had sudden spasms of longing for his more natural self.

The voluptuous idleness of his life since his arrival in Paris no longer satisfied him. He felt incomplete without his work behind him, he needed his theories of abstract drawing to sharpen his wits on. He missed the tranquillity, the familiar mental stimulus of his studio, and could not concentrate over a paltry sketch-book.

Each hour he became a little more dissatisfied, a little more moody. He was glad that Germaine would soon have to go back to England. For the time being he had sated his sex-appetite and had no further use for her. Presently, after a separation, the craving would come on him again and then he would be drawn back to her, but for the moment he had had enough. He was

bored with her. Without any consideration for the
wishes or feelings of his companion, he started to frequent
low cafés where he sat for hours carrying on argumentative conversations with mechanics, workmen and taxi-
drivers. Although a wealthy and cultured man, Gill
had a curious affinity with squalor of all descriptions.
Indifferent to his surroundings, unaffected by dirt or
bad smells, he seemed to gravitate naturally towards
the lowest point in his environment. Utterly careless
of his appearance, frequently unshaved and even unwashed for days at a time, he would go about in clothes
which would not have looked out of place on a tramp :
a habit which, originating in a form of exhibitionism,
had become an intrinsic part of his character.

Many people were repelled by his personal habits,
by his despotic disregard of others, and by the unrestrained profanity of his speech. On the other hand
there were certain people who seemed fascinated by the
strange fellow with the thatch of coarse, bleached-look-
ing, wiry hair, the bright blue, somewhat ghoulish eyes,
the savage, blasphemous tongue. Germaine Lewison
in particular was enthralled by him, though nothing
could have been more incongruous than the association
of the smart, fastidious woman with that slovenly,
eccentric figure. Dressed in her fashionable, expensive
clothes, looking handsome and sophisticated, she followed him meekly into the unappetising bedroom of the
shoddy little hotel he had decided upon. At first,
while he was happy and absorbed, she too floated through
the world in a dream of passionate bliss. Then, when
he began to tire, she endeavoured to re-enchant him,
she followed him submissively about, uncomplaining,

waiting patiently for him to return to her embraces. She tried, unobtrusively, to improve his appearance, and, when he cursed her interference, smiled back with a queer stuporous humility, as if drugged.

Now, on the morning of this spring day, when the air was fresh and invigorating outside and the hands of the church clock at the end of the street stood gilded in the sunshine at ten minutes to eight, she was lying beside Gerald Gill in the slatternly hotel bedroom. The shutters were closed and the stale air of the darkened room smelt of cigarette smoke and soiled clothing. The bed was tumbled and frowzy, the coarse sheets rasped Germaine's skin. She raised herself carefully on her elbow and looked at Gerald. Even in his sleep he had an uncompromising appearance. It was one of his minor eccentricities to sleep nude under the bed-clothes, and his exposed chest covered with light brownish hair looked hard as a rock overgrown with sea-weed. She sighed softly and lay down again on the hot pillow.

Noisy footsteps were approaching along the corridor and coming towards the bedroom door. Germaine listened to the boards creaking under the heavy tread. It must be the waiter bringing their morning coffee. But no, it was too early for that, and in any case the coffee was never brought until they rang for it. Gerald had given orders that they were not to be disturbed in the mornings. There was a loud knock on the door. It was not the waiter's knock. Germaine felt a pang of alarm. She started up in bed and turned towards Gill who had woken at once and was rubbing his face with his hands.

" Who the hell's that ? " he exclaimed crossly.

"Shall I unlock the door?" asked Germaine.

Gerald said roughly: "No." He called out in French to ask who was there. "The *patron*," came the reply. What the devil did the *patron* want at this time of the morning? It appeared that there was a gentleman downstairs waiting to see the English gentleman.

Germaine felt terror-stricken: a sense of impending catastrophe overwhelmed her. No one knew their address in Paris, there was no one who could conceivably call on them at eight o'clock in the morning. In vain she told herself that it must be one of Gerald's casual acquaintances, someone he had picked up the previous night and carelessly invited to call on him, who had chosen this unseemly hour for a visit. She knew it was not so. It was disaster. They were found out. In some unimaginable way they had been suspected and tracked down. In a flash she saw the end of her financial security, her social position, her life of leisure and comparative luxury: the end of everything. Her warm coloured face went pale with anguished foreboding.

Gill got out of bed and stood for a second scratching his chest and stretching his arms over his head. His gaunt, hairy, naked body looked huge in the dark, low-ceilinged room. A slender pencil of sunlight found its way in through the shutters and lighted up a fur of reddish down on his sinewy thigh. Next moment he had plunged into a pair of trousers, pulled a coat over his bare shoulders, turned up the collar and opened the bedroom door.

"Find out who it is," implored Germaine from the bed.

Beyond Gill she could see the white, fleshy face of the hotel proprietor floating uneasily against the background of the murky passage. The man looked sullen and slightly truculent. Her terrors increased. Gerald asked a few rapid questions. She listened with strained attention to the *patron's* surly replies. The stranger had come at a quarter to eight and demanded to be taken to the room of M. Gill. He was a foreigner, probably English. When the *patron* had refused to allow him to come up, he had insisted that a message be sent asking M. Gill to descend immediately. He had refused to go away and return at a more reasonable hour. He had refused to state his business. He had refused to do anything except wait downstairs. The proprietor shrugged his shoulders at the incomprehensible and unpleasant habits of foreigners, looked disapprovingly at Germaine, and marched heavily away. Gerald glanced at Germaine's pale and anxious face. " Brainless, provoking bitch," he muttered, as he followed the *patron* into the corridor. They were in for some bother, no doubt. But why couldn't the stupid woman keep her head instead of dithering at him with a face like a ghost at the first hint of trouble ?

Going downstairs with his loose, rather shambling gait he felt one or two qualms. He was none too easy in his mind over the deception of Martin. It was not the fact that he had slept with Martin's wife that troubled him, but that he had deceived his friend about it. Left to himself, he would have gone to Martin in the first place and talked the thing out with him. But Germaine had insisted on concealing everything. She had been absolutely determined on a clandestine affair, and he,

81

in unthinking anxiety to assuage his sex-hunger, had given in. He was suddenly furious at the thought that Germaine by her stupid bourgeois idea of caution might have come between him and the only man he cared about sufficiently to consider his friend. She wasn't worth it, that was a fact. No woman was worth the intimacy between two intelligent men. What fools women were. "Brainless, provoking bitch," he muttered again, with intense venom.

The staircase ended in a narrow paved hall which opened directly on to the street. On the left was the door of the little side room where the visitor would be waiting. Gerald Gill paused, abruptly aware that his throat was dry and that he wanted to smoke. Passers-by stared in amazement from the street at the big, dishevelled man standing barefooted on the paving stones and fumbling with a cigarette.

He had not formed any distinct expectation of whom he would see when he opened the door of the side room, but when he saw Martin Lewison standing near the window he was surprised. The genuine pleasure he always felt at the sight of this man came over him so strongly that for an instant he actually forgot the extra-ordinary circumstances of their meeting and held out his hand with a glad exclamation as though nothing unusual had happened.

"Wait a minute, Gerald," said Martin, in a constrained voice, deliberately ignoring the extended hand.

Yes, Martin had decided that he had been deeply injured and would behave accordingly. He had undertaken this filthy business of spying on Germaine and her lover, and he was in a thoroughly bad temper. He

82

was very fond of his friend Gill, but now Gerald had abused his friendship unforgivably, had deceived him in a disgusting manner and made him the laughing stock of all his acquaintances. That Martin did not really quite believe all these things, made no difference. He had trusted Gerald implicitly, and Gerald had taken advantage of his trust to seduce Germaine and involve Martin in all this loathsome bother. Because Martin was easy-going, everybody thought they could do as they liked with him. Now he would show them that they could not. He had stuck to Gerald although nearly everyone else was against him; he had always defended him loyally. But now that Gerald had turned traitor there was an end to Martin's loyalty. Gerald Gill was his enemy, and so was Germaine: everyone who took advantage of him was his enemy. He would show them that he was not to be trifled with any longer. All his life he had dreaded and avoided scenes, but since he had been pitchforked into this one he would stand up for himself and tell Gill exactly where he got off. He inhaled the smoke from his cigarette, and gazed stiffly at the barefooted man before him.

Gerald stood dazed for a few seconds after Martin had rejected his hand; he took a step forward with his hand still half extended, and then sat down unsteadily, so that Martin wondered if he had already been drinking, and rested his arms on a small table covered with a dirty check cloth.

"I suppose you know why I've come," Martin said. "This is a matter of business, not a friendly visit." He stared with a hostile and ironic expression at the ungainly figure in the disreputable, sweaty clothes.

The robust, well-nourished Martin looked more prosperous than ever in contrast to his companion. His large face with its green, attentive eyes was stiffened into a mask of estrangement. The room was airless and chilly at the same time. Gerald suddenly shouted to someone outside for coffee to be brought. He looked haggard and uncouth sitting there awkwardly in front of the well-dressed young Lewison.

Gerald Gill stirred his coffee as he listened to the other's curt, formal sentences. His usual aggressive high-handed manner was conspicuously absent. Martin's gesture of refusing to take his hand had shocked, almost appalled him. He would not have been more perturbed if his friend had assaulted him with physical violence. He felt that Martin had by this gesture failed not only him, Gerald, his friend, but had also failed himself in some way. Martin had allowed conventional standards and a sense of personal affront to overpower the dictates of intelligence. Gerald scarcely heard what he was saying. He nodded carelessly when Martin brought out the words, " So I have decided to start divorce proceedings," fiddled with the coffee spoon, examined his hands, of which the nails were bitten down to the quick, and did not attempt to conceal his pre-occupation. Martin was annoyed when he observed that Gerald was not attending.

" I wish you would condescend to listen to me," he said sharply.

Gerald suddenly became angry and began to make an attack. He had started by feeling guilty towards his friend, but the other's attitude filled him with an irritation that obliterated guilt.

84

"The reason why you're behaving so stupidly," he said to Martin, "is simply that you've allowed your intelligence to be swamped by a prehistoric instinct. The fact that I happen to have slept with your wife— in whom, by the way, you are not even remotely interested yourself—doesn't give you a divine right to come and abuse me and make yourself unpleasant. You treat me like a criminal and a cad because I have disregarded a convention which you have often described as obsolete and anachronistic when you weren't personally concerned with it. You're a poor muddle-headed devil; you can't put your theories into practice. But it's even more despicable than that; I don't believe you're even genuinely carried away by error. You're simply tricking yourself with a sense of righteous indignation because you think that's the easiest way of dealing with the situation and evading the real issue. Your attitude is far more criminal than mine; you're being dishonest with yourself as well as with me. You're too hopelessly evasive. Rather than come to an honest decision you'll bury your head in the sand and resort to every kind of low cunning and subterfuge. You're nothing but a damned moral coward of the bloodiest description. In fact, you're just an ordinary fool."

Martin Lewison grew rigid with anger, for he could not prevent himself from being affected by the last sentence, which had been spoken with quite a different inflexion from the rest—an inflexion of weary, contemptuous disappointment.

"I'm afraid there isn't time just now to enter into an analysis of my character," he said at last, falling back on an imitation of his father's artificial politeness, and

85

distantly returning the gaze of the blue, deep-set, accusing eyes. " It's unfortunately necessary for me to see you and Germaine in a bedroom together," he went on. " Some wretched formality. And there's a detective outside who is supposed to come up with me so that my evidence shan't be unsupported. Will you allow us just to look into the room for a moment? We shan't keep you more than a minute or two."

Somewhat to his surprise Gill did not flare up again. He did not burst out into a stream of profane abuse as Martin had anticipated. He seemed, rather, to have become suddenly deflated as though he had wearied of the whole affair and merely wanted to get it over as quickly as possible.

So he answered : " Oh, yes. Come upstairs if you must. I'll just go ahead and warn Germaine."

" I'll call in the detective," said Martin in much the same bored tone that his friend had used.

The two men left the room where the two cups of coffee, untouched, still steamed on the table. As Martin went out to fetch Claydon, who was waiting beside the church, he felt some uneasiness. Suppose Gill should take this opportunity of disappearing? It would be the devil's own job to find him again. At the same time, it would really be a relief if he did vanish. Martin also felt all at once horribly tired and depressed, sick of the whole business. His antipathy was so strong that he could hardly force himself to re-enter the dingy hotel and climb up the dark stairs.

When he and Claydon reached the bedroom, Gerald opened the door and then flung back one of the shutters.

" Good morning, Germaine," said Martin politely.

The colourless detective took off his hat and glanced observantly but impersonally about the squalid, untidy room.

Germaine was still in bed. She had put on a silk wrap over her nightgown. Martin recognised it as one he had seen before, and felt a sensation of shame. It was extraordinary and distressing to him to see the familiar garment in these sordid surroundings.

"Hullo, Martin," she said to him, with an hysterical spurt of laughter, stifled at its inception. Then she sat motionless and silent in the tumbled bed, watching the three men with a strained, nervous, painful attention. Martin turned away his eyes.

Gerald Gill planted himself on the edge of the bed, pulled off his coat with brazen effrontery, exposing his hard, hairy chest, and leaned against the pillows in an abandoned attitude.

"There, is that sufficiently suggestive for you?" he asked in a horribly loud, offensive voice. "Or would you like me to go further?" He actually started to unfasten his trousers, grinning with an unmistakably lewd expression at the detective.

"We have all the evidence we require, thank you," said the colourless man, calmly but severely pronouncing the words as he retreated through the still open door.

Martin stood where he was. He had a curious and embarrassing feeling that he was in the presence of two complete strangers.

"I'm sorry to intrude on you like this," he said in a low voice, unable to move, and conscious all the time of the half-naked man on the bed who stared at him with blue eyes uncannily gleaming, and a face filled with a singular blend of anger, contempt, accusation, disappointment and licentiousness. Incredible that this was the man who had been his intimate friend for many years, and with whom he had discussed subjects near to his heart which had never been mentioned to another soul.

Gerald Gill kept his eyes fixed upon Martin, and grinned his indecent, spiteful grin into that full, handsome face. There he lay, stretched out on the tousled bed, nude except for his dirty old trousers, showing the horny soles of his feet, which were nearly black with grime from the passage floor. Into Martin's eyes had come that look of rather pathetic bewilderment that was sometimes to be seen there. The three tormented ridges of flesh appeared on his forehead. He was once again overwhelmed with shame as he had been when his father insisted on reading aloud the copy of Gerald's letter to Germaine. And again, as on that occasion, he could not have told exactly why or on whose account he was ashamed, whether on other people's or on his own. He looked down at the carpet with its faded, threadbare pattern of what appeared to be serpents, red on one side and green on the other. The sunshine flooding in through the opened shutter fell in such a way that the chamber pot under the bed stood out clearly in the strong light, standing there on the ugly serpent design of the carpet. With the intentness of utter preoccupation Martin stared at the white china utensil in which a cigarette end was floating. His mind seemed, in those few moments, to explore the ultimate depths of human mortification.

Claydon came back and touched him on the shoulder, saying :

"We can go now. We have all the necessary evidence."

Martin looked up slowly, his puzzled, frowning face contorted : he seemed not to understand.

"We must be going now," said the detective firmly, leading him off.

II

Martin Practises Evasion

ONCE he had got rid of the detective on the morning of the day he had seen Gerald Gill and Germaine, Martin went back to the hotel near the Étoile where he had taken a room. He was surprised to find that it was still quite early. Although he had slept soundly till seven o'clock that morning, he had the sense of demoralisation and timelessness that is usually the result of sitting up all night. He took off his jacket and shoes and lay down on the bed. The three horizontal lines on his forehead looked deep and permanent as if they had been branded there with iron. For some time he lay on his back staring up at the ceiling, in the middle of which was painted a rococo design of cupids and full-blown flowers. He did not think of Germaine except for the passing thought that it had been strange to see her, whom he had always known as finical and luxury-loving, content with such mean surroundings. He did not really think about Gerald Gill. But the words which his friend had spoken—particularly the words, "In fact, you're just an ordinary fool"—kept recurring in his brain in hateful, devastating repetition.

89

He tried to concentrate, to submit Gerald's indictment to the arbitration of his own intelligence ; but for some reason or other he seemed quite incapable of consecutive thought. As soon as he tried to focus his mind, there arose before him, like an insane and hideous visitation, the image of the white china chamber pot which he could not even remember noticing, but of which his subconscious mind had retained a more than photographic impression, accurate in every detail. With loathing and nausea he was forced again and again to observe the floating cigarette end, the damp paper of which was becoming transparent and allowing the shreds of tobacco to escape one by one into the clear yellow fluid.

At last he fell asleep. He dreamed that he was a small boy again on the Cotswold farm where part of his childhood had been spent. He was walking along the edge of a field in which cattle were grazing, and quite near to a fence of strong wooden palings, painted white. Presently he saw with alarm that the cattle were much larger, nearer, and more minatory in appearance, and that they were all staring at him malevolently with faces resembling the faces of people he knew. He recognised his father's face among them. When he observed that they were moving towards him he was at first terror-stricken, but remembering his own small size he quickly slipped through the railings to safety. In spite of the satisfactory termination of the dream, he woke up feeling displeased with himself, gloomy and unrefreshed.

He went out to a restaurant, ate some food inattentively, and drank a bottle of Beaujolais. The wine, instead of cheering him, seemed simply to inflame the dissatisfaction he felt with himself and the whole world. To the annoyance of the waiter who wanted to clear the table, he sat on long after the other clients had departed, smoking one cigarette after another, crushing out the stubs in the saucer of his coffee cup and covering the table with grey ash.

He was still tortured by the recollection of Gerald's words. Perhaps it was true that he was the worst kind of moral hypocrite, deceiving himself in order to evade the responsibility of thinking things out. He was besieged now by remorse for having behaved so stupidly. If only he had not refused Gerald's hand. His heart turned cold, he seemed to fall into a black hole of shame when he thought of that petty, mean-spirited gesture. If only the interview could take place over again how differently he would conduct it. Should he go back now to Gerald and try to put things on a better footing ? The address of the hotel was still in his pocket, he had only to take a taxi or to walk a certain distance and he would probably come face to face with Gill. The waiter, watching more hopefully, saw Martin make a movement as though to jump up from his chair. But the picture of Gerald's face obscenely leering from the bed, the face of a complete stranger, came back to deter him. How could he expect to discover the familiar personality of his friend behind that lewd, impervious and alien face ? Not for another half-hour did the waiter see him leave the restaurant.

Martin walked blindly in the streets for some time. The afternoon sun shone down gaily, a fresh wind caught at the women's skirts, tram wheels squealed round the curves, the traffic spurted forward or jerked unwillingly to a halt in response to signals, taxi horns blared, brayed, tooted or squeaked discordantly. People wore flowers or carried flowers in their hands ; the flowering chestnut trees made a garden of the city street. Martin Lewison was unaffected by these things, and only noticed them subconsciously.

Finally he went into the Louvre. To stand before a picture and lose himself in it, to try and follow the journeyings of the painter's mind which had led to the finished work, to pursue the intricate paths of technique and craftsmanship, was usually a sure method of cutting himself off from personal worries. But to-day the charm would not work. He stayed for a long while in the Commando Collection, staring at the Cézannes of which he had always made a particular study. He gazed at the landscapes, the big masses, strong shadows and accents, the vigorous, methodical brushwork, the colour modelling harmonised by a blue, Arcadian mildness. He gazed at the still life in which the fruit appear in pure, limpid colours, their shapes rounded in a subtly graduated variation of tone. He tried mechanically to summon up the state of mind which these pictures usually inspired in him. To his astonishment and dismay he found that he could not do so. Between him and the canvas appeared spectrally the memories which afflicted him, Gerald's changed, indecent face, the white china utensil in which the cigarette butt nauseously floated.

Martin could not oust from his mind the self-doubts which Gerald's criticism had called up. He was not very analytical. It was not easy for him to follow the workings of his own brain. Some of the things Gill had said were certainly true. It was true, for instance, that he had no interest in Germaine, that he no longer desired her physically but, in fact, wanted to get rid of her. It was also true that the man Gerald Gill whom he had liked and admired till now was still the same man, no less likeable and admirable because Martin had happened to find him out in adultery. Martin glared at the pictures with unseeing, troubled eyes, frowning deeply and biting his nails meanwhile. But if Gerald were right, it became necessary that he, Martin, should admit himself in the wrong : and this his sense of unjury would not allow him to do. He had been grievously and shamefully wronged, there was no getting away from that. How, then, could Gill be in the right ? Only if Martin himself were being dishonest, if he were deliberately fostering his supposed grievance in order to evade the obligation of constructive thought. There was only one thing he could do to put himself straight in his own eyes and clear up this nightmare of confusion and uncertainty. He must conscientiously and dis-passionately hold an enquiry into his own motives and personal conduct. Yet all the time, even when he told himself this, he was only playing with the idea. He did not really intend to make the examination of himself. Subconsciously, he was still determined to evade the whole issue. He stayed so long in the gallery, glaring at the pictures, walking up and down and biting his nails, that the attendant began to watch him suspiciously.

At last he went out into the streets again. The late afternoon was already declining into evening, the change-over from daytime to evening activity was already begin-ning. The traffic was of a different type and flowed in different directions ; the pedestrians, too, wore different clothes, made for other objectives, and seemed animated by a new set of motives.

Martin went into the Dôme, sat down and ordered a Pernod. As he drank he became suddenly conscious of loneliness. Since early morning he had spent the whole day completely alone without speaking to anyone except a waiter. Gregarious by nature, he was struck by the thought that this uncommon isolation had something to do with his depressed mood. Suddenly he felt the necessity of surrounding himself with people, of telling them what had happened to him, and hearing their voices in reply. He searched the place with his eyes, scanning the strange faces with feverish eagerness and impatience. He seemed to know nobody in the café.

All at once someone touched him on the shoulder, a remarkable-looking gentleman, dressed in pale blue corduroy and crowned with prematurely white hair above a sunburned, gipsyish face, and followed by a very tall, imposing and pre-Raphaelite sort of woman. It was Kyria the Cypriot painter. He had recognised Martin from behind and come over to join him. He introduced his stately companion with classical simplicity as Antonia. They sat down one on each side of Martin who ordered drinks for them.

The arrival of these two was a godsend to the young man. The need to talk, to make a noise, to work off in words some of his sense of injury and shame had become a pressing, primitive urge. At last he had someone to talk to. There he sat between the two of them, the painter, Kyria, who watched him continually with soft, corrupt eyes like circles of brown velvet in his dark, plastic face, and the decorative Antonia who sat with her long, full black skirts flowing majestically about her. He poured out his woes to them. Antonia turned her impressive bosom towards him, and emitted sympathetic sounds from between her painted, pouting lips which she caused to quiver in a way somewhat reminiscent of a fish.

Martin ordered more drinks. He talked on and on, complaining about his misfortunes, reviling Gill and Germaine, justifying his own behaviour. Kyria nodded to some acquaintances who came over, were introduced to Martin and joined the party. Later on in the evening others came. Martin hailed them all joyfully, paid for drinks all round, and continued to talk about his sorrows, explaining the situation afresh for the new-comers' benefit. His flow of words seemed inexhaustible. It seemed as though he would never have talked enough. Yet he could not succeed in doing what he wanted to do, in banishing his own sense of guilty uneasiness. Like some poor hag-ridden wretch, he could not by any means escape from his torment. He began to drink as he had not drunk for a long time, not since the end of the war, drinking steadily and continuously in a deliberate attempt to drown his consciousness, still talking, talking meanwhile. The painter, Kyria, encouraged him with eyes softer than velvet. Antonia suggested food, but Martin refused to eat anything. The other members of the party looked on with varying expressions of amusement, apprehension and mockery. It was obvious that there would be an explosion of some sort before long.

Martin was swearing eternal friendship with Kyria. He took hold of the painter's slim, brown hand.

" We will never betray one another," he declared impressively, emotionally.

The other man smiled at him gently and assentingly, a smile of almost Oriental softness and guile. The very softness of the smile irritated Martin, who suddenly became noisy and argumentative. It suddenly seemed to him that the people at the table were in league against him. He looked round and saw a circle of strange, silent faces, staring at him expectantly. The faces expressed nothing but a cold, alert curiosity, rather obscene.

" Why can't you talk, blast you ! " he burst out in a loud voice.

He repeated this two or three times, growing increasingly angry and banging his fist on the table so that the glasses rattled. Attention was now focussed upon him. People in distant parts of the room stood up to see what was happening. The owner of the café appeared and requested Martin to make less noise. He spoke placably enough, but behind him loomed the threatening figure of his nephew who acted as chucker-out, an immense ex-boxer with the traditional broken nose. Martin was furious at this interference. His bewildered eyes gleamed despairingly in his flushed face. He stood up, raised his blurred voice another tone and shouted :

" Noise ! I must have noise ! I've come here on purpose to make a noise. Talk, you fools, talk, all of you ! "

With a sudden wild movement he snatched up all the glasses within reach and hurled them at the electric lights, then dived through the surrounding tables and made for the door, overturning on his way a trolley loaded with several dozen glasses and soda siphons. There was a moment of miniature panic in the café. Several people were sprinkled with fragments of broken glass, and the shattering crash of the breaking glasses mingled with exclamations and shrill, burlesque screams, half thrilled and half frightened. Martin found time to appreciate the uproar he had created as he burst through the circle of outstretched hands which seemed to spring up bodilessly around him. He actually succeeded in getting out on to the pavement before the ex-boxer caught him up and started to pummel him.

The painter Kyria had quietly faded out, all his companions had melted away; only Antonia, looking statuesque in her trailing garments, hurried to the rescue of Martin whose arms the chucker-out was twisting with brutal satisfaction. Followed by the café proprietor, and looking like the personification of an avenging goddess, she sailed up to the grotesquely interlocked figures, cursed the boxer in round terms until he released his victim, sternly reproved the proprietor for encouraging such brutality, handed over the small change remaining in Martin's pockets, together with his address and a promise to pay for the remainder of the damage on the next day. She then extricated Martin from the crowd which had collected round them and took him back to his hotel.

With her assistance he laboriously mounted the stairs. Swaying unsteadily, and supported by the faithful Antonia, he at last reached his bedroom. Firmly clutching a fold of her dress he leaned on the basin and vomited. In the intervals he persistently recapitulated his grievances. Antonia, who concealed a motherly and good-natured heart under her pre-Raphaelite exterior, undressed him and got him to bed. When she had left him he experienced a momentary lucidity. Lying on his bed under the frivolous gaze of the rococo cupids, feeling a little misty but otherwise rational, he realised that he had passed an eventful day. He had taken his wife and his best friend in adultery; he had failed for the first time in his life to appreciate Cézanne; he had babbled his most secret thoughts to a crowd of worthless and unsympathetic strangers; he had got disgracefully drunk and created a rowdy, vulgar scene in a café and been beaten up by a boxer with a broken nose. To-morrow he would certainly feel ill and humiliated: his arms would be painful for days: he would have to pay a sum of money to the café proprietor in compensation for the damage he had done. At the price of these painful alternatives he had evaded the responsibility of serious thought. He fell abruptly into a profound sleep.

12

The Man in the White Box

MATTHEW KAVAN, Assistant Locomotive Superintendent in the employment of the Shan States Railway Company, was out on line. That is to say, he was travelling along at a speed of about thirty-five miles an hour in his own carriage which was attached to the end of the Rangoon train. The carriage was not large, being about the size of the ordinary type of goods wagon to be seen on the English railways. Outside it was painted white with the words " Asst. Loco. Supt." in black letters on the door. Inside, the confined space was divided into three compartments : the kitchen at one end in which his servant travelled and cooked his meals, the cupboard-like central compartment containing a square zinc bath like a large biscuit tin and the lavatory stool, and the so-called " office " in which he was now sitting and in which he slept, worked and ate during the fourteen days out of every month which he was obliged to spend in travelling over his district.

It was five o'clock in the afternoon. At twenty minutes past five the train was due to reach Thazila where the carriage of the assistant locomotive super-intendent would be uncoupled and shunted on to the siding where it was to remain all night. Matthew Kavan detested Thazila, a dirty, tin-pot, poverty stricken little town, sweltering there in the middle of the scorching, interminable plain. There were no British residents and therefore no club, no rest-house, no civilised amenities of any kind. Unfortunately, it happened to be a junction and he was forced to visit it fairly frequently.

He took out his handkerchief and wiped the sweat from his forehead with a gesture that was purely auto-matic. It was a gesture he had made some thousands of times during the three years he had been in the country. The wooden carriage seemed to attract and absorb every possible fraction of heat. Although the sun would soon be setting, it was still unbearably hot in the cramped compartment. Kavan leaned over and pushed up one of the wire screens that covered the

carriage windows.   An immediate gust of dry, burning
air struck him in the face, covering him with gritty
fragments of cinder blown back from the engine ahead.
He shut down the screen with a bang.   The train
panted breathlessly on across the endless, arid, colourless
plain of the Central Shan States.

It was early summer and in England people would be
getting into lighter clothes, thinking about holidays, and
hurrying home from work to play tennis or cricket, or
walk, or lounge out of doors in the long, mellow evenings.   Punts would be out on the river, passing the
bottom of the garden of his mother's house at Rich-
mond ; young fellows in flannels and pretty girls lying
on piled-up cushions.   Pretty girls everywhere, wearing
thin, gay summer dresses : in cars and boats and on the
seashore, in city streets and country lanes, in gardens
and woods and fields, in restaurants and theatres and
shops.   The puritanical Matthew Kavan could not
drive out of his mind the thought of all these fresh young
English maidens with rounded sturdy limbs and bloom-
ing complexions, so different from the shrivelled Anglo-
Indian matrons whom he met at the club.   In a moment
his brain had become a riot of buxom, bare arms and
legs, of hair and dresses disordered by the wind, of
flushed cheeks and soft, inviting mouths.   He contemplated this seductive revue chorus of imaginary beauties
sitting on his hard bunk in the swaying white box-like
carriage, around him a folding table, a chair, a mosquito
net, an oil-lamp with a cracked chimney, and a siphon
of luke-warm soda-water.   His neat, small-featured face
was damp with sweat, his eyes prominent, his mouth
slightly open ; he did not look puritanical now.

He had not seen his wife Anna for two years. During those two years he had remained completely chaste. To the utmost limit of his ability he had striven to keep the thought of women out of his mind. He had refused as far as possible even to think about Anna. But now, in the broiling carriage, on the line between Thazila and Minzi, her image thrust itself upon him. The thought of Anna would not leave the sex-starved man who sat sweating in the moving white box which was his home for fourteen days out of every month. He saw her before him, standing with casual grace—her body always unconsciously assumed most graceful poses—her face smooth and childlike, really the face of a little girl, with smooth, lustrous hair that fell by its own weight into a graceful curve; her eyes blue, with that dreamy, absent look which he had never been able to fathom. He would not think of her eyes as they had been in anger, hard, grey and stony, like her necklace of cold metal beads, steely. He would not remember that she had left him in anger. It was extraordinary that she should have wanted to leave him; that had always been incomprehensible to him; he refused to think about it. He loved her; that was enough: what more could any woman desire? It was impossible that she should not love him in return.

After she had gone he wrote to her in his round, legible handwriting long, rambling, somewhat incoherent letters in which he announced his willingness to let bygones be bygones, and to make a fresh start in the future. In return he received from time to time cool little non-committal notes which he kept carefully in his pocket-book, encircled by an elastic band.

For two years he had lived on by himself, in the heat, in chastity, in loneliness, in discomfort of every kind, complacent, self-righteous, sure of himself, supported by the prospect of a sentimental reunion. Now the prospect of reunion was coming near. In six months his leave would begin. Six months : that was roughly one hundred and eighty days. Only one hundred and eighty more days of this existence : the rattling, stifling journeys in the white box, cramped quarters, inadequate baths standing up in a square tin with a few cupfuls of brownish, gritty water, ill-prepared meals of the eternal curry and rice, tepid drinks, smells of goats' meat cooking in rancid butter, choking smells of smouldering charcoal, of cinders, of oil and axle grease, and unwashed Asiatic humanity ; always the cringing, dishonest *babus* to deal with, the thieving, lying, shifty subordinates and the short-tempered, tyrannical superiors.

The train was slowing down as it approach Thazila. In a moment he would have to get out and give orders about shunting his carriage on to the siding. He would have to start interviewing people ; Eurasians, native drivers, firemen, clerks, sweepers, chuprassies and the fat, indolent, self-important station master. He would have to inspect water supplies and measure up stacks of wood fuel, all in the relentless heat, in the dust and bad smells. Later on it would get dark, and he would sit in his carriage with the oil-lamp heating the stagnant air and the wire screens over the windows to keep out the insects, working at papers which must be ready to go back to his office on the up-train at nine forty-five. At eight o'clock he would have his evening meal. Perhaps he would tell his servant to set up the folding table outside under the tamarinds that grew near the siding. It would be cooler out there, but the crowds of insects would be a tormenting plague, and the pariah dogs would come sneaking round after scraps, snapping and snarling just out of reach of his foot. At nine forty-five the up-train would come in, and he would walk over with a chuprassi carrying his office box, to see the papers safely on board. Perhaps there would be another railway officer on the train and they would have a glass of whisky together before it moved off. Then he would go back in the darkness, stumbling over rails and sleepers and yelping pariahs, back to the lonely, suffocating discomfort of his cramped carriage and the tantalising voluptuous dreams which he hated but could not banish from his uneasy sleep. Another of the one hundred and eighty days would be behind him, wiped out.

The train began to pull up in a series of nerve-shattering jerks. He made a mental note that the Westinghouse brake was being carelessly applied or else was not functioning properly : one more job for him to attend to. The train stopped. In the stationary carriage the air at once became heavier, more oppressive. Kavan stood up in his grubby, crumpled suit of white tropical drill. His damp shirt stuck to his back and made him uncomfortable. He pulled the limp material away from his flesh and put on his battered old topi. Immediately his head became horribly hot and started to throb unpleasantly, the heavy topi felt like an iron weight on his brow.

He opened the carriage door ; heat, dust, noise and odour fell upon him with full force. A chuprassi with a sash and a metal badge was forcing himself through the jostling, shouting crowds towards the white carriage. Matthew Kavan stepped out on to the swarming platform and acknowledged curtly the chuprassi's salaam.

13

Result of Visiting a Bedroom

THE large, quietly luxurious lounge of the Mont Boron Palace Hotel, Nice, was always fairly full after dinner. Now, because the winter season was over and the summer season had not yet begun, there were fewer people than usual : but still, a good number of men and women in evening dress had distributed themselves among the palms and flowering plants and the richly upholstered furniture. A string quartet in one corner was filling the room with subdued, decorous music which served to blend the chattering voices into a harmonious undertone without being loud enough to disturb the bridge players.

Lauretta Bland, a charming, beautifully gowned little lady with cleverly tinted hair, and looking, in a favourable light, not much over forty, pushed back her chair from the green-topped card-table. For once in a way she was quite glad to take her turn as dummy and to leave her partner to play the hand. She was growing tired—not, of course, of bridge itself as a game—but of the particular society and environment in which she had been playing all the evening, and for a great many previous evenings as well. She had spent the whole winter at the Palace Hotel.

Lauretta, who usually found her evening game of bridge so enjoyable, was discontented to-night. The atmosphere of the high-class hotel enveloped her with unostentatious luxury, the soothing music floated through the room, smoothing out into a melodious murmur the voices, the laughter, the susurrant fall of cards, the tinkle of coffee cups and liqueur glasses. The dinner had been excellent, the menu exactly suited to her taste; her new gown was a success, simple and yet sumptuous, with a skilful slimming line that minimised her worrying tendency to a diaphragm bulge: her bridge partner was a man of adequate experience, they were winning from their opponents steadily but not too easily. All through the winter, evenings of this description had satisfied her completely; seated contentedly at the bridge table she had played her reliable game with more cunning than at first appeared, and a delightful vivacity had emanated from her *soignée*, discreetly scented person. But to-night, after the first few hands had been dealt, she had actually become abstractedly silent, beginning to feel flat and bored. She was quite relieved when she could let her attention wander away from the game.

There were certainly fewer people than usual in the lounge. Her wandering gaze missed several familiar faces. The season was over, nearly all the nice people had left the hotel or were leaving in a few days. She herself would have left for England a week ago if her tiresome niece, Anna Kavan, had not just then appeared on the scene. It was like Anna, who always contrived to do something inconvenient and unexpected, to join her aunt just when the latter was preparing to go back home. A petulant expression appeared on Lauretta's delicately rouged and powdered face. It was really too bad the way Anna continually managed to worry her. Ever since she had adopted her dead sister's child the girl had been a perpetual trial. Anna had always been independent, self-willed and unsatisfactory; quite lacking in sense of duty or natural affection. There was something abnormally cold and hard about her, she was neither girlish, nor dutiful, nor loving, nor amenable, nor any of the things which Lauretta would have liked her to be. And her conduct since her marriage had been dubious and eccentric, to say the least of it.

Frowning querulously, Lauretta Bland thought about her niece's scandalous and incomprehensible behaviour. Other people had girls who married well, were happy and affectionate and obliging, a credit and a comfort to their relations. But how did Anna behave? She ran away from her husband, who was a perfectly nice fellow, to live with some flashy-looking girl whom no one knew anything about. There they were, the two of them, leading heaven knows what sort of a shady existence in London, ignoring their families, and paying no attention whatever to convention or decent feeling. Next Anna persuaded her aunt to advance the money which was to start the shop in Beauchamp Place. Then, just when Lauretta was beginning to hope that the girl was getting some idea of stability and serious conduct, she threw the whole thing up, abandoned the business without a penny to show for her aunt's original capital, and came to join Lauretta in Nice without waiting for an invitation or even troubling to announce her arrival.

Lauretta tapped the toe of her satin slipper peevishly against the leg of the bridge-table, so that her partner looked up from the cards and asked if she disapproved of his method of playing the hand. She smiled and told him " No." The petulant frown returned to her face as soon as he looked away. Really, it was insufferable of Anna to plant herself here, unasked, detaining her in Nice when she was eager to get back to her house in the Chilterns. The garden at home would be at its best now. She did not in the least want to take Anna back with her : the girl was nothing but a nuisance in the house, loitering about unsociably by herself and refusing to fit in anywhere. Yet she could not very well leave her alone in a town like Nice.

She sighed, and looked crossly round the room. Where was Anna now ? One would think that having upset all her aunt's plans she would at least attempt to behave agreeably and becomingly. But no, without troubling to consult Lauretta's wishes or convenience, she was always going off on her own, talking, most likely, to that wretched little Jew boy with whom she had struck up an acquaintance. As she thought of Adrien Bloch, quite the most undesirable person in the hotel, Lauretta's indignation became so strong that it forced her on to her feet. Speaking some words of apology or explanation to her companions, she left the table and walked quickly across the lounge.

In the drawing-room she discovered Madame Bloch, the mother of the unfortunate Adrien. Her son, a boy of nineteen, had just done his term of military service and had been sent home to her seriously ill with congestion of the lungs. She had brought him to Nice to recuperate, and he and Anna, almost the only young people in the hotel, had quickly become friends. Stout and mild looking, the Jewish lady sat reading in a corner of the quiet drawing-room. She raised her large dark eyes to Lauretta, placatory and rather surprised. Looking tranquil, heavy and somehow archaic beside the vivid, modish, angry Lauretta, she replied pacifically to all her questions. Her son had been feeling tired, his head ached, and she had sent him to bed. Yes, Anna had come later to ask her where Adrien was. She had told her, and the girl had gone upstairs to say good night. Possibly she was reading to him in bed. All the other woman's scandalised indignation proved ineffectual against the Jewess's static, unassertive serenity.

Lauretta left Madame Bloch in disgust and took the lift to the third floor. She walked along the thickly carpeted corridor. The light of battle illuminated her; her small, dainty feet in their satin slippers flashed in and out of her skirts and planted themselves with warlike determination. In her clear pink and white face her bright eyes darted hither and thither with birdlike fierceness.

She rapped on the door of the young man's room. He was in bed. His dark hair on the pillow, his thin neck rising from the open collar of his pyjamas looked immature and pathetic. He turned big, apprehensive, shadowed eyes on the pugnacious Lauretta who ignored him completely. Anna, sitting on the edge of the bed, regarded with composure the fashionable, outraged figure of her aunt who, standing in the doorway, said in a cold and threatening tone:

"Please come with me, Anna. I want to speak to you."

The girl rose at once, gave her hand to Adrien, who clasped it eagerly in his thin fingers, and followed Lauretta from the room. The two of them walked down the long, warm corridor in perfect silence. Reaching her own room, Lauretta shepherded her niece inside and shut the door.

"Really, I don't know what to say to you," she began at once, in a sharp, malicious voice. "You seem to be utterly devoid of any idea of decency."

Anna stared at her and said quietly:

"I don't understand you. What are you talking about?"

Lauretta Bland looked at her and saw that her eyes had turned grey and distant and that a sort of film had come over her face, making her look oddly fixed and unreal; almost doll-like. The older woman remembered the same look on her niece's face when she had scolded her as a child. It was as if the girl let down a protective shutter between herself and distasteful reality and, safely removed behind it, became invulnerable. Lauretta found it exasperating.

"I'm talking about your shameless conduct," she said, sharply accusing; "spending the evening in the bedroom of a strange young man. The whole hotel will be gossiping about you. We shall have to leave the place now."

Lauretta suddenly saw a chance of using the situation for her own ends, but this, far from mollifying her, made her feel more vindictive. She glanced at her niece with real hatred in her bright bird's eyes.

" You make a mistake if you think I'm going to allow this sort of behaviour while you are with me. If you want to associate with decent people you must behave decently yourself. Otherwise, you would do better to go back to your Bohemian friends in London."

" I'm not a child any longer. You've no right to talk to me like this," said Anna in a low tone. She looked steadily but remotely at her aunt and added : " If you don't want me I can go away again. I came to you because I had no one else to go to."

" I suppose even that Howard girl couldn't endure you and turned you out in the end," Lauretta exclaimed, her voice shrill with anger and an uncontrollable, triumphant malice.

" I can go away. I ought not to have come to you. I'm sorry : I made a stupid mistake," said Anna, still in the low tone that sounded distant and stubborn.

Lauretta had worked herself into a little frenzy of bad temper, malice and righteous indignation. All her long-repressed grievances now began to take the air.

" How can I have you living in my house, never knowing from one moment to the next when you're going to shock everybody ! " she exclaimed. " How can I introduce you to respectable people ! "

Anna stood with that queer indescribable film over her face. The cruel stupidity, the mock-righteousness of the woman : the senseless antagonism : the obscene pleasure in bullying. She would have nothing more to do with her aunt. She would not stand here any longer to be bullied and reviled.

But she did not move. Instead she turned her grey, critical, speculative eyes upon her, eyes that seemed already old with disillusionment, and said quietly, a little hoarsely :

" Where am I to go then ? Back to Matthew Kavan ? The voyage would be expensive, and he is coming home on leave in a few months."

" Matthew Kavan ? " Lauretta repeated. " I only hope he will be willing to take you back again after the way you've treated him and the scandalous way you've been behaving during his absence. You'll have to alter your habits, you know, if you want anyone to put up with you. You'll never find anyone willing to live with you as you are now."

Anna turned in silence, almost stunned, away from the angry woman. The spate of harsh words bewildered her, paralysed her mind. She went to her own room and opened the shutters. A light, fresh wind was blowing up from the sea. The nocturnal world was like the interior of a black bowl upon which an irregular pattern of stars had been splashed in luminous paint : the bright constellations pricking the black sky above, the warmer lights of Nice strewn on the darkness below. For a time this dark, impersonal, star-sewn world consoled her. She felt a gentle melancholy that was without pain. But soon the image of Lauretta Bland rose again to destroy her peace. The small, sharp, darting gestures, the wounding offensiveness of her words. It was as if the air around her were filled with cruel, bird-like sounds and movements. She had done wrong to come to her aunt; she must leave her as soon as possible. But where was she to go ? What was to become of her ? The responsibility of directing her own life seemed to weigh too heavily upon her. She felt sad,

uncertain, lost.   Was it perhaps true that no one would
put up with her ?   She had an instantaneous vision of
herself, a critical, detached, unlovable egoist, avoided
by everyone.   Well then, she must remain alone.   But
she did not want to be quite alone.   She suddenly felt
frightened of her own isolation.

Meanwhile, Lauretta, changing her dinner dress for
an orchid-coloured negligée, once more looked bright,
contented and altogether charming.   Draping the becoming folds of the wrap about her figure she hummed
a gay little tune.   She had scored a victory over Anna
and at the same time thought of a way of disposing of
her niece without herself appearing heartless or neglect-
ful.   Very soon now she would be back in her English
home ; and she would not have to endure the presence
of that troublesome girl, either.   She smiled approvingly
in the mirror at her reflected face with its delicate make-up
and artfully dyed hair.

PART II

Partners

WILLIAM LEWISON was on his way to pay a
visit to his partner, Mr. David Fairbrother,
who was seriously ill in his house in Bennett
Street, St. James's. As he turned the corner from Piccadilly by the side of the Ritz, William tried to reckon
up Fairbrother's age. The old boy must be getting
on for eighty. It was a good many years since he had
taken any active part in the affairs of the Cray River
Development Trust (Canada), but although he was
only a sleeping partner he had always maintained an
alert interest in the business. Recently he had had a
stroke and was failing; it was doubtful whether he
would last much longer.

Walking briskly along in the pleasant sunshine, the
spruce, vigorous William reflected on the declining
powers of his associates. Old Fairbrother, the monu-
mental, almost legendary figure of business integrity,
was rapidly sinking, the lawyer Quested was looking
worn and ill, several others were drifting into sickness
and old age. Soon he, William, would be the only
one left of the original group of business men to which
he belonged. Younger men, men like his other partner,
Byrne, who did not really belong to their epoch at all,
would be taking the place of his familiar acquaintances.

But William Lewison was not going to be superseded just yet. True, he had often toyed with the idea of retiring, but when he saw how the old brigade were all giving way, being pushed into obsolescence, a stubborn arrogance took possession of him. He would put these modern upstarts in their places. Not one of them had the thorough-going, conscientious application of the old-fashioned school; no, nor the cunning, either, he thought with a smirk. He could be modern enough when it suited him; modern enough to take advantage of all the newfangled ideas, at the same time preserving what was serviceable in the old. He had kept himself pliable, adaptable, without losing his sense of proportion. With cool unbiased judgment he would decide when it was most profitable to fight the moderns with their own weapons, when to resort to older methods of warfare. "There's plenty of life in the old dog yet," he thought, lightly stroking the ends of his moustache with an upward movement of his bent forefinger in its spotless wash-leather glove.

In Fairbrother's house he was shown into a little sitting-room on the ground floor. The narrow, anti-quated house was always half dark inside, even on sunny days. The walls of the room were covered with old steel engravings, part of Fairbrother's collection of portraits of dead and gone business men, famous indus-trialists and pioneers of commerce and finance. The old man's sister came in, managing and important, and conducted William upstairs.

He found Fairbrother on a couch with a plaid rug over his legs; the skin of his face looked a dirty yellow against his patriarchal white hair and beard. William

Lewison talked sympathetically in his pleasant, soft voice, assuming his charming, simple manner for the benefit of the invalid and trying not to look too complacent or too robust. All the same, it gave him a pleasant feeling of superiority to be sitting there, alert, well dressed, full of mental and physical vigour, while his aged partner lay on the couch exhausted and played out. The poor old chap was breaking up fast; he hardly looked as if he would last through the summer.

William sat up straight in his chair and talked away with sympathetic optimism. In his elegant attire, slenderly yet wirily built, he smiled under his neat moustache, and gazed patronisingly at the sick man out of black, dissembling eyes. He was surprised when Fairbrother interrupted his sickroom chatter with the remark :

"I hear that boy Martin of yours has been getting into difficulties."

William crossed his legs. Checked in his flow of sympathy, he looked at the other more critically. There appeared to him to have been something almost impudent in the old man's last remark.

"A little domestic trouble," he answered lightly. "It will probably mean a divorce : we are all convinced that it will be for the best in the end."

"Very disagreeable for you," said David Fairbrother, gazing at William with eyes whose whites had the same dirty yellow tinge as his skin.

This time there was no mistaking the insolence of his tone. William felt angry, then pityingly contemptuous. Of course, the man's brain was affected; he wasn't responsible for what he was saying.

" The suit will not be defended," he said smoothly. " There will be no publicity at all."

Soon after, he took leave of his partner and stepped out into the sunshine feeling pleased with himself and his visit. It had done him good to feel his superiority to the rambling, broken Fairbrother whom he had once held in reverence. Now the poor old fellow was a complete wreck—even his brain had gone.

Suddenly he observed a familiar figure coming down Bennett Street towards him. Could it be, yes it certainly was Hubert Byrne, his other partner ; no one else had such long thin legs under such a protuberant stomach. The two men met in the middle of the pavement and exchanged greetings. Yes, Byrne was just going to call in on poor old Fairbrother, who, he had heard, had taken a turn for the worse. The suave, elegant William studied this badly proportioned Canadian of forty-five with his sallow, clean-shaven, longish face that had two deep creases running from nostril to jawbone, giving the effect of a bloodhound's dewlaps, his big, ugly belly, his spindly legs. He listened attentively to his partner's dry, plausible, discreet tones. He was wondering whether he ought to trust the man so implicitly, whether he was making a mistake in leaving England for a few weeks as he intended to do. Was Byrne completely trustworthy ? This private visit of his to David Fairbrother looked rather odd. Impatiently he thrust such thoughts out of his mind. He was being absurdly over-suspicious. It was just nerves ; he needed a holiday to set him up. Surely a man could call to enquire after an invalid without arousing his partner's suspicions. Byrne had never given him the slightest grounds for mistrust : on the contrary, he had always shown himself as utterly reliable, circumspect and prudent, lacking rather in enterprise. William, priding himself on his grasp of psychology, felt convinced that Byrne lacked the initiative necessary for disloyalty.

" So you're off to France soon," the other was saying. " Lucky man ; how I envy you."

" It's mostly on Martin's account," William responded. " It will do him good to have a complete change of environment just now. Things have been difficult for him."

" I shall be surprised if you stay away long," Byrne said. " You don't trust any of us to look after things in your absence, do you ? I believe you think we're all a lot of incompetent muddlers who can't get along without you." He laughed his dry, rustling laugh, adding : " And upon my soul, I do believe we shall feel lost while you're out of the country."

" How dare you flatter me in that shameless way ! " said William, chuckling.

He walked on cheerfully, his confidence quite restored. Byrne's words were not the words of a man premeditating a breach of trust. It would be sheer stupidity to suspect him.

Meanwhile the sick man lay on his couch weak and excited, filled with thoughts of confused venom. He thought with fury of William Lewison sitting up in his chair, dapper and assured, patronising him. The conceit of it, condescending to him just because he was ill and his head was not as clear as it had been !

His sister, the domineering, fussy old woman, came

in to announce disapprovingly that another visitor had
called. She did not want to admit Hubert Byrne to
the sickroom ; but Fairbrother, who knew why he had
come, insisted upon seeing him.

2

A Wrist-Watch Lover

A VERY low, new, rakish-looking grey coupé with an
abnormally long bonnet was nosing its way through the
afternoon traffic of Knightsbridge. Young Tony
Quested, who was alone in the car, insinuated its elon-
gated nose between other vehicles, sent it shooting
forward at the first gleam of the green lights, and forced
it past every obstacle, giving a display of brilliant and
somewhat dangerous driving that was by no means
appreciated by the other drivers on the congested road.
Darting forward in the first instant of release from a
traffic block, he swung the long grey snout of the car
into Sloane Street, slid smoothly through a comparatively open space, and pulled up with a spectacular
curve in front of a confectioner's shop.

Inside the shop, behind a window full of wedding
cakes, *petits fours* and expensive chocolates, Gwenda
Lewison was sitting at a little green table finishing a
muscat water ice. Dressed in creamy yellow, her dark,
glossy hair showing under the fashionable small hat
which she wore on the side of her head, she looked
striking and artificial, like a yellow orchid in a florist's
vase that is perfect in itself but without the beauty of
naturalness. Her small, pale face with its enquiring

nose was carefully made up according to the last fashion of the moment, her eyes were enhanced by artificial lashes half an inch long. But in spite of this sophisticated exterior she was nervous and over-wrought, fumbled with the clasp of her bag when she paid for the ice, and gave an extravagantly large tip.

As soon as Tony Quested appeared in the doorway she jumped up and went over to him. Her face lighted up and became more natural beneath its subtle mask of powder and paint. They went out together to look at the new car. Gwenda stood on the pavement admiring it ; she had not seen it before. A vague disquietude stirred in her as she remembered that she had provided most of the money with which Tony had purchased the long grey monster. The car had cost a good deal and she had been left with a serious overdraft at her bank. It would be awkward if her father discovered the overdraft and asked inconvenient questions. Fortunately he hardly ever enquired into her financial affairs. She banished the uneasiness from her mind and smiled appreciatively. It was certainly one of the smartest cars on the road.

" Get in," said Tony, opening the door for her.

" Good heavens ! What do you steer by—the stars ? " she exclaimed laughingly, settling herself in the low seat. Visibility had been sacrificed to the rakish build of the car, the windscreen was phenomenally narrow and afforded only a restricted view of the road.

He, too, laughed gaily, flattered because she was impressed, and eager to show off his brilliance as a driver. Entering some quiet residential streets where the police supervision was less stringent, he proceeded to display his powers, leaving behind him a trail of indignant and vituperative persons upon whom he bestowed compensation in the form of an airily waved hand. Gwenda Lewison sat beside him admiringly, happy simply to be near him. She was completely under the spell of the dashing, empty-headed young man.

Tony Quested owned a tiny flat in Ethelbert Place, a quiet, tree-bordered cul-de-sac in South Kensington. Several of the old-fashioned, two-storied houses had been let off as flats but no attempt had been made to convert or modernise them. The street had a quiet, pleasant, neglected air and was difficult to find. As they climbed the rather steep stairs to the second floor Gwenda wondered, as she had often wondered before, where Tony got the money to pay the rent of the flat. It was far from clear to her how he managed to indulge his expensive tastes on the moderate allowance made to him by his father. The lawyer did not even know of the existence of the flat in Ethelbert Place. Tony kept it as a secret base from which he carried on his active, slightly mysterious private life.

The young man was in a gay, triumphant mood, pleased with the car, pleased with Gwenda's obvious admiration. With youthful arrogance he praised her appearance, showing a connoisseur's appreciation of dress. He himself looked smart and debonair with a sea-green tussore silk tie and a shirt of exactly the same shade. The room was pretty and comfortable, even a touch of luxury was afforded by a spray of speckled lilies in a fine alabaster vase. " How in the world does he do it ? " thought Gwenda. " Where does the money come from ? " Jealousy pricked her happiness with its spiteful point, a hundred vaguely suspicious circumstances flocked into her mind : was he being supported by other women ?

With relief she allowed all these doubts to melt away when he took her into his arms. She felt that she had been waiting for him for a long time, and enjoyed his embraces feverishly and with rapture. When his mouth touched hers she forgot how elusive and unsatisfactory her lover was.

She lay beside him on the wide divan, comforted and satisfied, glancing at him through the heavy silken fringe of her artificial eyelashes. He smiled back at her, relaxed and friendly, a bit impish, smelling faintly of chestnut blossom. Why couldn't he always be like this, she thought, contentedly intimate beside her ? " Stop thinking," she told herself. " Enjoy the moment for what it is." She forced her mind into quiescence, and suddenly felt sleepy. Her thoughts grew pleasantly confused. Tony's arm pressed against her shoulders uncomfortably, but she did not move. Stray words and sentences from her novel floated before her. She had been working at the book in a desultory way for eighteen months or more. When the externals of her life were favourable she wrote well and fluently ; when things went against her the manuscript was neglected. Just now it was going fairly well. She closed her eyes, feeling again in imagination Tony's caresses. If only she need not go away to France, just now, when she was getting on so well with him. She hated the thought of leaving him behind in London while she was away. What would he be up to in her absence ? With whom would he be sharing the secret of the little flat in Ethelbert Place? His face hovered before her closed eyes, smiling, impertinent and strangely empty. Was it, perhaps, a trifle vicious as well?

Opening her eyes again she saw his real face close beside her. It was a young, pleasant face with delicately formed, rather pointed ears which gave it a faunish look. There he lay, breathing gently and exhaling a faint fragrance of chestnut flowers, his eyes clear and without guile. It seemed absurd to accuse such a being of viciousness. She raised her hand to caress his fair, ruffled hair. At exactly the same moment he also moved and looked at his wrist-watch to see the time.

Because she was sensitive and unsure of herself Gwenda was humiliated by the gesture. Her sense of inferiority made her feel angry with him. She felt cheapened and betrayed, and all at once was in one of those passions of raging, impotent, wounded pride to which his slighting behaviour frequently stirred her. She gave herself to him, she surrendered herself passionately to him, and five minutes afterwards he was looking at the time, scarcely bothering to conceal his boredom. She jumped up furiously, flinging off the hand which he stretched out lazily to detain her, and went into the bathroom to dress.

While she put on her clothes her heart raged against Tony. Doubtless he was laughing to himself, thinking how he had scored over her, that he could treat her as badly as he liked, and that still, like a tame dog, she would come running to him whenever he chose to whistle. His conceit was beyond all bounds. She was risking a good deal for his sake. Her father disapproved of Tony and would be furious if he were to learn of her liaison. She was always afraid of being seen about town with the young man. Not that there was much danger of that, she thought bitterly. He had too many other private interests to spend much time with her. Any woman with a trace of personal pride would cut herself adrift from such an off-hand and insolent lover. She suddenly decided to break with him, to walk out of the flat and never see him again. But at the same time she knew that she could not do so. Tony was in her blood.

Re-painting her face with rapid, mechanical skill she heard him moving about in the next room. He was dressed and smoking a cigarette at the window when she went in. Without turning round he called her to come and see how well the car looked from above. Instead of answering him, she stood at the door, pulling on her gloves, and said :

" Good-bye, Tony. I'm going now."

" Right. That suits me exactly. I'm going back to the West End myself. Where shall I drop you ? " he said, careless and irrepressible, as he turned to face her.

" Don't bother about me." The girl tried to make her voice sound matter-of-fact. " I'll take a taxi."

" Why so up-stage ? " he said, smiling, and making a move to accompany her out of the flat.

Gwenda stopped him, repeated her good-bye with stiff lips, and closed the door firmly behind her. This time he made no attempt to follow or detain her. He moved his feet in an intricate dance pattern and carelessly called out " Good-bye ! " Then he went back to the window, watched her emerge from the house, walk to the corner of Ethelbert Place and vanish from view.

When she was out of sight he went downstairs himself, started the car and drove off with his usual verve,
whistling quietly all the time. As he drove he thought
casually of the girl who had just left him. He knew he
had offended her and was quite unmoved by the fact.
Gwenda was quite amusing to sleep with, but on the
whole he was bored by her. He liked to be always
pursuing new women, savouring the long-drawn,
reluctant yielding of a fresh quarry to his irresistible
charms. This girl had fallen like a ripe fruit into his
hand : she was always ready and waiting for him, ready
for his bed or for anything he liked to propose, always
following him about adoringly. She was the wrong
age, too, he reflected; twenty-seven was neither old
enough nor young enough to suit his taste : it was
neither one thing nor the other. She was not exciting.
He took a cigarette from the gadget on the dashboard
which also presented a match automatically, and lighted
it with one hand. He had to remind himself that
Gwenda was useful. She had plenty of money and no
objection to spending it. It was obviously politic to
remain on good terms with her. Some day he might
even find it expedient to marry her. He smiled over
the wheel as he thought how such a marriage would
enrage old William Lewison. His own father, too,
would be very astonished. How aghast the two old
boys would be if they knew of the intrigue that was
going on under their noses.

Pulling up at a flower shop he ordered a bunch of
yellow roses to be sent anonymously to Miss Gwenda
Lewison. She would know well enough where they
came from.

3

The Invisible Umbrella

AFTER the quiet magnificence of the Mont Boron Palace Hotel, Nice, the Bellevue Hotel at Bandol-sur-Mer seemed primitive with its bare, carpetless stairs and corridors, its dining-room overcrowded with tables, its one small sitting-room filled with stiff, uncomfortable pieces of furniture. Lauretta Bland, acutely aware of the contrast, felt a slight qualm. Was Anna making comparisons, too, and mentally stigmatising her meanness? Lauretta was particularly susceptible to the reproach of meanness.

She felt a little uneasy in her conscience; but she would not admit that she might have acted differently. No, no, she could not condone or overlook Anna's disgraceful behaviour, she could not take the girl back to England, into her own home. That was asking too much; Anna had no right to expect that of her. So she had arranged for her niece to stop here, at the Bellevue Hotel, Bandol, with Mary Graham, an old friend of her own who happened to be staying there. The thought of Mary Graham had come to Lauretta like an inspiration; how fortunate it was that she had kept her address. She did not know Miss Graham very well, and what she did know of her she despised. The woman was an elderly spinster, rather foolish, rather good natured, impressionable, sentimental, and very full of admiration for the wealth and charm of her friend whom she rarely saw. Miss Graham would be perfectly willing to keep an eye upon Anna while she stayed at the Bellevue.

To her aunt's surprise and relief, Anna herself agreed indifferently to the arrangement. Lauretta felt that everything had been satisfactorily settled, for the time being, at any rate. If the hotel was rather poor and uncomfortable it was only what Anna deserved. It would do the girl no harm to live simply for a while : she had been unappreciative enough of the luxury with which she had been surrounded at Nice.

Anna went into her new bedroom and looked round. It was quite small, quite clean, and bare, almost stark. With its plain green-washed walls, its floor of polished tiles, its austere, narrow bed, it reminded her of a convent cell. On the whole she was pleased with it. This austerity suited her better than the stereotyped luxurious-ness of an expensive hotel. She felt vaguely that it was symbolic. Without troubling to understand her own thought, she had a hazy idea that her life was to be like the small room, quiet and solitary.

When Lauretta had gone Anna went for a long walk by herself. She walked through the little town, past the few shops and cafés, along the quay where the gaily painted rowing-boats rocked gently on the deep-green, glass-clear water, past the ugly casino, and on to a long, dusty, winding road that skirted the sea. The road was disagreeable for walking ; cars and lorries kept flying along it, raising clouds of dust and honking dis-tractingly ; in places it was so narrow that pedestrians were forced into the ditch every time a car came past. Still Anna plodded on, not walking fast, but moving with determination through the hot afternoon sunshine. She was making for a certain point, for a small peninsula that jutted out, always just ahead of her, into the dazzling sea. She wanted to sit down somewhere, absolutely alone, far from everybody, and think. And for some reason it seemed to her that the peninsula was the only place where she would be able to do this. The peninsula had become her goal : in spite of heat, dust and the noisy traffic she progressed steadily towards it, obstinate and unthinking, with regular and unhurried steps.

At last she was able to turn off the main road. She had reached the peninsula. With a sense of relief and relaxation she followed the stony track that ran through pinewoods and open spaces fragrant with rosemary, always within sight and sound of the sea. At first there were a few villas scattered among the trees : she passed them and came to an aromatic solitude of thyme and rosemary and clumps of wind-contorted pines. It was peaceful, sweet-scented and beautiful, the sunshine poured over everything in a warm flood. Anna observed the beauty, smelt the fragrance, and felt the sun warm on her face and on her bare arms. Nevertheless, she was divided from these things. An obscure mental distress separated her from the enjoyment of peace and beauty. She felt as though she were carrying about with her an invisible umbrella which isolated her in a small circle of shade. The sunshine lay bright and golden on the breast of the world : but wherever she moved the circle of shadow accompanied her ; she was the centre of that circle and could not come out into the sunshine.

Just as she had trudged along the main road, as if travelling towards an allotted objective oblivious of the dust and the traffic, so she now walked steadily onwards,

making for the extremity of the point. Her feet rose
and fell to the accompaniment of a schoolroom phrase :
" A peninsula is a piece of land nearly surrounded by
water." The words fitted themselves to her footsteps,
kept time with her pace, and repeated themselves in her
head, which felt light and empty of sensible thought.
" A peninsula is a piece of land . . ."

Suddenly she came to a standstill. As the movement of her feet was arrested, the foolish words which
had repeated themselves so many times over died out
of her brain as if she had never known them. She had
come to the end of the peninsula, to an open space at
the top of a rocky cliff. A small desert of an open space,
with bushes and many stones, sun-soaked and lost and
a bit desolate, as if stranded there in the blue, between
the sky and the blue sea. The sky seemed to have
come close, and the sea muttered below, and the bit of
waste ground in the middle hung there forsaken, between
the two. It was not a very high cliff.

She went to the edge and looked down. Isolated in
her circle of invisible shade, she stood on the very brink.
Below, not really far down, swung the slow, heavy,
blue-green bulk of the sea. The sun shone warmly,
and Anna stood on the edge of the cliff, looking at the
light glittering in a swarm of dazzling points on the
nearer water, and the horizon gleaming blue in the
distance, and the green-banded depths, and the dark
places where the water flowed thinly over the rocks.
It seemed to be watchful, it seemed to be waiting for
her, to catch her in the trap of its ponderous, muttering
jaws.

Anna sighed and stirred uneasily in the warm sun.

Why had she come to this place? Thinking of her long walk she almost felt that she had been drawn here. She sat down on a rock and thought of the night of her twenty-fifth birthday when she had resolved to take control of her life. Certainly since then she had made an attempt to decide things, to take responsibility for herself. And where had the attempt led her? Apparently to a piece of waste land jutting into the Mediterranean, to loneliness and a haunting circle of gloom through which she could not break.

She thought of all the people she had known, of Lauretta and Catherine, Sir Edward and Matthew Kavan; even of the boy Adrien Bloch who had liked her and pressed her hand. She had never made contact with a single one of them. Not one of them had ever really meant anything to her. She had been right to cut herself off from them. But what remained, then, in her life? She received a few pounds a week from her aunt, a small allowance also from Kavan : that, of course, would cease when she finally broke with him as she fully intended to do. She had never been taught any profession, she had no outstanding proficiency in any special direction. At school she had had that fatal sort of facility, brilliance almost, that succeeds without effort or satisfaction and never seems to lead anywhere. She did not consider herself beautiful. With her smooth, bright hair, her rounded, dreamy, somewhat childlike face, her abstracted equanimity, her distant, cool, critical glances, she seemed frightening and indifferent, frightening people away. This appeared to be what she wanted subconsciously; to frighten people away from her.

But all the same she felt that she was a failure. Her life so far had consisted of twenty-five years of procrastination and incapacity. She had never really been able to adjust herself to life, to get herself going, as it were. It seemed so incomprehensible : she was a person who might have done almost anything. And she had done nothing at all. She did not want to do anything. She felt herself empty, like an empty vase. At the very middle of her being something essential seemed to be lacking.

What was this thing that she lacked ? The will to succeed, perhaps. Or something more vital even than that, something without which life became really meaningless, mad, a sort of lunatic game which one played against oneself. It almost seemed to her that she willed her own destruction, willed life to go against her. She seemed deliberately to seek out situations, to set in motion trains of events which in the end would lead inevitably to her downfall. She refused absolutely to compromise with the world. If life would not come her way, let it go. She would rather die than make any compromise. At this point she began to think of a book she had read recently. It was by a German writer named Feuchtwanger and contained a passage referring to the habits of ibexes which, rather than adapt themselves or submit to human influence, rushed up to the tops of mountains and stood poised there, motionless, in the deathly cold, not even condescending to move when their ears became frost-bitten. Smiling a little bitterly, she wondered if she were not following the example set by the ibex. But at least the ibex, presumably, was actuated by some powerful impulse, some heroic spark of haughty exclusiveness which drove it to such extremes of self-detriment. Whereas she, lacking any specific conviction, seemed to be behaving like the ibex simply out of social and moral inadequacy : which was merely stupid.

So Anna pondered, vaguely and gloomily, sitting on the sunlit cliff. She thought of her future, and the thought frightened her. She looked down at the vast, primordial bulk of the sea, and that, too, caused her a pang of fear. It was so massive and cold, so destructive, so opposed to humanity. The water was clear, jewel-clear and brilliant, of a wonderful sapphire colour ; the rocks were like pools of wine under the glaze of the water ; and there were translucent patches of pure emerald. She got up and looked at the great cold mass of the sea. She felt its fascination, its cold magic. It was so heavy looking, portentous, with its rhythm of slow-heaving waves, and the white foam, corpse-like, floating at the feet of the rocks, and the rocks themselves, so dark, iron-dark, like red-black iron.

She leaned forward over the edge of the cliff and looked down at the water beneath. A few stones, dislodged, bounded away, down to the rocks below. The sound of their impact was lost in the noise of the sea. There it was, the huge, hulking body of water, cold, and the foam clots like naked, drowned bodies among the dark, glistening rocks at the foot of the cliff. She stared and stared at the sea, in a queer daze.

Suddenly there was a noise above the noise of the waves, the sound of someone walking quickly over the stones and the rough ground behind her. Anna looked round and saw a large young man quite near

133

her and rapidly coming closer. She had been so sunk in herself that the sudden return to reality gave her a painful shock. Like a somnambulist who has been too abruptly awakened, she started violently and almost lost her balance as the loose stones moved under her feet. The young man grasped her arm to steady her, and drew her away from the edge. He was well dressed, and had a full, tanned face that seemed vaguely familiar to her.

"I thought you were going to fall over the cliff," he said in a pleasant, rather drawling voice. "I'm sorry I startled you."

Anna stood quite close to him, almost leaning against him, as if she needed his support, her face rather pale, more upset than the occasion appeared to warrant. The fact that she half recognised the young man increased the confusion of her mind. She had that disconcerting sense that the whole incident had taken place before somewhere; perhaps only in a dream.

"You're all right, aren't you?" he asked. "There's nothing wrong, is there?" He gazed at her in some perplexity, frowning a little. "Perhaps you don't understand English?" he added in a more anxious tone.

"Oh, yes. I am English," said Anna, pulling herself together. She stood up straight, pushed back a strand of hair that was blowing across her cheek, and smiled at the stranger.

"You frightened me because you appeared so suddenly," she explained to him. "I thought I was miles away from anyone. In fact I came here to be quite alone."

"Then I'm sorry I disturbed you," he said. "But really you shouldn't stand so near the edge of the cliff

during your meditations. If you happen to be interrupted again I'm sure you'll fall over." He looked at
her confidentially, cocking his eye at her, rather winning.

Anna had to smile at him again.

" It's not very high. I shouldn't have been killed
if I had fallen over," she said, glancing down once more
as she spoke. The rocks looked ugly and grim with
the water sucking at them. It was suddenly incomprehensible to her why she had stopped so long on the
cliff edge. The spell of the sea was exorcised. She
now wanted to get away from it as quickly as possible.

" You'd certainly have broken an arm or a leg," he
remarked ; " and heaven knows how long it would
have been before you were picked up. Very few people
come round this point."

" What are you doing here, if one may be permitted
to enquire ? " Anna asked. She began to feel animated,
almost gay ; the invisible umbrella had floated off into
the empty air.

" Oh, I was making drawings ; looking for something to paint," he replied off-handedly.

She now observed that he carried a sketch-book
under his left arm.

" So you're an artist," she said. " Are you well
known ? Have I seen you before ? Perhaps I've seen
photographs of you. I seemed to recognise your face
when you first appeared."

" I'm afraid my face isn't yet familiar to the public,"
he answered, smiling. " Perhaps you're mistaking me
for a cricket professional or a film star. My name is
Martin Lewison, by the way. I don't flatter myself to
the extent of imagining you may have heard it."

No, she could not recall it; but the conviction that she had seen him somewhere persisted all the same.

"My name is Anna Kavan," she said, after a pause.

They were now walking away from the extremity of the headland, the noise of the sea had sunk to a subdued grumbling. Across the blue water, the little town of Bandol lay palely strewn along the shore, in the slanting rays of the setting sun. It looked a long way off: the blue curve of the bay was in between. At the nearer end of the town, the opposite end to the Bellevue, was the large white mass of the hotel where he told her that he was staying, the best hotel in the place.

"I shall have to walk faster than this," she said, "or I shall never get back before dark."

"Let me drive you," he offered at once. "I've got the car just near here, and I'm going back to Bandol myself now."

"A car . . . near here?" she said, in surprise.

"Yes. There's a road of sorts up the middle of the peninsula. You followed the track by the sea, I expect, and didn't notice it."

They passed through some trees and came to more level ground. Sure enough, there stood a big dark blue Sunbeam, looking towny and out of place in so wild a setting.

"Better come back with me," he said. "It's a long walk, and you must have had enough solitude for the moment." He smiled again, so that his face looked boyish. He opened the door of the car and stood waiting.

She looked at him, noting his massive torse, a little too heavy for the lower part of his body, his strong, ugly hands. He hesitated a moment, then climbed into the driving seat and started the engine. She stood there uncertainly.

"I think I'll walk back," she said. And added, smiling : "I've always been told not to accept lifts from strangers."

"Perfectly right," he replied. "All the same, you'll probably pay for keeping to the path of virtue by getting a blistered heel or something disagreeable of that sort." He took off the hand-brake and the car glided forward a few inches.

"I hope you're wearing comfortable shoes," he said. And as she laughed, he added : "I've always understood that the path of virtue was a hard and stony one ; now I see it for myself. I think you'd better abandon it." He beamed at her with his friendly, slightly teasing eyes.

"Well, it really would be nicer to drive," said she, stepping on to the running-board.

"Much nicer and much more sensible," he replied amiably, as she sat down beside him and the car slowly started off over the rough road.

4

No Gentleman

GERMAINE LEWISON stood at the bus stop in King's Road waiting for the number 19 bus which would take her to Piccadilly Circus. She had an appointment to meet Gerald Gill at the Café Royal at nine o'clock. It was a warm, cloudy evening, the air felt moist and

enervating. Standing under a lamp and against a
darkened shop window she saw herself as if in a black
mirror, her body fashionably and becomingly clothed,
her face carefully and rather heavily made-up under the
smart little hat. She had taken particular pains with
her appearance and had dressed herself in the clothes
which she considered most likely to meet with Gerald's
approval.

A 19 bus came in sight. She got in and sat down
in the nearest vacant seat. It was so long since she had
been under the necessity of travelling in buses and tube
trains that she felt slightly self-conscious in the public
vehicle. As she handed her fare to the conductor, it
seemed to her that the man must be wondering why
she had not taken a taxi. She took her ticket from him
mechanically, and began to consider the coming interview. She would have to be tactful, she must keep
herself well under control. Although Gill had behaved
abominably, leaving her in Paris without a word and
consistently avoiding her when she followed him to
London, it would not do to reproach him. If the
divorce went through, as it seemed certain to do, was
not Gill her last hope? She must not antagonise him
with accusations or demands, but on the other hand
she must be careful not to display too much affection
or he would construe that into an assertion on her part
of a claim upon him. Her face looked worried under
its coating of rouge and powder, and less self-possessed
than usual: the pupils of her small bright eyes contracted to black pin-points.

If only Gerald were not so intractable, so terribly
difficult to deal with. He was so utterly devoid of

decent feeling, too ; not like an ordinary respectable man who could be shamed into marrying her. For that was what it came to : Gerald had somehow or other got to be shamed, bullied or cajoled into marrying her as soon as she was free. The problem was to decide which method to employ. Her troubled preoccupation increased to such an extent that one or two passengers glanced curiously at the smartly dressed woman who sat there frowning into space and twisting her ticket in her gloved fingers.

Had she done the right thing in following him to England, in telephoning to him repeatedly and refusing to be put off until he had agreed to meet her ? Sitting there in the bus, she felt almost ill with uncertainty. Her easy life with Martin had softened her, she was out of condition for struggling with a harsh and unsympathetic world. She had been so long accustomed to having everything her own way. Now she was suddenly faced with the necessity of wresting something vital to her very existence from a brutal, unwilling, and incalculable man. Earlier in her life the prospect would not have daunted her ; but now she felt herself unequal to such a contest. It was too bad that she, who had already worked hard to achieve financial stability, should have to begin all over again. It was going to be a damned unpleasant business, dealing with Gerald. How was she to tackle him ? How could one extract marriage from a man who acknowledged no obligations ? She felt that her whole future depended on the result of this interview ; it was like entering for an examination which she knew was beyond her powers.

She might have reflected that the situation was entirely

due to her own misconduct and carelessness. That was
certainly true. But who could have imagined that the
casual, indolent, unsuspicious Martin would find out her
infidelity, and, having discovered it, would actually
insist upon a divorce? It was not Martin's normal
behaviour. No, she could not have been so mistaken
in her estimate of his character. It was the old man
behind him, the father, who had egged him on and been
responsible for the whole thing. William Lewison
had always loathed her as a daughter-in-law and been
determined to get rid of her. Germaine's anger flared
up against William Lewison. It even appeared to her
that by his machinations he had driven her into Gerald's
arms in order to free his own son.

The bus stopped at the Piccadilly Hotel; she got
out and made her way quickly up the little side alley and
across Regent Street. The café was already crowded,
the air was full of noise, smoke and the smell of food.
At first she saw no sign of Gerald. The crowded,
noisy, smoky room impinged violently upon her senses,
making her feel dazed for a moment. Supposing he
did not keep the appointment he had made so reluctantly? Then she caught sight of him. He was wearing
his old greasy, spotted clothes, and sitting on one of the
red velvet seats near the wall, talking to another man
whom she did not know. He did not rise when he saw
her, but ducked his head and studied her out of his deep-
set, distrustful eyes as she sat down at the table. Then
he muttered some introduction and continued his
conversation with the other man, ignoring Germaine
completely. She saw at once that things were going
to be even more difficult than she had feared. Quickly

becoming angry at Gerald's rudeness, she repressed a desire to force his attention by speaking loudly and indignantly, and ordered herself a glass of brandy.

Reluctantly she felt the attraction of which she was always conscious in Gerald's proximity. As she sipped her brandy, her sharp eyes noted with a rush of emotion that was half disgust a huge tear near the neck of his shirt, the collar of which was practically torn away. On his jacket she recognised the same dirty marks that she had longed to remove in Paris. Of course, he hadn't shaved for two or three days. What on earth was it that drew her to the man? He was dirty, amoral, boorish and uncouth. Yet she had been swept off her feet by him. She sat beside him on the red seat and smelt the odours of sweat, beer and tobacco that emanated from his person. Suddenly she felt revolted; the whole café seemed crammed, like a rag and bone shop, with soiled, evil-smelling masculine garments. She fought back her rising hysteria and ordered another brandy.

Gerald and his friend were still involved in their discussion, drivelling on about the foundation of æsthetics. Possibly such things really were important to him. He had nothing more serious to think about. He was fortunate, he could afford to play with his ingenious theories, which, after all, were only so many childish games of make-believe when compared with the realities of existence. Why did she sit here, meekly listening to this puerile chatter instead of forcing the brute to attend to her? Here was she, her whole future at stake, and he insulted her by talking a lot of incomprehensible nonsense to some chance acquaintance whom he had picked up, or who, more likely, was simply sponging on him for a few drinks. He was keeping the man here in order not to be left alone with her. Did he think he could get away with such a transparent ruse? She was not going to be put off so easily.

She opened her bag and looked at her face in the mirror. Her cheeks were shiny and red, inflamed by the brandy and the hot air of the room. She applied a coating of powder, but still her face looked puffy and overheated. It was the last straw. She was insulted and injured and now she also found that she was looking ugly. Losing control of herself, she suddenly exclaimed in a loud and emphatic voice: " I want to speak to you alone, Gerald." Turning to the stranger, she looked him full in the face and added distinctly: " Please go away."

Astonished by the angry voice with the pronounced foreign accent, the man hastily departed. To Germaine's surprise Gerald did not protest. She looked at him nervously, feeling that she had taken the first false step. How was he going to react? From his scowling face with its strange eyes she could learn nothing. She felt an hysterical desire to scream, to throw things about and to abuse him in filthy language. The big, disreputable man beside her finally opened his thin lips and said:

" Listen, my good woman. For some time you've been pestering me to meet you. Now that we have met, kindly tell me as quickly as possible what it is you want."

Germaine knew that Gerald was completely without consideration, but the cold insolence of his tone came as a shock to her and shocked her into silence. She looked at the tall man sitting there with his morose, indifferent, arrogant air, and reflected hopelessly that she was dependent upon his mercy. She could not think how to approach him, and in her uncertainty retorted angrily:

"You ought to be ashamed of speaking to me like that."

Gerald was looking critically at Germaine. The desire for her had not yet revived in him; she represented nothing but the cause of the breach between him and his best friend. He saw her red, round face with its small, shrewish eyes, the face of a scolding peasant housewife. He felt no interest whatever in her, and he felt no obligation towards her because they had slept together in the same bed. If this red-faced peasant woman had got herself into a hole, why should he be expected to pull her out?

After a moment he said uncompromisingly, in a cold, flat voice:

"I suppose you want to talk about the divorce. I have nothing to say about it. Only, you must understand, it is quite useless to expect any assistance from me or to depend on me in any way. Martin, I presume, is making you an adequate allowance for the present."

Germaine's narrow eyes glared at the man beside her, filled with inexpressible fury, resentment and humiliation. Scarlet, outraged and almost speechless, she managed to exclaim:

"Then you don't mean to marry me in the end?"

"Certainly not," retorted Gerald Gill. "Nothing would be more repugnant to me."

" You vile, unspeakable cad ! " Germaine burst out, jumping up from her seat. " I might have known you wouldn't behave like a gentleman. You've never done a decent action in your life." Obscene phrases of the lowest description rose to her lips, sentences which she had heard years before in her father's café during some workmen's brawl. She checked herself abruptly and turned her back on him.

Although she knew she was behaving stupidly and throwing away her last chance of success, she turned away from him and walked out of the café. Gerald watched her till she was through the door, and then went on drinking his beer.

Germaine hurried out in rage and despair. It had started to rain, the pavements were greasy with a thin blackish slime. She longed for a taxi : but no, she must save every penny now, as much as possible of Martin's allowance must be saved up for the grim future. Trembling with fury, feverish and nearly in tears, she waited for the bus that would take her back the long, wearisome journey to the Oakley Street boarding-house where she was living. She was furious with herself because she had not handled Gerald more tactfully and exploited him to some practical end, an immediate gift of money at least. But she was still more furious with Gerald with his cold, indecent, insulting brutality. Yet she could not help admitting that she was wounded, cruelly hurt and humiliated by the callous way in which he had repudiated her.

5

Some Nocturnal Activities

THE elderly spinster Miss Mary Graham was undressing for the night in her tidy, bare little bedroom on the second floor of the Hotel Bellevue. Her room faced south and was slightly larger and slightly more expensive than that occupied by Anna Kavan which was on the floor below and had a window at the back of the building. Miss Graham's window commanded a highly decorative view of the harbour with a whole flotilla of brightly painted rowing boats moored in the foreground : but at present the shutters were closed lest some late fisherman should catch a glimpse of her chaste preparations for bed.

Miss Graham, busy and harmless as a cheerful, insignificant sparrow, flitted briskly about among the pieces of cheap furniture which scantily garnished the hotel bedroom. On a glass shelf over the wash-basin stood a jar filled with wild red tulips which she had bought that day from a market stall. On the night-table beside her bed was a small, faded photograph of her mother in a frame of beaten silver, a well-used prayer book bound in imitation vellum, a tooth-glass half full of water, and an orange which she had saved from the dinner-time dessert and intended to eat in the morning.

As she plaited her hair into a thin pepper and salt pigtail she reflected how glad she was to be able to be of some service to her brilliant friend Lauretta Bland whom she had admired at a distance for many years.

145

She was delighted at the opportunity of chaperoning Lauretta's niece. Moreover, it was really a pleasure to her to have the girl as a companion. Anna seemed quiet and unexacting, she did not always want to be racing about on expeditions as some young people did, she did not interfere in any way with the placid monotony of the maiden lady's routine. Neither perspicacious nor inquisitive, Miss Graham accepted Anna at her face value, and rejoiced that the girl was content to get up late in the morning, to sit about quietly in the sun and to go for long, solitary rambles on the slopes of the hills.

Tying the end of her pigtail with a narrow ribbon that had once ornamented a chocolate-box, Miss Graham switched off the light and then threw open the shutters. Sure enough, there were two fishermen in a boat just opposite the hotel, one of them rowing slowly while the other stood up with the long-pronged implement for spearing the fish, near the bright light fixed in the front of the boat. Safe in the concealing darkness, she stood at the window for a minute, watching the slow-moving boat with the dazzling light reflected in the black water, the statuesque silhouette of the man with the spear, outlined in the hunter's immemorial pose. The languid plosh, plosh, of the oars reached her at long, measured intervals. Whole archives of ancient Mediterranean civilisation were embodied in the simple chiaroscuro scene. Miss Graham stood there watching, not without appreciation. She was always careful to make a note of beauty when she saw it. Then she took off her dressing-gown and got into bed. She lay with her white cotton nightdress drawn well down

over her bony knees. Soon she was fast asleep, breathing evenly and peacefully and occasionally snoring
a little.

While Miss Graham was watching the fishermen,
Anna Kavan was also standing at her bedroom window
which overlooked, instead of the picturesque harbour,
a narrow, unfrequented road which ran round the back
of the hotel. Anna had not begun to undress. On
the contrary, she had combed her smooth hair and re-
powdered her face as if in preparation for some further
activity. Presently she heard footsteps approaching,
and Martin Lewison appeared in the deserted road.
He stood in the light from her window and smiled up
at her. She had arranged to go out with him that
evening. Turning off the light, she let herself down
from her window to the flat roof of a store-room below.
The hotel was built on sloping ground and it was an
easy drop from the roof of the store-room on to the
dusty roadway.

" Clever girl," he said happily, as they walked off
together. " In your place I should have left the light
burning. And then if anyone had happened to be
looking out they couldn't have failed to see us.

" What about Suzy's at Toulon ? " he suggested.

Anna cheerfully agreed ; it was a modest little *dancing*
they had visited before.

The car was waiting at the end of the lane. Martin
drove skilfully and rather too fast. His broad shoulders
looked tremendously massive in the darkness ; he was
in good form, talkative and stimulated. Anna had
already been out with him at night several times and
had also met him during her long daytime walks, but,

preoccupied with her personal problems, she had not been acutely aware of him. To-night she was much more conscious of his personality and willing to listen to his voluble theorising.

Bravery, he propounded, as he drove the car along the winding coast road, bravery generally indicated that there was something lacking in the individual who displayed it. He himself was displaying recklessness, which, of course, was a variation of bravery, in his relations with Anna. It was essential that his name should not be connected with any woman while his divorce was going through. The slightest suggestion of impropriety on his part and the King's Proctor might intervene to prevent the decree from being made absolute.

Anna replied that she was surprised, then, that he had deliberately sought her company, since the divorce was obviously important to him.

Martin glanced sideways at her. The reason was that he was a fool, he said coolly, taking a sharp bend too quickly. He was one of the fools who got a kick out of danger. He was the sort of man who whilst flying a fast 'plane would say to himself, " Oh well, I've got to die some day, so what does it matter if I run a few risks now ? " and would then proceed to give a display of bravery by doing all sorts of foolhardy stunts in the air.

In the small glow of light from the dashboard his hands on the steering-wheel showed strong, thick and somewhat simian with their ugly, sensitive fingers. In his faintly illuminated profile the nose was finely curved and impressive with clean-cut, delicate nostrils ; he had

148

the profile of a later Roman emperor with his big nose, his heavy, fleshy chin, his full, sensual lips that formed a perfectly shaped Cupid's bow.

"I don't mind admitting I'm a fool," he remarked in his pleasant and rather mocking voice. "Nobody really minds owning to the stupidity of bravery. One can at least get some fun out of the heroic attitude. So I've no objection to telling you that these outings are very stupid from my point of view. A flashy exhibition of heroism or bravado, whichever you like to call it; a sentimental playing with fire. But my behaviour seems at any rate more defensible than philosophical bravery. I've no patience with the philosopher who loses a fortune and stoically maintains that it's unimportant since he still has a roof over his head and enough food to eat. The philosopher's bravery is worse than mere stupidity; it's a joyless evasion. He's simply using a false argument to blind himself to disagreeable realities. He's trying to make life tolerable to himself by camouflaging the intolerable. I'm an evasionist myself, so I've got a specially deep contempt for evasion. But at least I'll see that I get some amusement out of my sophistry. Let's make an agreement, Anna, to condone one another's evasions and have a good time together."

They had supper at Suzy's bar : *foie gras* sandwiches and a sweetish champagne *nature*. The place was packed with naval officers and their partners ; the door stood wide open and the air came in with a faint salty tang of the sea.

Afterwards they danced on the crowded floor. Martin did not expend much energy, but slid his feet lazily, scarcely troubling to move round the room. He smiled down at Anna, and looked rather like a chubby, precocious schoolboy.

"Don't you like me at all?" he asked. "You don't tell me anything about yourself."

She explained her resolution to direct the course of her life. To Martin all this cerebration sounded academic, false and somewhat infantile. The idea that one could control one's fate by being self-conscious about it struck him as a comic superstition, for self-consciousness alone was merely restricting.

"Of course it's true that you can't control your activities without being conscious of them," he said, "but you've got to have an extremely analytical brain before the consciousness will be of any use to you."

This was the sort of conversation that went on between Martin Lewison and Anna Kavan in Suzy's *dancing* at Toulon. The girl felt more alive than she had done for months, amused and flattered by his attentions, and stimulated in her mind by his half-frivolous theorising. It was three o'clock in the morning before they got back to Bandol.

"You do like me a little, then, don't you?" he asked in a whisper as he was helping her up to the store-room roof and so back to her room.

"Very much," she answered sleepily from the window-sill, looking down at him with drowsy approval.

6

Hubert Byrne goes out for the Evening

WITH William Lewison out of England, Byrne felt
jubilant. Things were arranging themselves according
to his wishes, and William, that wily old bird, was going
to walk neatly into his snare. In a few days the transaction with David Fairbrother would be completed,
Fairbrother would have sold out his interest in the
company, and he, Byrne, would have acquired Fairbrother's shares, thus achieving a controlling interest in
the business over Lewison's head. He smiled quietly
to himself as he thought how simple the trap had been
to lay and how accommodatingly William had stepped
into it. It was fortunate that the agreement which
prohibited any one of the three partners from buying
shares in excess of those held by the other two had
contained this one loophole. The wording of the
agreement referred explicitly to the buying of shares
from outside sources : there was no mention of a pro-
hibition with regard to transactions between the parties
themselves. Fairbrother, the old dodderer, had given
no trouble at all. It was a real bit of luck that he had
been nursing a secret grievance against Lewison all
these years. He had been only too glad to fall in with
Byrne's plan, there was no danger in it for him, for the
agreement referred explicitly to the buying and not the
selling of shares ; and once he was out of the partnership, who would be likely to attack the aged man on
his bed of sickness ? How furious William would be
when he came back to find Byrne in possession of

majority shares. With only a third interest left he would be obliged to resign the chairmanship.

It had needed a lot of manœuvring. Conferences with lawyers, secret confabulations with Fairbrother in his dark old Bennett Street house. Plotting here, planning there, deciding just what risks might be taken. The Canadian was sailing a bit near the wind, and had no intention of being caught out on a charge of fraud. Sharp practice was well enough, but anything which might legally be termed swindling must be carefully avoided. And all this had to be got through at top speed, before William reappeared on the scene. Once back in London, the old boy would be certain to smell a rat ; it would be impossible, even with the utmost secrecy, to conceal from him what was afoot. Byrne had been working against time and had nearly run himself off his thin legs in the warm weather. He had lost five pounds in weight. But now he had got everything in train, there was nothing more to worry about. Unless something utterly unforeseen were to occur, he would pull it off. He was in command ; the great Lewison would have to take a back seat in future.

At seven o'clock in the evening in the St. John's Wood flat where he lived alone with an elderly housekeeper, Byrne suddenly decided to stand himself a good dinner. He would have a celebration, a night out. He had certainly earned it. He smiled, his long jowl creased into heavier folds as he took up the telephone. An amusing idea had occurred to him : he would have a chat with the son or the legal adviser of the man he was outwitting. It would be both entertaining and instructive, and he would be able to make sure that nothing was suspected. Which should he visit, the son or the lawyer? Finally he made appointments with both Quested and Cedric Lewison. He put on his hat, buttoned his coat over his prominent stomach and went out to dinner at Simpson's.

About two hours later he was in a taxi, driving towards the club where the lawyer spent most of his evenings. Byrne had dined well, in leisurely fashion, on the dishes that pleased him, large, thick, juicy portions of underdone meat accompanied by strongly-spiced sauces and a pint of excellent red wine, followed by ripe Stilton cheese. Feeling well fed and complacent, he entered the impressive, dingy old building.

The smoking-room of the club was even more old-fashioned and dim than Fairbrother's dark little parlour. As he opened the door Byrne looked in that antiquated setting like a Dickens character drawn by Cruikshank with his long, sedate, bloodhound's jowl, his pendulous belly and his long black, spindly legs. He looked round; it was a few moments before he could recognise any of the comatose figures in the big chairs. The members of the club were digesting their dinners, drinking coffee in small white cups or brandy in huge bell-shaped glasses, and smoking imposing cigars. Many of them held evening papers in front of their faces.

Yes, there was the man he wanted to see, Mr. Anthony Quested of Laurence Poulteney Hill, solicitor. As he sat down beside him, Byrne was wondering how the lawyer would react to the discovery of William's discomfiture. Old Quested was close, devilish close and secretive, but Byrne had a shrewd suspicion that his

heart would not break at the humbling of his school
friend's pride. Queer, when one thought of it, how
Lewison managed to put everyone's back up. He
looked so charming and smooth with his smile and his
simple manner, as though butter wouldn't melt in his
mouth : and yet every one of his so-called friends
cherished a secret hope of his confusion.

Byrne's spirits rose. He looked at the man beside
him. Quested with his neat white death's head of a
face obviously suspected nothing whatever. In his
prim, legal fashion he was cordial to his guest, and
insisted that he should drink a glass of the club's special
old brandy. He himself, alas, on account of his dyspep-
sia was forbidden to touch the stuff. The two men
talked amicably in their low, discreet, pedantic voices,
smiled occasionally a brief, unrevealing smile, drank,
one his brandy, one his coffee, and sat stiffly in the vast,
shabby, comfortable chairs amidst the hideous early
Victorian furnishings of the room.

To Byrne, Anthony Quested, though reassuring, was
rather a bore. He was out of date really, a back number. But that was all to Byrne's advantage. There
was nothing to fear from him. What an old dug-out
the fellow was, though. He would really have preferred dealing with someone nearer his own measure
even if it meant taking increased risks. He was overcome by contempt, a bored sense of drowsiness. It
wasn't worth while talking to Quested. The evening
was falling flat. All at once he excused himself, said
good night, and walked out of the room, carrying his
stomach before him.

A short stroll brought him to the Garret Club where

he had agreed to meet Cedric Lewison. The Garret was a small, quite respectable artistic, literary, and theatrical club. Most of the members belonged to one of those three professions. Martin Lewison had joined the club but hardly ever visited it. He had got Cedric, who had slight artistic leanings, elected to membership, and Cedric was frequently to be seen there, refreshing himself in an atmosphere of mild Bohemianism after a day spent among business men.

Although it was early the small club room was full and several couples were dancing. Byrne joined Cedric Lewison and his wife and sat down. As he tasted a tankard of the nut-brown ale for which the club was celebrated, he began to feel pleased with himself again. Keeping one eye on the dancers he drank and with precise jocularity supported Jean Lewison who was arguing against her husband that women were safer drivers than men. He spoke confidentially to Cedric and congratulated him on a new line of advertising he had just put out. Cedric was friendly and responsive. As he talked to him, Byrne had a return of the contemptuous feeling which the lawyer's unsuspecting attitude had aroused. Looking into the dark eyes which were so like William's and yet so lacked William's vigorous astuteness, he reflected that the son was not a patch on the father.

Suddenly, as if he had spotted a new quarry, he asked, watching the dancers:

" Who is that young man ? I seem to know him by sight."

An elegant youth had just danced past them with intricate, professional-looking steps, and a pleasant, curiously empty face.

155

" That's Tony Quested," said Cedric. " I wonder who his latest conquest is."

" He's dancing with Nancy Mallalieu, that girl who's always having her photograph in the *Tatler*," Jean Lewison said. " I simply can't understand what those society girls see in him. He's not specially attractive and he hasn't an idea in his head."

" Is he the son of Quested the lawyer ? " asked Byrne.

" Yes," said Cedric. " He's in partnership with the old man now, but I don't believe he ever does a stroke of work. One never even sees him in the office."

Byrne was intrigued by the thought that this dashing, perfectly dressed creature with the beautiful society girl in his arms was actually the son of the old fogey whom he had left half asleep in his chair in the club smoking-room. The dance ended in a faint outburst of clapping. They talked of different things.

" Do you know him well ? " Byrne asked later.

" Who ? " asked Cedric.

" This young Quested."

" No," replied Cedric. " Jean doesn't like the chap, do you, Jean ? "

Nevertheless, when the young man presently crossed the room on his way to the bar, Cedric stopped him and introduced him to Byrne.

" A bright lad, isn't he ? " said Cedric Lewison, when Tony, after a few casual remarks, had left them with a smile on his young, impertinent face.

" Is he going already ? " asked Byrne, watching across the room the conspicuous fair-headed youngster assisting his partner into her wrap.

" Yes," grinned Cedric. " We're too dull and quiet

for him at the Garret. He only puts in a short time here on his way to the Carolina Club. I expect he's off there now. He dances there most nights, I believe."

Byrne went on talking to Jean Lewison. He kept his good temper and was amusing in a restrained, sardonic style. On his way home to St. John's Wood he continued to feel pleased with himself. He made a resolve to enquire about the membership regulations of the Carolina Club and possibly to join it himself. He decided to keep an eye on young Tony Quested and strike up an acquaintance with him. He had had it in mind for some time.

7

Tribulations of a Chauffeur

THE chauffeur George West could not sleep. Night after night he lay awake in his room which faced the railway embankment at the back of the Bandol hotel, and listened to the trains passing at intervals. Just round the curve of the embankment, only a hundred yards or so from the hotel, was an enormous viaduct, and George West had grown skilful in distinguishing the different types of train by the noise they made in crossing the viaduct. The goods trains crossed the bridge with a long drawn out rumble that seemed to re-echo interminably round the encircling hills, the expresses panted breathlessly across, their long-snouted Mallet engines hissing impatiently and emitting sharply truncated staccato whistles as they came to the bridge, the local trains fussed, rattled and clanked their way over, whistling lengthily and importantly on a falling cadence.

George had lived most of his life in London just off the noisy Euston Road, and it was not the noise of the trains that kept him awake. In point of fact, he was rather glad to hear them as he lay there in the dark; they gave him a sense of companionship, assuring him that he was not the only wakeful creature in the black world; he knew approximately the times when they were due to pass, and waited for them expectantly. For the expresses, particularly, he had a friendly feeling, because some of them were going right back to the northern coast, to Calais, to link up with boats which in turn would link up with English trains, and thus formed a sort of link with Winny his wife whom he had left at home.

George West was homesick. He had never been out of England before, he had never left Winny for more than two nights at a time since they had been married. He had hated leaving her now with no one to help with the children and all the worry and weariness of this new pregnancy upon her. But when William Lewison had told him to drive the car down to the south of France he had had no option but to obey. George was not unreasonable; he saw that William could not be expected to forgo his foreign holiday because his chauffeur's wife had become pregnant, and he felt no resentment against his employer. But in the night his nostalgia became overwhelming. If only Winny could be there, lying beside him with her arms round him: that, and that alone, he felt, would send him to sleep again.

158

A mosquito buzzed inquisitively up to his face and he struck out at it in the darkness. No matter how carefully he searched the room before going to bed one of those annoying insects always seemed to be hidden there, tormenting him with its irritating whine as soon as he turned out the light. Now there would be no rest for him till he had tracked it down and killed it. He switched on the light and got out of bed. Standing there in his cheap cotton pyjamas he surveyed the room without catching sight of the mosquito. The heavily patterned wall-paper made an effective hiding place. He picked up a towel and flapped it fiercely once or twice, slapping it against the wall.

Suddenly he sat down on the bed. His pyjamas had shrunk from their many washings so that the arms and legs were too short for him, and this combined with his brown, puckered face and rumpled hair to give him the appearance of an unhappy small boy. Still holding the towel in his hand he sat there and stared frowningly into space. What on earth was the matter with him, getting all worked up like this over a mosquito? Why the hell was he so miserable? Any other young chap would jump at the opportunity of seeing the world and earning good money at the same time, yet here was he mooning about as if he were attending his own funeral, and worrying himself to death over Winny instead of having a bit of fun while he had the chance. Hang Winny, for once. She must look after herself, like other women. He was going cuckoo, worrying about her like this; soon he would be completely off his rocker if he didn't look out.

The trouble, he told himself, was that he didn't feel

well. The greasy Provençal food didn't agree with him, he had no stomach for it, nor for the rough, blackish wine that was served with his meals and tasted to him like vinegar. A pint of beer, now; that would do him a world of good. But the beer they sold in the cafés was poor stuff, insipid and very expensive.

No, he wasn't feeling well, he said to himself, rubbing his forehead with the back of his lean brown hand. This not being able to sleep was getting him down. His eyes felt hot and strained in the daytime, his head often ached abominably, and the queer boring pain over his right eyebrow had become so frequent that he hardly noticed it any more. There were times, though, when it became acute and forced itself on his attention; generally when he was driving through one of these crazy French towns where the drivers made no proper signals but raced about like demons and lunatics, honking all the while and jamming on their brakes.

The chauffeur George West who had driven cars automatically since he was twelve years old, who knew the big Sunbeam as he knew his own body, now had sudden spasms of nervousness when he was at the wheel. He had never really got used to driving on the right side of the road, for one thing. And he was beginning to be haunted by a very disturbing, quite irrational fear: he was afraid of running over a child. He could not remember when the dread had first entered his mind nor whether there was any real cause for it. The French children did not play in the roads or behave more recklessly than English children; if anything, they seemed to have more road sense than the kids at home. Yet he was becoming obsessed by the fear, his brief hours of sleep were made horrible by dreams in which crowds of small creatures, no bigger than dolls, rushed out just in front of him as he drove, and were mown down by the wheels of the car.

He rubbed his eyes impatiently and looked round the room. He really ought to lie down again and made a determined effort to get to sleep. But the bed, though he had slept in much more uncomfortable ones in his time, did not please him : it was a wooden bedstead, and George had always slept on an iron one. The un-English bedroom with its curtainless window and lurid wall-paper was hopelessly inhospitable and un-familiar. The recollection of the hundreds of miles of roads over which he had driven and which now lay between him and the English Channel made him feel lost and nostalgic. How stuffy the room was. There wasn't a breath of air though both window and shutters were standing wide open. Of course, the breeze came from the other side of the hotel, from the sea. He suddenly decided to go out into the fresh air for a few minutes ; perhaps then, when he came back, he would be able to sleep. Putting on a pair of trousers and a jacket over his pyjamas he softly opened his bedroom door and let himself out by the back entrance of the hotel.

It was much cooler outside and not very dark. The lights which were left burning all night here and there in the grounds illuminated weirdly the scabrous trunks of palm trees, leaving one side in black obscurity. The stirring palm leaves cast shadows like the pinions of gigantic birds. From force of habit George strolled up to the garage. To his surprise he saw the door wide open, the vacancy yawning behind like the mouth of a deserted cavern. The car was out, then. Martin must have taken it. Neither the old man nor his daughter would be out at this time of night. A flicker of curiosity, faint as the shadow of a dream, as to what Martin could be doing passed through the chauffeur's mind beyond his personal distresses, and was instantly swallowed up. He stood still. The discovery of the empty .garage had disconcerted him. He now felt unable to walk down to the sea as he had originally intended to do, or to go back to his room. In a curious state of indecision he loitered beside the open door of the garage, his hands in his pockets, his frowning face ghastly in the livid light of a solitary electric bulb.

It was not long before he heard the sound of an approaching car, the familiar, unmistakable hum of the Sunbeam engine. Yes, there it came, pursuing the powerful beam of its own headlights, swinging recklessly off the road, taking the sharp turn into the drive with hoarsely screaming tyres, and plunging through the chequered shadow and light like some prehistoric monster charging an enemy.

" He's a bit tight by the look of it," George said to himself, watching with some disapproval. He had no personal objection to dangerous driving, but he disliked seeing the car for which he was responsible treated to such rough handling. " Fine dust-up there'd be if I was to drive like that," he thought. " I'll bet he's strained the chassis, braking on corners and crashing into the kerb."

Instead of driving into the garage Martin overshot the mark slightly and jerked the car to a standstill under the palms. George stepped up to him and looked through the open window.

"If you'll just leave her here I'll put her inside," he said, raising his hand in an automatic salute.

Martin climbed out of the car and stared at him in amazement.

"What the bloody hell are you doing here?" he asked good-humouredly. "Do you know it's nearly four o'clock?"

It was true that he was a bit lit up. The evening had been long and pleasant at Suzy's. The presence of the chauffeur did not surprise him as much as it would have done had he been perfectly sober.

"There's an Indian proverb which says that only fools and liars walk in the moonlight," he went on cheerfully: "I know you're no fool, George, and I hope you're no liar, so you don't seem to fall into either category. But I see there isn't a moon just now," he added, looking up at the sky where a faint pallor of dawn was already perceptible.

"I couldn't sleep," said George, "so I came out to have a walk round." He sounded a trifle sulky, but Martin did not notice.

"Can't sleep—you must be in love." The pleasant jocular voice had more of a drawl than usual.

George West said no more. An infinite gulf seemed now to separate him from this large, friendly, slightly intoxicated man who talked cheerful nonsense about moonlight and being in love. He wished Martin would go away. To think that he had once contemplated confiding his private worries to him! He still saw that Martin Lewison was a good fellow, hardly like one of the employer class, but now he recognised that some other fundamental difference existed between them. Without realising what it was that divided them, he felt the profound division of the flippant, sceptical, volatile mind from the slow, inquiring, serious, idealistic mind.

Martin yawned, and looked with vague compunction at the chauffeur's boyish, troubled face which appeared strangely distorted by changing shadows as the suspended electric bulb oscillated slowly in the sea breeze. He dimly remembered noticing that the young fellow had not been looking up to the mark lately, and a feeling of self-reproach that was half irritation came over him. He was always meaning to have a talk with George, to draw him out a little, and see if he was in any difficulty, but somehow he never actually did so. He was beginning to feel almost conscience-stricken about it. Yet the funny thing was that he really liked the chap and wanted to help him. Why did he keep deferring the conversation?

He yawned again, audibly. This, at any rate, wasn't a suitable occasion for a heart-to-heart talk. At four o'clock in the morning of some other day he might quite likely feel in the mood for it. But just now he was at the point when the stimulating effect of drink was giving way to an overpowering desire for sleep. The dance tunes to which he had listened all the evening repeated themselves drowsily in his head.

"Well, if you'll see to the car I'll be turning in," he said, starting to walk away. "And I advise you to go to bed too. You'll be dead beat to-morrow if you don't get some rest."

When Martin had gone George got into the car. In the driving seat, with the familiar switches and levers around him, he felt more at ease. He was aware of a comfortable sense of familiarity and security which seemed to emanate from the car along with the faint, characteristic smells of petrol, oil and upholstery. It was peaceful. There were no children here, trying to get themselves run over. He switched off the head-lights, stretched his arms over the wheel and rested his head upon them. A pleasant somnolence overcame him. Before his closed eyes floated a variety of pic-tures : himself as a thin, freckled boy, smeared with grease and dirt, following the mechanics about in his uncle's garage and admiring them ; then getting his first job as a chauffeur, dressing up in the new uniform ; then meeting Winny, hearing her cheeky, gay laugh and kissing her for the first time.

Suddenly he started up with a feeling of fright. He had actually been dozing there over the wheel. What was happening to him that he did such queer things, walking about in the foreign darkness and falling asleep in his employer's car when he ought to have locked it up in the garage ? He hastily started the engine and reversed until he was opposite the garage door. But then, instead of driving inside, he put the gear into neutral and sat still with the engine quietly ticking over. He didn't want to leave the car and go back indoors, that was the fact of the matter. Well, why should he ? It was already getting quite light, it would soon be five o'clock.

Making up his mind in a hurry, he straightened up the wheels of the car, switched off the engine and got out. In the pale, watery dawn light he carefully examined the tyres to see if they were wearing unevenly.

" I'll bet he's strained the chassis, swerving round corners like that," he muttered to himself, bending nearly double over the tyres. Presently he stood up again, and taking some string from his pocket started to make a painstaking test to see if the wheels were out of alignment. Two early rising maids whose window overlooked the garages stared with suppressed giggles at the lean, melancholy looking young chauffeur who was working so intently with his measurements and his ball of string.

George West, for his part, toiled on laboriously, obliviously and sadly until he was surprised by a strange illusion. The car seemed to be moving away from him, but this was impossible for the brake was on and he had not started the engine. Yet it was moving faster and faster, and he was pursuing it as though it were his last hope in the world. The chauffeur George West pursued his car through several eternities. It was a good car, he had driven it some thousands of miles, and he knew it as he knew his own body. He did not want to lose it, he did not want to be left behind. But he could not catch up with it as it raced into a horde of little creatures no larger than dolls who vanished under the wheels with a thin, shrill screaming. He was obliged to let the big Sunbeam race out of sight into darkness and to fall into darkness himself.

When the two maids saw George drop down beside his car and his length of string they were thrown into a panic. They shrieked loudly and attracted the attention of the waiter next door who was just getting out of bed. Accompanied by various other members of the staff whom they collected on the way, they went out and surrounded the fallen chauffeur. George West lay motionless in the dust with a stern, reflective expression on his boyish features, and the end of the string still tightly grasped in his hand.

The people came forward to look at him, there was all at once quite a crowd ; besides the hotel employees, some workmen had come in from the road to see what was happening, and a boy on a bicycle followed them. " What's happened to him ? " they asked eagerly. " Is it a faint ? A stroke ? Some kind of a fit ? " Presently the head waiter appeared, dispersed the on-lookers and had George West carried back to his bedroom where water was splashed on his face and head and an ineffectual attempt made to pour brandy into his mouth. None of these measures having any effect, a doctor was sent for and some time later entered the room accompanied by the hotel manager and by William Lewison who had been informed of the accident and appeared looking more exotically elegant than usual in an emerald green silk dressing-gown with small black spots.

The three looked down at the young man lying on the bed. He lay without movement, hardly seeming to breathe. In spite of the water which had plastered his hair to his forehead in sodden wisps and the brandy which had trickled from the corners of his mouth, he still looked palely severe and reflective. The doctor made his examination. He could not say anything definite, but it seemed possible that there was a tumour on the brain or that a small blood-vessel had ruptured there. He spoke of sending him to the hospital at Toulon, but the jolting journey over bad roads contra-indicated this. Finally it was decided that George should be taken to the Bandol doctor's own clinic which was close to the hotel.

Martin was still asleep when the rickety local·ambulance came at ten o'clock and carried the chauffeur away.

8

News of a Death

GWENDA LEWISON was not enjoying herself at Bandol. The neglected manuscript had not even been unpacked from the bottom of her trunk. As she dressed in her large, airy bedroom, a corner room and one of the best in the hotel, she derived no pleasure from the bright morning sunshine or the vista of blue sea which sparkled gaily outside. Instead, she felt stupidly gloomy and depressed; stupidly, because the immediate reason for her depression was such an inadequate one. The previous night in the lounge an elderly French lady with whom she had struck up an acquaintance had offered to tell her fortune with a pack of cards. Gwenda, sceptical and preoccupied, had looked on without much interest till a curious grouping of black cards caught her attention. "News of a death," the Frenchwoman had said, and Gwenda remembered no more of her prognostications. The foolish, sinister phrase, however, stuck obstinately in her head and had haunted her half through the night. In the night hours, all the dormant superstition in her character, which in daylight she would have repudiated indignantly, rose up ominously in grisly forebodings.

"News of a death." Whose death could it be? Not her father's, for she had never seen him in better health than he was at present, cheerful, active and enjoying his holiday. Surely not Martin's or Cedric's. There remained only one person whose death would be a matter of real concern to her. Before her eyes appeared a certain impudent face with a cynical, indifferent smile that would sometimes change to a charming, intimate, impish grin. Tony Quested. The thought of his reckless driving filled her with terror. A dozen times she envisaged the fatal crash, the new car smashed out of its elegant proportions, going up in flames, the body of Tony Quested lifeless, crushed, charred, mutilated, blood matted in the rope-coloured hair. With the morning light these horrible visions faded, she reproached herself for ridiculous superstition; but an aftermath of depression persistently lingered.

Her dressing did not take very long, the three simple garments she wore were soon adjusted: a handkerchief-shaped bodice that left back and shoulders bare, a pair of shorts, and a skirt which wrapped round her waist and fastened with a single large button at the side. Suddenly, as she was painting her face, a change came over her; the worried lines disappeared from her forehead, she smiled and looked all at once five years younger than before. Of course, it was the death of the chauffeur which the cards had foretold. Idiot that she was, not to have thought of it sooner. George West had been lying seriously ill at the little clinic for several days now, and Gwenda had never regarded his illness as anything except a minor annoyance. Now it suddenly became a godsend. She felt more friendly towards George West than she had ever done in her life.

Humming a tune to herself, she went along the corridor to her father's room. But as she reached his door her face clouded again. Gwenda Lewison was very fond of her father. As his only daughter and his youngest child she had been accustomed all her life to be spoiled and petted by the old man, and had spent far more time with him than either of his sons had done. She had grown used to being alone with him and to monopolising his attention. Now she suddenly found that she was to share his company with Martin. It seemed to her that William, in his satisfaction at winning back his son from Germaine, was taking altogether too much notice of him. Gwenda resented this. She admired rather than liked Martin, and she preferred to admire him from a distance. It now appeared likely that he was to become a permanent rival for William's affection. Gwenda was jealous. She definitely wished Martin out of the way.

With her head full of these thoughts she opened the door. At first her father's room seemed to be empty; then she caught sight of the vivid green dressing-gown on the loggia outside the window. William's slender figure reclined on a long chair in the shade, only his ankles and his feet in their thin green leather slippers were exposed to the sun. His face with its dark, gleaming eyes looked the picture of benevolent contentment. It was pleasantly warm on the loggia. Through the deep rose-coloured arches the indigo sea glittered and ruffled itself in the light breeze. William greeted his daughter, offered her a cigarette from a box beside him, took one himself, and lay back with the tortoiseshell holder in his mouth, watching Gwenda approvingly. He was thoroughly enjoying himself, at peace with the world, and the sight of the girl with her brief, provocative dress and her skin tanned by the sun to a warm gold increased his enjoyment. He smiled benignly upon her as they talked.

Gwenda smoked her cigarette and listened to her father's agreeable chatter. She threw in a careless remark now and then, gazed at the sea till her eyes became dazzled, shifted her position and tapped her sandalled foot on the floor. When there was a pause in the conversation she said sharply :

" Do you know, dad, that Martin goes out somewhere nearly every night? I couldn't sleep a few nights ago and went to his room for a book at one o'clock in the morning. He wasn't there. The next night I heard a car at about eleven and looked out. I can see the gate from my balcony and I'm sure it was the Sunbeam driving off; I could see the G.B. on the back distinctly. Last night I heard it again."

Without putting down his cigarette William replied courteously :

" That's very interesting."

Then he got up and asked Gwenda to help him move the chair for the sun was too hot on his ankles. It exasperated her that the old man took her revelation so calmly, and she remained sulkily silent. William took a few puffs at his expensive Egyptian cigarette, while Gwenda threw hers away half smoked. Then, casually and amiably, the father remarked :

"Aren't you going to have your sunbath on the beach this morning?"

As though this were what she had been waiting for, she turned away abruptly and went down to the beach in a bad temper. There were several people there whom she knew, but she avoided them and walked alone to a more deserted spot. Unfastening her skirt, she spread it cloak-wise on the sand and stretched herself upon it, lying in the hot sunshine with tightened lips and an anxious, ill-humoured frown.

Meanwhile, William Lewison continued to recline on the loggia, comfortably arranged, in his light heelless slippers, and with his green dressing-gown with the black spots draped becomingly around him. He intended to rest there for another half-hour before getting dressed. He was thinking of what Gwenda had told him about Martin. As it happened, the news had not come as a surprise to him. Some trivial incident, some trifling series of coincidences, he could not have told what, had led him to suspect that something of the sort was going on. He had deliberately refused to follow up the suspicion, not wishing to disturb the delightful tranquillity of the holiday. It was tiresome of Gwenda to have thrust the matter under his nose like that. Now he would be obliged to pay some attention to it. He sighed, and the peaceful benevolence of his expression was a little disturbed.

There was a knock at the door and Martin came into the room behind him. He had brought up some papers which had just arrived, and handed them to his father. William liked to read the French newspapers, and in London he was often to be seen with *Le Matin* or *Le*

Journal de Paris. He told people that he was interested in French politics : it was a little affectation of his. Now he laid the papers down on the chair at his side and glanced with indecision at Martin.

He felt it incumbent upon him to question his son, or, at any rate, to let him see that he knew of his erratic behaviour. But he did not want to say anything that would upset the serene cordiality of their relations. The old man's lips curved into their winsome and not quite honest smile under his neat moustache as he said by way of preliminary :

" You're not getting into any mischief, I hope, Martin ? "

Without waiting for a reply, he went on :

" I hear rumours of your having become rather a night bird lately. You know me well enough to be sure I don't want to interfere with your liberty in any way or pry into your concerns, but I hope you are remembering that there is a special need for discreet behaviour in your present circumstances." The disingenuous William could not refrain from putting a sardonic emphasis on the last four words of the sentence.

The son, whose look of protective affability had become fixed as a mask from the start of the conversation, smiled unrevealingly and spoke in a careless voice.

" Don't worry," he said. " I shan't forget the King's Proctor."

" Perhaps you think he can't see as far as the Mediterranean," William said jokingly ; " but I shouldn't rely on that. He's probably got a telescope to his eye at this moment."

The meditations of William Lewison were no longer

peaceful after his son's departure. His mind was filled with uneasy doubts concerning Martin. What was the boy really up to ? Had he taken offence at his father's words, or, on the other hand, had he failed to take them seriously ? The secretive young dog dissembled his feelings so thoroughly that one never knew where one was with him, reflected William, half irritably, half fondly.

A knock at the bedroom door interrupted his train of thought. This time a telegram was brought in. He tore open the flimsy blue strip and read the type-written message. Then, with the remnants of his benign repose wiped as if with a sponge from his face, and his dark eyes frowning, he rose from the chair and stood up in the gay dressing-gown which now looked frivolous and out of keeping with his troubled expression. The telegram was from Quested, stating that David Fairbrother was dead and asking William to return to London at once. Its phraseology was like that of all telegrams, impersonal, imperative and abrupt ; there was a mistake in the spelling of Fairbrother's name.

All thoughts of Martin vanished instantaneously from William's brain, which was now occupied by images from his business life. David Fairbrother as he had last seen him, old and failing, with his austere white beard and his yellowish face, then the familiar picture of his own office, then a spider's web representation of the far-flung range of his activities and interests, intricately interwoven, and held together by an elaborate structure of artful, brilliant and sometimes dubious threads. Then there was the question of the telegram

174

itself to perplex him. Why had it been sent by the lawyer, instead, as would have been more natural, by his remaining partner Byrne? All this filled his mind with disquietude, ousting the thought of Martin and his affairs.

Uneasy alarms disturbed the measured rhythm of his heart and made his hands shake as he dressed.

As soon as he was ready he sent off a telegram to the solicitor. He would return to England immediately. "There's something wrong somewhere," he thought, as he wrote out the words on the form. " But perhaps I'm imagining it all," he thought next. He would go back and make sure, anyhow.

9

An Iron Cross equals George West

DR. HENRI RIMBAUD was intensely interested in the case of George West. Although an obscure country doctor, the plump little man with his black hair and bad complexion was really gifted in his profession. Behind him lay the ten years of hard work, of patience and of unremitting conscientious effort which had finally enabled him to open his clinic. The small white building perched on the side of the hill which sloped steeply down to the sea was the high-water mark of achievement in his career. It had been a triumphant moment for him when he installed the chauffeur—by far the most interesting and unusual case which he had treated there—in one of the quiet, cell-like rooms of the clinic.

Now he stood by the narrow bed, his greasy southern skin looking darker than ever by contrast with his white overall, his stethoscope dangling over his chest like part of some Æsculapian insignia, gazing down on the rigid form of the patient. Really a most absorbing case, he reflected, scraping with his forefinger the stubble of beard on his chin which he had not shaved that morning. How interested Professor Duclos of Montpellier would have been. He would have liked to have his old master's opinion. Diagnosis was extremely difficult, but he still inclined to his original theory of a tumour or a slight cerebral hæmorrhage. On the other hand, it was possible that the whole condition was of psychological origin, and in the nature of a flight from reality. It was all excessively obscure.

The doctor scraped away at his chin, making a rasping sound in the silent room, and gazed at the immobile patient who lay like a corpse with half-open eyes. What was going to happen to him, that was the absorbing question; what would the next development be? Would he just linger on in insensibility until his heart gave out? And, if he recovered consciousness, what sort of consciousness would it be: the consciousness of the normal young man, George West, or some dubious shadow state, more or less imbecile? Pre-supposing improvement, what were the chances of another hæmorrhage following almost immediately? Was it justifiable to contemplate the possibility of anything like a permanent recovery?

"Anyhow, he's out of it all now," thought the doctor. "He's not worrying about anything at present."

176

But, as it happened, Dr. Henri Rimbaud was wrong:
George West was not out of it all, and though he was
not worrying about any definite thing, he passed much
of his time in a condition of confused, anxious distress
not far removed from actual worry. True, there were
immense successive periods of oblivion into which he
tumbled as if into a chain of black, smothering lagoons.
But between the deaths, in the indeterminate space-
time between one lagoon and the next, something
afflicting happened, somewhere in the general void
something stirred and trembled painfully towards the
fringe of awareness, and that something was himself.
Just in line with his half-open eyes the iron rail of the
bedstead with its intersecting perpendicular support
formed roughly the shape of a cross, and sometimes it
was a cross, strangely detached from all association,
grotesquely magnified to the dimensions of the universe,
that seemed subjected to some nebulous torment. And
this cross also was George West.

Martin Lewison came to visit the chauffeur and stood,
frowning unhappily, just inside the door. The little
doctor, looking like a grocer's assistant in his none-too-
clean overall, stood beside him and talked volubly and
somewhat incomprehensibly, breathing an odour of
garlic into the visitor's face.

" Don't worry. He can't hear us," he said, as Martin
replied in a lowered voice.

But Martin was not really listening to the doctor's
elucidation of the case. He was staring at the prostrate
George with a feeling of acute, helpless discomfort.
He had watched the rapid emaciation which had taken
place in the patient during these few days, and it was

not the slack concavity of the once firm and hard-looking cheeks, nor the greyish pallor, nor the stiff, immovable limbs which perturbed him so deeply : it was his own sense of guilt. It was ridiculous, but he could not rid himself of the idea that if he had made friends with George West, if he had had a talk with him as he had always intended to do, the chauffeur would have been well at this moment. If he had stayed in the garden talking to him that morning at four o'clock it would have sufficed. George would not be lying there, corpse-like, upon the bed. He knew he was not to blame ; that the blood vessels of George's brain would not burst or remain intact according to the behaviour of Martin Lewison. It was utterly irrational that he should feel guilty. Yet guilty he felt.

Down the steep stairs, taking quick steps, he made for the door of the clinic. This sense of guilt was almost more horrible than the shame he had felt over his treatment of Gerald Gill. He turned the wrong way, and had to be shown out by a nurse. Through an open door he caught sight of a dark little room which seemed to be hewn out of the side of the hill and looked like an *oubliette*.

He hurried out into the sunshine and walked quickly away, inland. Among the olive groves and the orchards of carefully pruned almond-trees he began to think about Anna. If he were to tell her of his guilty feeling it might be exorcised. Really, she seemed to have power to comfort him. He needed her support; a pity he couldn't see more of her. Well, to-morrow, after his father and sister had taken the train back to England, what was to prevent him from seeing as much of her as he liked? He called up a mental picture of the slim, graceful girl. After the deathly immobility at which he had just been looking, she seemed wonderfully vivid and alive. She attracted him strongly: she was dangerously attractive to him. A sudden access of prudence overtook him. Hadn't he been extraordinarily stupid to spend so much time with her? He felt very disturbed, all at once. The wisest thing would be for him to see no more of her at all. Should he, too, go back to England? His father would be pleased if he decided to travel with them. He thought of going to the Wagon Lit agency to reserve a place on the night train.

But he did not go to the agency. Instead, he walked on towards the hill path where he expected to meet Anna.

10

"Dare, I say unto You"

ANNA was travelling towards Toulon where she was to meet Martin Lewison. Immediately after the departure of his father and sister Martin had proposed that he and Anna should go away together for a time, and she had agreed forthwith. As a slight concession to prudence, they had decided to leave Bandol separately and to meet at Toulon. Anna was excited and tense as she had never been in her life. She had dressed herself carefully for the journey, in her most becoming clothes. As she looked out at the sunlit, picturesque landscape her eyes were blue and warmly contented: the numerous delays of the local train did not annoy her. Lauretta Bland and the fatuous Miss Graham, only yesterday so large in her life, were now small and dim; she had not forgotten them nor had she decided to flout them; they had simply become unimportant. She had written two short letters, one to her aunt, one to Mary Graham: the wording of these two communications was practically identical and stated briefly and politely that she had got tired of Bandol and had decided to travel about for a while. With the sealing of the two envelopes she laid aside the thought of her past life as if it were a winter coat of which she had no present need.

When Martin had first suggested the plan she had felt uneasy at the risk he would run, and had started to argue against him. It would be a serious matter for him if the escapade were discovered: she was astonished that he should run into danger so lightheartedly. With smiling airiness he had quoted to her: "Dare, I say unto you, my children; dare and dare again." In spite of his previous sardonic perorations on the subject of bravery, she was filled with admiration for his attitude and with real affection for him. The Nietzschean quotation repeated itself with high-sounding *éclat* in her brain. She herself was all eagerness to dare everything.

But, after all, she thought, she wasn't daring a very great deal. What in the world can a person like Anna, who doesn't seem to belong anywhere, really risk, whatever she does? She thought of herself as she felt wherever she went, always slightly left out of things, like a foreigner who doesn't quite grasp the subtler significance of what is going on; a foreigner everywhere. She always seemed out of her element; as much among the Bohemians and intellectuals as with the conventional people. A bit of an outsider. There was a little droning song she often sang to herself, and she sang it now, under her breath, sitting in the slow local train. It was in German, and the words, coming from heaven knows where, seemed to epitomise the feeling of isolation. " A stranger I came to your town, I left it a stranger still."

The first hope of an anchorage which she had ever glimpsed in these seas of strangeness was her friendship with Martin Lewison. Something about the big, smiling, amiable man with his intellectual quickness, his rather superficial charm of manner, and his physical appeal had touched a sympathetic chord in her. She could not believe that this man, too, was of an alien race, speaking another language. He did not make her feel like a foreigner. For the very first time in her life she felt at home with a fellow being. Martin surely would not let her go away a stranger still.

He was waiting for her in the café outside Toulon station where they had arranged to meet. When he saw her come into the room, his brown and handsome face lighted with such sudden pleasure that she felt a real emotion, as if, meeting him, she had at last come home in life. Martin's face could be extremely expressive when he did not trouble to conceal his moods. Now there was no more mockery in it, no bravado. It was the face of the real Martin, the charming, natural, playful, high-spirited man.

He knew he was behaving recklessly in going away with Anna. His action was really foolhardy. There were so many ways in which it might be found out, so many accidents might happen to give him away ; the King's Proctor might easily get to hear of what was going on. It would be dreadful if the divorce failed to go through and he was left tied to Germaine in the end. His father would never forgive him if that were to happen. But the strong element of danger in the situation stimulated him instead of making him nervous. The risk he was taking cancelled out his haunting sense of guilt with regard to the chauffeur, George West. He had not consciously considered the matter. He did not allow himself to think that he was running away with Anna mainly to escape his own sense of guilt. He felt strong, excited and very much alive ; much more intensely alive than he had felt for a long time.

At the sight of Anna he became radiant. He gazed at her smooth face, really striking now in its rare animation, and at her figure which, no longer listless, appeared more graceful than ever. He told her that she was beautiful. This made her happy.

They sat for half an hour in the café, waiting till it should be time for the train which would take them to Italy. Anna felt no surprise at being there with Martin. The only surprise she felt was at having lived without him for so long. She looked at him. She could not imagine how she had lived all these years of her life not even knowing of his existence. No wonder her life had seemed empty and meaningless. Now, all at once, it had meaning. She looked at him, and she liked him enormously, and she knew she would never like anyone else half so much. It would have been idiotic and wicked if they had not gone away together.

And Martin looked back at her and was violently attracted, and he was glad that he was rash enough to chance everything with her. Each of them felt that both had been living in inauspicious circumstances, and each was delighted by the thought that these circumstances were going to be altered.

The train was not due to start for some time. It was really too early to go on to the platform. But they strolled up and down arm-in-arm and bought foolish bunches of flowers and looked at the magazines on the stall.

"I hope you feel suitably appalled by your immoral conduct," Martin said with his teasing smile.

And Anna replied cheerfully :

"I feel I'm doing the first really good and sane action of my life."

With that, the train having arrived, they got into a carriage, so absorbed in their new happiness that they were oblivious of their fellow-passengers, but noticed and envied by everyone, even by the porter and the restaurant-car attendant.

It was pleasantly calm in the carriage and they sat there happily.

"You've had too many worries lately, Martin," said Anna. "It will do you good to forget them all for a while."

"I've forgotten them already," said Martin, "and I don't mean to be reminded of them for a long time. Did you think I was going to send my address to everybody ?"

"Where are we going ?" asked Anna.

"To Italy," answered Martin.

"But where in Italy?" said Anna. "For what station have you bought tickets?"

"Wait and see," replied Martin, adding: "As I'm escorting you on the road to perdition, you might as well leave the travelling arrangements to me."

"A psycho-analyst wouldn't have much trouble with you," said Anna. "Anyone can see you're just a bad little boy showing off and rebelling against authority."

"I protest against being called a rebel," Martin retorted. "I'm really the most law-abiding person. I even pay taxes uncomplainingly in support of a government which prohibits the spreading of information on birth control while large sections of the community are enduring unemployment and semi-starvation as the result of over-population."

While they were chattering their way towards the Italian frontier, Dr. Henri Rimbaud, in his private room at the Clinique Miremont, was writing a letter to his old master, Professor Duclos of Montpellier, telling him of the interesting development in the case of the young Englishman who, after lying like a log for eight days, had suddenly recovered consciousness. Everyone in the clinic, both nurses and patients, was delighted at this turn of events. One man alone was not delighted: he lay in bed weak and helpless, partially paralysed, with his mind unhappily active. An emaciated young man with a week's growth of beard, and boyish, distracted, homesick eyes: George West, the chauffeur, with whom Martin had never found time to talk, and who was now left alone at Bandol.

II

Hubert Byrne goes out for the Evening Again

WHEN Hubert Byrne received the news of Fairbrother's death he became thoughtful. The transaction regarding the shares was completed ; the control of the Cray River Development Trust (Canada) was now in his hands. Nevertheless, he felt that the old man's death was inopportune and might lead to unforeseen complications. Two of the three copies of the partnership agreement were safely in his possession ; his own copy, and the copy which Fairbrother had handed over to him with his shares in accordance with their pre-arranged plan. The third and last copy of the agreement was, of course, in the keeping of William Lewison. It was this third copy that was exercising Byrne's mind. He thought about it a good deal, and was interested not merely in the document itself but also in its whereabouts. He wondered whether it was in the safe at Starling Hill where some of William's private papers were kept, or whether it was at the lawyer's office, or whether it was lodged elsewhere.

Byrne was very inquisitive. He tried in various ways to nose out the place where the document was deposited. He went about and talked to a number of people, in offices, in restaurants, in private houses. Sometimes he made a suggestion or took a note of some piece of information. But generally he was listening, inclining his heavy jowled face gravely towards the speaker, not saying much himself. His clumsy body in the dark city clothes moved unobtrusively and with

a certain subterranean determination from one rendez-
vous to the next.

Now, after Fairbrother's death, he reviewed the
situation with care. William was on his way back
from the south of France. Byrne wrote a letter to his
partner requesting William to notify him as soon as
he arrived home, and addressed it to Starling Hill.
When he had sent the letter to the post he went out
and bought himself a new dress tie.

After he had finished dinner that evening he sat for
some time reading the *Standard* in the sitting-room of
his rather comfortless flat. He was in full evening
dress. Not until the housekeeper had gone to bed did
he go to his own bedroom, carefully re-arrange the new
white tie in front of the mirror, and collect his hat, his
silk scarf, and the light-weight overcoat that he wore
in the evening. Then he telephoned to the rank for
a taxi and was driven to the West End.

The Carolina Club was having a gala night. The
brilliant dance room was transformed for the evening
into a jungle scene. The huge wall mirrors were concealed behind a cunningly painted *décor* of serpentine
boughs, fantastic tree-trunks and exotic foliage : great
ropes of creeper writhed across the star-spangled ceiling,
in the middle of which a crescent moon now diffused
eerie light. The artist had intended everything to be
weird, grotesque, sinister and distorted, like a madman's
dream or the vision of some drug addict. Hubert
Byrne's respectable Dickensian form moved inappro-
priately through this imaginative riot to a table
almost hidden behind the fronds of an exaggerated,
nightmare fern. From here he could get a good

view of the room without being open to observation himself.

No one recognised the quiet, middle-aged Canadian by the fern or paid any attention to him. The waiter brought him his wine and hurried on to attend to more promising customers. Byrne sat there unobtrusively, gravely watching the dancers and occasionally eating a mouthful of smoked salmon or taking a sip from his glass. At midnight a carefully planned cabaret show was produced, a sort of jungle fantasia, full of extravagant scenic effects, dances of wood nymphs, negroes, serpents, tigers and jungle demons. Shapes which had hitherto appeared to be part of the decorative scheme suddenly came to life and joined in the weaving mesh of intricate rhythm. From the orchestra came strange sounds, at once desolate and exciting, wails from the nethermost hell, the real jungle howl of uttermost desolation. An incongruous figure, Byrne sat there in a stiff and decent attitude, his long face impassive, among dryads, wild animals, dancing devils and the sensation-seeking patrons who crowded the expensive night club and filled it with an atmosphere which was at the same time blasé, feverish, corrupt and inane.

It grew later and later. Byrne had almost finished his bottle of wine. He was tired. He had had an exhausting time lately with all his worries, his investigations, his countless enquiries. Yet he sat on in a stiff attitude, watchful and inconspicuous, in front of his half-empty glass and sheltered by the fronds of the gigantic fern. When at last he caught sight of the face he was waiting for, his own expression did not change in the least. With his silver Eversharp pencil he wrote a few words on the back of a visiting-card and sent a waiter with it across the room.

Tony Quested was with a party of well-dressed people, sitting in a negligent pose between a dark-haired lady and a vivacious blonde, both of whom were twitting him, not without a hint of malice, on his bad temper. He was refusing to respond except by an irritating smile : he really was in an ill-humour. Since Gwenda's departure he had had a run of bad luck which was unusual for him. The Mallalieu girl with whom he had been enjoying an ardent flirtation had suddenly thrown him over as if he were a garment which she had worn once and decided to give away. In spite of all his wealthy acquaintances he was seriously in debt and hardly knew where to turn for ready money. He had approached his father for an advance, but the old man had made a terrible fuss and accused him of being a spendthrift and a good-for-nothing, and, instead of money, had given him a long lecture on the subject of morals and hard work. The financial situation threatened to become really ugly for Tony at any moment. He was in a desperate mood as he sat there smiling provokingly and almost rudely at the sallies of the two women.

Receiving Byrne's card, his attitude suddenly changed. Instead of feeling harassed and quarrelsome he regained in a moment his normal self-confidence. It was a good sign that that dried-up old stick across the room wanted to speak to him. If he knew anything about business, there ought to be money in it, Tony thought : it would not be his fault if the money failed to find its way into his empty pockets. Smiling confidently now, he entertained his companions with a display of his usual careless gaiety. It was astonishing how quickly his mood had altered. After intentionally keeping Byrne waiting for some minutes, Tony excused himself to his friends and went over to the table behind the fern.

12

The Token

ANNA and Martin Lewison were having lunch under an awning on a terrace that jutted out like the prow of a boat right into the pale waters of the lake. This love affair of theirs at Gardone had been a tremendous success; day after day of warm and unforced happiness. They swam in the lake, sat about lazily in the hot sun, and wandered along the steep hill paths where the sound of bells floated up drowsily from the modest brown churches below. Always there was the big, shining lake, the bright sky, the line of the mountains, jagged and rather unreal, shutting out the world. In England, not many hours' journey away, Martin's troubles were piling up for him: the divorce suit, his father; he hardly gave them a thought.

He was simply entranced by Anna in these first days, completely and utterly captivated, as though under a spell. He had even ceased to think about painting. He didn't care if he never opened his paintbox again. She was so extraordinary to him, so different from any-one he had ever encountered. For once in a way he let down his defences, the real Martin emerged and touched another human being, and it was the most thrilling, enchanting contact. Anna had a powerful glamour for him with her intelligent receptivity, and her elegance that was not the acquired elegance of sophistication but something unconscious and innate, an integral part of her personality.

And Anna was delighted with him : more than ever now that he had succumbed to her so completely. She felt that she had never had a real emotion before, never wanted anything until she wanted Martin. And she had got him, she had got what she wanted. She seemed to have found herself at last. The two of them had a marvellous time. They positively radiated happiness. People stared at them wherever they went. Martin really thought he was happy. He thought he was in love with Anna, he *was* in love with her. But the usual evasiveness was at work in him, working away underneath, to undermine his devotion. He wanted to be devoted and engrossed in his love affair : but he didn't want to be caught. There was a reservation somewhere.

They sat at lunch on the terrace that jutted into the lake. He smiled lazily at her ; his face had gone darker with the sun, a reddish brown which made his eyes show up greener. He looked fresh, contented, good-hearted. But because he was an extreme individualist there was a certain reluctance behind his contentment. He was just a trifle resentful of Anna, feeling that she was encroaching upon his independence. He felt apprehensive, although he was devoted to her. She sat facing the water, but from his seat he could see the pale, undistinguished curve of the shore, with vineyards and a few sparse-looking trees beyond the last of the houses, a band of shingle edging the lake, and clothes spread out to dry on the stones. A cloud covered the sun, and all at once his resentment became conscious, and Italy seemed a bad place to him.

" There's something unsatisfactory about this country," he said. " Most of the show-places are just flashy and artificial, a lot of flashy sideshows arranged for tourists. Once you get away from the sideshows there's nothing much left but squalor. I've never been anywhere so artificial. All the spontaneous life of the place seems to have been trampled out by Cook's tourists."

Anna looked at him and then went on with her lunch : she was disconcerted and did not follow his changing mood. This man whom she loved was so incomprehensible to her. Why, in the midst of their peaceful happiness, did he suddenly become antagonistic ? She did not understand that that was how his ego asserted itself, in little spurts of uncalled-for viciousness now and again. He was inconsistently resentful in spite of his independence, and inconsistently selfish in spite of his amiability, and inconsistently vicious if anything troubled him. Suddenly, at that moment, he started to loathe Italy. " Dictator-ridden, musical-comedy country," he thought, catching sight of a black shirt in the distance. He suddenly had a feeling that something bad was coming to him out of Italy, previous raptures notwithstanding.

Later on, when they were strolling through the village, his dissatisfaction increased. The streets were too narrow, the houses overhung too steeply, the passers-by pushed too rudely and stared too impudently, the foreign voices sounded strident and contemptuous. Suddenly, he couldn't endure the streets or the noisy, brazen, cheerful people. The very sight of a Fascist walking along with a conceited swing of his tight-trousered thighs filled Martin with disgust.

"Let's go out into the country," he said, feeling his nerves on edge.

They left the houses behind and followed a sandy path that skirted the vineyards. The day had turned to one of those still, oppressive afternoons when colours are blanched to an even, uninspiring brightness. There was no one at work among the vines, no one in sight, only some lean goats that started and scrambled away. It was sultry and breathless, and the barren brightness was wearisome to the eye. Anna wanted to sit in the shade, but there were no trees except a few olives carefully fenced in with barbed wire. Martin longed to get away from it all. The barbed wire looked ugly and sinister to him. But Anna kept on, wandering along with a vague, loitering gait that seemed as if it would never get her anywhere at all, on and on, till they came down to the edge of the lake again. And here there was more barbed wire shutting off the vines, and the pale tepid-looking water sucking apathetically at the tiny beach which was part dust and part stones and part refuse cast up from heaven knows where. In front, the vacant, eye-searing, watery glare, and behind, the dusty, inhospitable sweep of the land. To Martin it was the abomination of desolation to-day. Yesterday he would have thought it pleasant enough.

He looked at Anna and wondered what was in her head. Her eyes looked mild and dreamy, staring over the vines which writhed out of the ground, strangely contorted, like brown serpents.

"Look," she said, "there's an empty house over there : it's got a queer look about it, don't you think ? It seems deserted : and so lonely : miles from anywhere."

"Yes. Shall we go and look at it ? " he asked, seeing the old house, a ruin perhaps, standing back in the olive-trees, half hidden. His voice sounded lazy and joking ; but there was that curious resentment in him, which made him seem in opposition to her.

They found a gate, roughly boarded up. One of the boards was loose and it was easy to get through into the olive grove. Under the trees the quality of the afternoon seemed to change. The place felt secret and remote, the sunshine lay in the spaces between the trees as in some ancient garden of the forgotten past.

"How quiet it is," said Anna.

She stood there, under the silvery trees, in the birdless silence, seeing the sunshine swim between the trees, feeling she had crossed some boundary. She stood with her hand on the great, gnarled trunk of an olive-tree. Martin waited beside her. Wind came stirring through the leaves. They waited beside the big tree-trunk for the rustling approach of the wind.

Between the grey foliage and the huge twisted trunks the abandoned house gleamed vacantly. The white shell of the house was intact, but the windows were empty black holes and part of the roof had fallen in. Some planks were nailed over the door. Anna felt uneasy, it looked so desolate in the bright, unbreakable hush and loneliness of the afternoon. Martin was beside her, gazing at the place with an odd sort of half-feigned playfulness. His eyes had taken on a strangely hostile and secretive look. She did not understand him. Standing in front of the empty house she felt almost nervous of the secret look in his eyes.

" I wonder if there's a Token inside," he said to her.

He began to go forward towards the house. With vague uneasiness she watched him walk up the steps to the boarded door. Coarse brownish grass grew in the crannies of the crumbling stone steps.

" What is a Token ? " she asked.

" A kind of ghost," he answered, still withdrawn from her in spite of his teasing smile.

She watched him lounging carelessly in front of the nailed-up door. He looked frank and easy-going, with his broad shoulders, and his face so naïve and brown. Yet there was that peculiar reservation about him ; he was not quite all that he appeared to be. He looked now as if he were playing a childish game. He put out a hand to knock on the fastened door, then let it fall again, changing his mind.

" What does the Token do ? " she asked him. " Does it always live in an empty house ? "

" It lives in an empty house, and no one ever sees it," he said.

" Then how do you know if it's there ? "

He smiled in a playful way that was not quite sincere, not quite spontaneous.

" It comes to the inside of the door if you knock," he replied. " You can hear it coming up to the door."

" What an eccentric ghost," she said, smiling. But she was slightly uneasy. Something about the silence, and the empty house, and Martin's behaviour was discomforting to her.

"Yes," said Martin, "a Token is a queer sort of ghost, and its got a queer sort of power, too. It's got power to give the person who knocks the right of taking someone else's troubles on himself. If I knock on that door now, and the Token comes, I can take all your suffering, mental and physical, upon myself for the rest of our lives."

This statement was made in the lighthearted tone that rang just a little bit false. Martin had that curious manner just then : he seemed to be smiling misleadingly on top of his real thoughts, not giving himself away at all.

"Would you do that for me ? " she asked.

And with that baffling, secretive smile he answered :

"Of course I would. . . . Shall I knock ? "

"No, don't," she said quickly, taking a step towards him.

There was a pause. Both were watching silently the desolate house, the immemorial grey olive grove. The situation was rather unreal.

"Shall I knock ? " he asked again, his face brown and teasing with the false smile.

"No. Come away," she said.

Slowly he came down the steps and moved off beside her. Anna now wanted to get away from the place. By walking away she wanted to escape the sense of unreality that was closing in on her once again. A shadow seemed to have fallen upon her ; she felt strange as if she were dreaming. She felt like a sleeper who struggles against a depressing dream. She looked at the massive figure of Martin, with his ruffled hair, walking under the trees, looking towards the lake, shading his eyes from the slanting afternoon sun. How friendly he looked, and charming. An emotion stabbed at her heart. She was in love with him. Yet there was that evasiveness in him, and that spiteful quality that was beginning to depress her and to rouse her resentment. She had a diffused sense of sadness, disappointment. She wanted so much to go on being peacefully in love with him. The days had been cloudless till now. Now the old shadow had fallen on her again ; the shade of the invisible umbrella. A yearning that was almost intolerable came over her at the thought of her past happiness. Why must things change, why must she lose her happiness ?

" What are we doing ? " she exclaimed suddenly, intense.

But he, with the smile hiding his thoughts, replied in the familiar tone of fictitious lightness :

" We're going back to the hotel, I suppose."

Anna stopped and looked at him : so he, too, stood still. They were out of the olive grove now, near the edge of the lake. The empty house behind them showed wan through the branches. He stood there with his hands in his pockets, smiling lazily. The deceptive smile was starting to irritate her.

" Why are things going wrong between us to-day ? " she asked in her quiet voice.

This time he did not smile. He felt some nervous shrinking.

" Are they going wrong ? " he said vaguely, shrinking away from the question.

196

The everlasting evasion : she felt a weariness in her heart, the weariness of his eternal avoidance of responsibility. She met his eyes, green, penetrating, somewhat mournful. The secretiveness had gone out of them. Three deep furrows appeared on his forehead.

" Don't you like me any more ? " he asked, naïve, appealingly absurd. It was true, the secret look had vanished, but there was still a resentment somewhere.

" Of course I like you," she said. " That's why I want you to do something."

" What am I to do ? " he asked, puzzled and frowning.

" Our happiness is going—can't you feel it ? " she said. " It's beginning to drift away from us. We shall lose it altogether if we don't make an effort. I'll do all I can, but that's not enough. You must do something, too."

She put back a strand of hair that had fallen across her cheek. In the sunset light, with her face smooth and intent, she was beautiful.

" Let's make an effort to keep our happiness," she said. " Our love has been a good thing. Don't let us lose it."

Watching him closely, she saw the protective mask cover his face, the impenetrable look of extreme, deliberate dissociation. He was dissociating himself from her words. He stiffened, and absented himself, turning the affable, sunburned blank of his face towards her. He didn't want to listen to her appeal : he didn't believe in so much dangerous analysis. Fundamentally, he didn't want to be serious.

" How long will it be before your decree is made absolute ? " she asked him. " I could get a divorce, too, and we could be married next year. These temporary affairs are never any good. We need some stability if we are to keep our happiness."

She watched him, watched the astonishment appear over the impersonal detachment on his face. He stood beside her, astonished.

"I didn't know you were so conventional," he said finally.

"I don't think I'm particularly conventional," she answered. "But I realise that happiness can't be built on a basis of impermanence."

There was a pause. Then:

"Will you marry me when we are both free?" came her voice out of the silence.

He waited some moments, then his voice sounded softly, constrained and unhappy.

"No," he said.

"Why not?"

"It would be wrong."

"Why would it be wrong?"

He did not answer. She stood perfectly still, watching him. She had become very remote. In the yellow sunlight her face was set dreamily, as if in abstraction. The strand of hair, fine like gold, blew across her cheek. She put up her hand and brushed it away.

"Let's go back now," she said at last.

They began to walk back together, the way they had come. Martin did not look at Anna. He wanted not to see her; he wanted to blot her out of his consciousness. Yet he could not be unaware of her casual elegance as she moved beside him with the soft, straying movement of her limbs that made him want her more than anything in the world, more even than his own peace.

"You were willing to call up the Token for me," she said, smiling and half reproachful.

He felt the wistful smile like a knife in his heart.

"Yes, I would do that," he answered, muted. "But the other thing—that's altogether different: that's something considerably worse than a lapse from ethics. It's an affair of wronging one's own soul; like the sin against the holy ghost—whatever *that* may mean."

She reached out and caught his hand and held it in hers.

"But you do love me, don't you?" she insisted. "I'm sure you love me. Then why not marry me? Let's keep our happiness intact." She gave his hand an urgent, small clasp.

He was almost persuaded. He was really in love with her. A part of himself was all the devoted lover, devoted to this strange, alluring woman, the object of his desire. But another part of him wanted to escape, to get about other business. He had a soul to save as well as a body.

"No," he said. "I can't marry you. It would be hopelessly wrong."

And he gently disengaged his hand and began to walk on more rapidly, his face brown and obstinate as an unhappy mask with the three deep frown lines upon it.

PART III

I

A Talk at the Breakfast Table

WHEN William Lewison telephoned to his
partner to announce his arrival in London
and to arrange an interview, Byrne responded
with veiled offensiveness that if William wished to see
him next day he hoped he would not object to coming
to his flat at breakfast-time ; he had not got another free
moment. William was furious at this slighting treatment, which filled him with grave forebodings. He
replied ironically : " Please don't put yourself out in
any way on my account."

Next morning, while he was driving in a hired car
to St. John's Wood, he felt tired and worried and not
in the least like the film actor, Adolphe Menjou. The
journey from the south of France had exhausted him,
and on top of that he had been unable to sleep, even in
his own bed at Starling Hill. A sense of impending
trouble and uncertainty as to what had actually occurred
during his absence rested like a heavy cloud on his
mind, depriving him even of the comfortable pleasure
he usually felt at the sight of his carefully chosen furniture, his library and his rare alpine plants. He had
told no one, not even Cedric, of his arrival, but had spent
the previous evening quite alone, speaking only to the
butler, Flood, and going to bed soon after ten o'clock.

He had a feeling that until he knew just how matters stood he could not be bothered with anyone. It would be showing himself at a disadvantage, he felt, to appear in front of Cedric before he had mastered the facts and formulated a method of dealing with them.

Now, however, in the chill of a grey English summer morning, he almost wished that he had got Cedric to accompany him to the interview with Byrne. Sitting there in the car, which did not run nearly so smoothly as the Sunbeam, he found himself nursing an unwarrantable sense of grievance because not one of his children had come forward to support him at this troublesome time. Impatiently, he forced himself to realise how unreasonable such thoughts were. He was alone by his own deliberate intention, not because of any neglect on the part of his sons, one of whom he had advised to remain in France, while the other did not even know of his return, or of his daughter, who had gone, with his full consent and approval, on a visit to friends in Devonshire. Such weak vapourings were the result of sleeplessness followed by unaccustomed early rising. It was all Byrne's fault for appointing this ridiculously early hour for their interview. Confound the fellow, what did he mean by such impertinence? William would make him pay for it, sooner or later. But first he must find out exactly what had happened; that was the immediate thing. He was a dangerous chap, after all, this Hubert Byrne. William's instinct to distrust him had been a sound one: a pity he hadn't followed it. Well, he had the man taped now, at any rate. He wouldn't trust him again in a hurry.

As he climbed the three flights of stairs which led

to Byrne's flat he felt breathless and so weary that it was an effort to raise his feet from one step to the next. A vague sinking feeling, something between faintness and nausea, attacked him as he stood waiting for the door to be opened. It seemed to him that this sensation came because, tired as he was, he did not feel a match for his partner.

Hubert Byrne received him in a bleak little dining-room with large, ugly furniture and an electric fire. With an air of equality, even with a suggestion of patronage, he apologised to William for the informality of the meeting. The clumsy figure of the Canadian sat awkwardly at the table in front of the breakfast dishes. His prominent stomach looked huge under the glossy white napkin which he had spread over it. The room was full of the smell of fried bacon. Hubert Byrne asked William to sit down, rang for fresh coffee, and went on spreading butter on a triangular piece of toast. The elegant William looked frail and old as he sat there facing his munching partner.

The housekeeper brought coffee for the visitor and took away some empty plates. She had hardly closed the door after her when Byrne started to speak. William Lewison stirred his coffee mechanically as he listened to the other's discreet circumlocutions. The small room was too warm; the smell of bacon hung in the air; the ponderous furniture with its heavy scrolls and bulbous excrescences sprawled round the walls; a knife clinked on a plate. The long smooth jowl of the younger partner rose and fell; William's dark eye rested dismally upon it. He felt paralysed by the heat of the room and by the sound of the dry, pedantic voice which seemed to be holding forth on the subject of business enterprise. His shoulders sagged slightly. He was tired, tired. Why was he sitting here listening to this man? What was he doing in this over-heated, unappetising room, surrounded by half-empty plates and hideous furniture? He felt exhausted, listless, and irritated to the point of stupefaction by all this apparently meaningless verbosity. At the same time he was uneasily conscious of his own lack of concentration at the moment when concentration was most necessary. His head was strangely heavy, his brain felt like cotton-wool. He must make an effort and pull himself together.

The other man's long peroration seemed to amount to this : that in business dealings a young head was generally to be preferred to an older one ; that in many cases it became necessary for the ultimate good of the firm to make use of methods which, if judged apart from their object, might possibly be considered un-worthy ; in other words, that the end justified the means.

William wanted to interrupt, to make him come to the point, but for some reason he could not speak. This damned fellow, this Byrne. It was intolerable ; he dragged him out of bed at an unearthly hour of the morning, and then forced him to sit in front of a lot of greasy plates while he talked away interminably and wiped egg from the corners of his mouth. What a dirty feeder the man was ; his napkin was rapidly getting covered with yellow smears. And how unjust life was. A few days ago William had been sitting peaceably in the sun, happy with his son and daughter. And now he was shut into this mean and stuffy room and every-thing seemed curiously far away. An ugly, pot-bellied man was wiping his mouth on a napkin and talking and talking; and meanwhile he, William, was sitting on this horrible chair, unable to say anything or to concentrate on what the other was saying.

But Byrne was now saying something astounding. His quiet, expressionless voice announced : " You need feel no anxiety. I am a younger man than you, and now that through the purchase of Fairbrother's shares I have come into control of things, I intend to re-organise the business. I will relieve you of all responsibility. You will have nothing to do but to draw the profits."

At that William suddenly shook off his lethargy.

" What do you mean ; now that you have come into control ? " he asked with an incredulous intonation.

It was suddenly borne in on him that something terrible had happened, a disaster far worse than anything he had imagined. The man Byrne was guilty not just of disloyalty but of downright swindling. He, William Lewison, the infallible, had actually been tricked and swindled by this worm, this shameless serpent before him. A wild indignation bubbling like blood in his throat almost choked him at the realisation of how he had been duped.

" I mean that I now hold majority shares," replied Byrne deprecatingly, " and that, I suppose, you will prefer to resign the chairmanship."

" I shall do no such thing," said William, gazing at Byrne with hatred.

Byrne shrugged his shoulders, crumpled his napkin into a ball and laid it on the table beside his empty plate.

" I quite understand how you feel," he said smoothly. " This has naturally come as rather a shock to you.

When you have had time to get accustomed to the idea I have no doubt that you will see that it is all for the best. Everything can be arranged amicably and without dispute."

"I don't intend to settle anything amicably," said William in a furious voice. "I intend to settle with you in a very different way. I refuse to regard the transaction as legal. I shall consult my solicitor at once."

"Then you mean to fight me?" said Hubert Byrne with a sneer.

"Yes," said the older man, getting up and going to the door. "I will fight you to my last halfpenny if necessary."

"You are over-excited," said Hubert Byrne.

2

A Man cries out in the Dark

THE marshy ground that lay between Matthew Kavan's bungalow and the station was infested by leeches. On the road there was frequently to be seen a pool of blood where some native had discovered a half-gorged leech on his leg and torn it away from the flesh. Matthew Kavan had a shrinking horror of leeches, and the necessity of walking along this particular road almost spoiled the pleasurable relief with which he escaped from his white travelling box on the line. He had a superstitious feeling that if he were ever to discover a leech fastened upon his body he would go out of his mind with horror. He always walked along the road at top speed, keeping

his eyes on the ground.   Afterwards, when he was back
in his bungalow, he felt ashamed, and invented other
reasons for his haste.   When he came in on the night
train at about nine o'clock he had to walk along the road
in the dark, and this was even more disturbing, for what
chance was there of seeing and avoiding a leech by the
feeble light of a chuprassi's lantern which was all he
had to guide him?

He walked as fast as he could.   The chuprassi could
hardly keep pace with him, and finally proceeded at a
half-trot, stumbling frequently into the deep ruts worn
by the wheels of bullock carts in the soft surface of the
road.   There were no carts as late as this.   Nobody
was about.   Only once a group of natives passed them
going towards the station and singing loudly in queer
twanging voices to keep off the evil spirits of the marsh.
As they came into the feeble, flickering light of the chuprassi's lantern, the brown faces turned towards Kavan
were strangely blank, and the singing stopped for a
moment.   Kavan knew that the natives detested him.
This did not displease him, and he returned the compli-
ment by despising them heartily.   A feckless, useless
crew.   As he passed the brown men on the road he kept
his face rigid, ignoring them, and the hairs in his nostrils
quivered as if he were disdainfully spurning them.   But
when the weird singing, yelling, burst out again behind
him, he winced and walked faster than ever.

To-night he did not have to seek out excuses for
hurrying; several plausible reasons lay to hand, ready-
made.   To begin with it was late, he was tired after five
days' travelling on line, he wanted to get a bath and a
good night's rest.   Besides that, the English mail would

have come in during the day, and he would find the weekly batch of letters and papers waiting for him at the bungalow. Mail day was the most important day of the week. The letters from home were more precious than rubies. Matthew Kavan opened them slowly, one by one, and lingered over every word.

When he discovered an envelope addressed in Anna's writing among the letters, he put it on one side to be read last. The rest of the mail was uninteresting and he had soon finished with it. He turned to his wife's letter and scrutinised it, the oblong envelope with the familiar handwriting, the foreign stamp in the corner. Anna. In a few weeks now he would see her again. He did not think what would be likely to happen when they met. Reunion, reconciliation; a fantasy of these things occupied his mind continually. He lived now on his expectations. Certainly there would be a sentimental reunion and they would live happily ever after. He had endured the discomforts of heat, of his unsatisfied body, of leeches, of the white travelling box; and the approaching reunion was to be his recompense for all this. Taking the still unopened envelope with him, he went upstairs, undressed, and washed himself thoroughly in the iron bath tub. As he sluiced the water over his tough, sinewy limbs he thought all the time of the letter waiting for him on the table. At last, wearing his shabby cotton pyjamas, he stood by the glass shade which protected the candle from insects, and tore open the envelope.

The letter was short and only covered one side of the paper. Kavan read it through twice before the meaning of the words penetrated to his brain. In writing made somewhat spidery by a too pointed nib, Anna informed him politely and impersonally that she did not intend to live with him again, that she was living with another man, and that when Matthew returned to England she would meet him to discuss the advisability of a divorce. She added, as an afterthought, that doubtless Matthew himself would agree as to the futility of trying to patch up a relationship which had already shown itself such an obvious failure.

The glass candle shade was a flimsy thing and easily upset. Matthew Kavan knocked it over with an uncontrolled jerk of his arm as he finished reading the letter for the second time. A stifling darkness enveloped him which seemed to emanate from his heart rather than to be the natural result of the candle's extinction. His heart was black, and in his brain everything was pitch dark. He knelt down and felt round with his hands for the candle. He found that the floor was covered with sharp fragments of broken glass. His pyjamas stuck to his flesh; the heat suffocated him; when he stood up again the sweat ran off him like water. He took a few random paces, fumbled about and grasped some piece of furniture. The feel of the wood stirred a reflex in his brain and he began to shake the thing of which he had taken hold. Suddenly it plunged forward on top of him, bearing him to the ground. It was only a light hanging cupboard made of canvas and thin strips of wood, and he was unhurt. Nevertheless, he cried out in a loud and agonised voice. No one answered him. The servants did not hear or did not want to hear. He did not cry out again, but lay on the floor crumpled under the wardrobe, whimpering quietly.

For some time he failed to realise anything, except that he was in heat, darkness and misery, crushed down by an oppressive weight. He thrashed out blindly with his arms, and though the cupboard could easily have been moved by a well-directed effort, his undisciplined movements failed to dislodge it. For what seemed an eternity he lay there in the stifling darkness, feeling nothing except despair. All at once he remembered where he was and what had happened to him. He raised the cupboard with his shoulders and stood up, sweating, his limbs cramped and bruised, intending to re-light the candle. He could not find it; the broken glass was scattered all over the floor but the candle had vanished: finally he lay down on his bed in the dark. He fell into a doze of exhaustion.

When he came to he felt in a murderous rage; he was glad that he now felt only anger in place of the black desolation which had overwhelmed him while he lay under the wardrobe. He thought: " She has deceived me, the bitch, the whore. All this time I have been faithful to her, and she has laughed at me with her lovers. While I was slaving for her in the heat she was lying with another man." He also thought: " If she could have seen me pull the cupboard down on top of me she would have been sorry." He called Anna's image before him. He thought of the different things he would like to do to her body. This gave him some gratification. All the same, it was insufferable that at this very moment while he was lying here and the heat was tormenting him, somewhere in Europe she was taking her pleasure with an unknown man.

That she had betrayed him was bad enough. That

he was to be cheated of his sentimental reunion was bad enough. That he had remained so long chaste for nothing was bad enough. But the worst thing of all was that she had made a fool of him. He lay bathed in sweat, and stared into the oppressive darkness, and hated Anna with all his heart.

He did not know how long it was since he had read the letter, how soon morning would come. He began to wish eagerly for the time to pass, for daylight to come again so that he could take some decisive action against Anna. He wanted to go at once and take some violent revenge : he would have liked to go there and then to wreak some violent vengeance upon her ; perhaps to kill her.

His rage lasted all through the night.

In the morning, when he went to his office, he was outwardly composed. But his temper was villainous, he inflicted fines and punishments on his subordinates without reason, the clerks were afraid to approach him. When the head clerk brought in some papers for signature, Kavan stared at him with such glassy venom that the man was aghast and felt for the amulet which he wore as a protection against the evil eye.

3

Every Dog has his Day

CEDRIC LEWISON sat at the mahogany desk in the library at Starling Hill reading through a pile of papers which all required careful attention. His progress was very slow. Not only were the matters of which the docu-

ments treated complicated in themselves, but his mind
was not really concentrated on his work, and he found
himself constantly lapsing into thoughts of his father's
illness, and of the strangeness of sitting at his father's
desk. He did not feel at ease in the room. The
presence of William Lewison seemed to lurk in every
shadow, and Cedric could not rid himself of a childish
feeling of trespass, as though he had no right to be
there and might at any moment be interrupted by a soft,
sarcastic voice asking him what he was doing. The
sense of his own unaccustomed responsibility troubled
him. He had always longed for independence of action,
for freedom from his father's domination ; but now when
he tried his freedom he found it strangely demoralising.
At any rate, he felt unable to cope with these papers.

It was nearly eight o'clock. In the ordinary way
he would be at home now in the comfortable, familiar,
unpretentious house that Jean ran so smoothly, saying
good night to the youngsters and getting ready for
dinner. Afterwards there would be friends dropping
in for bridge perhaps, or perhaps he would take Jean
out to a cinema, or perhaps they would just spend a
quiet evening alone, reading and exchanging occasional
remarks about everyday affairs. The thought of this
tranquillity affected him as poignantly as if he had lost
it for ever. He wished most intensely that he had not
decided to stay the night at Starling Hill. There was
really no need for him to have done so. He was not
even allowed to visit William in the big bedroom where
he was being efficiently and expensively kept alive by
doctors and day and night nurses. There was no
reason for Cedric to stop in the house. There was no

point in it. Yet he could not bear the thought of the old man being left quite alone there in his illness, to the care of strangers. Supposing he should suddenly ask for his children and find that not one of them was near him?

Cedric sighed, put his fountain-pen into its jade green tubular container, and passed his hand wearily over his forehead and his short, dark, brittle hair. Everything had gone wrong so suddenly. He thought of the shock with which he had heard of William's serious heart attack, and of the secondary shock of Hubert Byrne's treachery. The fact that he, Cedric, had not even known of William's return from France did not seem to exonerate him from responsibility for his father's collapse. If he had been there to support him he felt sure the old man would not have been taken ill: and if he had earned William's confidence he would have been there. He blamed himself severely and drove himself on to do all the things which he imagined William would wish him to do. He spared himself nothing. Since first he heard of the disaster he had hardly rested a moment, but had rushed from interview to interview, trying to find out the extent of the damage. With old Anthony Quested he had had a particularly long and unsatisfactory interview. The lawyer had sat staring sombrely out of his office window at the little courtyard, looking peaked and dehumanised, and repeating in his dry voice that it was impossible to be sure of anything until William recovered sufficiently to attend to business. William Lewison had always liked to keep everything in his own hands, and there were many questions of which even his legal adviser knew nothing.

In spite of his non-committal attitude and formal phraseology, Quested managed to convey the impression that things were pretty bad ; perhaps worse than anyone realised yet. Cedric came away from Laurence Poulteney Hill feeling alarmed and discouraged, convinced that Quested did not think much of him as a business man and was deliberately avoiding serious discussion with him.

No matter how hard he tried to attain his father's standard of efficiency he always seemed to fail. Failure was all that could be expected from a failure. He had failed to win William's confidence. He had failed to make anything of his interview with the lawyer. Now that the whole responsibility of the multiple Lewison interests rested upon him, he was failing to rise to the occasion.

He got up and rang the bell. His throat felt uncomfortably dry. He ordered a long drink from the butler, and when it came sat down again at the desk with the tall glass in his hand, his pleasant face clouded, his lips flaccid, and his eyes devoid of lustre. Sitting alone there in the handsome room he looked limp and defeated.

The attempt he had made to get in touch with Martin had failed too. Of course he did not know how to tackle that problem, either. At the first news of William's illness he had sent a prepaid telegram to his brother at Bandol asking him to return at once. Seeking for some inspiration he took out of his pocket-book the reply he had received from the hotel after an unaccountable delay. " Monsieur Lewison left here some days ago. Address unknown." He fixed his dark,

melancholy eyes on the telegram as if he were reading
it for the first time, although he already knew the wording by heart. He was completely baffled by it, and did
not know what to do next. Ought he to tell someone,
Quested, for instance, and have enquiries made ? How
did one set about tracing people who disappeared on the
Continent ? And supposing Martin were up to something disreputable : it would not do to have his conduct
made public. Martin was an irresponsible sort of
blighter. At the thought of his brother's amiable,
evasive smile, Cedric felt an overwhelming need for
some kind of moral support. He folded up the telegram
again and put it carefully back in his wallet.

If only he could confide in someone, ask someone's
advice. For a moment he thought of going home and
unburdening himself to his wife of the whole worrying
business, but immediately afterwards he decided that
this would not be fair either to Jean or to Martin. He
finished his drink and stood up. He did not want to
dine alone under the lugubrious eye of Flood who
would be sure to question him about William's condition in a hushed, graveyard voice that was insupport-
ably irritating. He did not want to go on working, or
to go upstairs to the sickroom to hear the nurse's pro-
fessionally optimistic report. The only thing he felt
he must do was to confide in somebody, and he suddenly
decided to get in touch with his sister and tell her to
come back to Starling Hill at once. William, in his
first half-conscious moments, had asked for Gwenda,
but had afterwards said that she was not to be told of
his illness or recalled from her visit. Still, he might
ask for her again at any time. It was only right that

she should be in the house. Cedric went to speak from the telephone in his bedroom where he could be sure of complete privacy.

But he was not to be allowed the relief of sharing his troubles. At the moment when the telephone operator was making the connection between Starling Hill and the Devonshire country house where she was supposed to be staying, Gwenda Lewison was setting out a cold supper on the table of Tony Quested's flat in Ethelbert Place. She had come back from France full of longing for Tony, and this opportunity of spending a few days with him had seemed too good to be missed. Gwenda had a natural aptitude for intrigue; and it was simple for her to let her friends think she was at Starling Hill while William imagined her to be in Devonshire. In self-justification she argued that she was hopelessly in love with Tony, and couldn't be expected to miss a chance like this of getting him all to herself for a time. She had done her best to be pleasant and to make her father's holiday a success: he had had his amusement; now it was her turn.

Tony sat smoking a cigarette while she went to and fro between the living-room and the tiny kitchen, fetching plates and cutlery and arranging the things they had bought at the cooked food shop round the corner. Gwenda was not in the least domesticated; but for once in a way it amused her to play at preparing a meal, and so they had brought home half a cooked chicken, some thin pink slices of ham, bread, butter, cheese, olives and a bottle of pale Rhine wine. As she fetched the glasses from the cupboard, she reflected how tiresome it was of Tony's father to want to see him

this evening. Surely the old man had plenty of oppor-
tunities at the office of saying anything he liked to his
son without making demands on his free time as well.
But to-day he had insisted that Tony should spend an
hour with him after dinner to discuss some urgent and
private affair. She wondered with vague curiosity
what the matter could be. No doubt Tony would tell
her about it when he came back. He had promised to
get away as soon as possible and to take her out to dance
during the later part of the evening.

Tony finished his cigarette and sat down at the table.
He held out his plate for a slice of ham, and reflected
that it was pleasant to have Gwenda there in his flat,
waiting on him, and looking decorative in her gay
summer clothes. He was cheerful and did most of the
talking. He was enjoying the situation. It amused
him to think that he possessed private information about
Lewison affairs of which Gwenda knew nothing. He
had it in his power to astonish and horrify the girl at
any moment, should he feel so inclined. It was a
piquant situation, one that he found most congenial.

She looked so contented, serving the food, amused
with her domestic pose; he had half a mind to tell
her about the business disaster which had overtaken her
father, just for the fun of seeing her expression alter.
But no; he was enjoying himself too much to upset
things at the moment. Let the intriguing state of
affairs go on a little longer. Time enough to spring his
mine when he began to feel bored.

They sat together at the table in the quiet flat, desul-
torily talkative, thinking of other things from those of
which they spoke. Gwenda was glad not to be dining

in a restaurant. It gave her a delightful feeling of
intimacy with Tony to be sitting down beside him to
a meal which she had got ready. She thought of the
meals she shared with her father in the bow-windowed
dining-room at Starling Hill: there was no sense of
intimacy about them, with Flood hovering between
the sideboard and the table and William silently ruminat-
ing over his food. William was a dear, she was really
fond of him, but he was not much of a companion for
her. He was a bit of a monomaniac, always preoccupied
with business affairs. But why shouldn't he have his
mania? Everybody had some private obsession. Hers
happened to be Tony Quested.

Tony went out as soon as the meal was finished.
He had arranged to meet his father in the smoking-room
of the club, and the old man was waiting for him
in his usual corner, his arm-chair turned unsociably
away from his neighbours. He was glad to see his
well-dressed, fair-haired son walking towards him,
but merely remarked sardonically that he regretted
having been obliged to interfere with Tony's evening
engagements.

Old Anthony Quested was in a bad temper. He
had always loyally defended the Lewison business interests; yet now, because William had come to grief, he
felt extremely uncomfortable, almost guilty. He ought
to have suspected Byrne. At any rate, William ought
to have had more sense than to have been taken in by
the scoundrel. But whether William or he himself
were to blame, the damage was done, and Hubert
Byrne had nicely diddled them both.

On top of all this came the additional complication

of William's illness. Cedric was no more capable of taking his father's place than he was of flying to Mars. The fellow seemed to have no initiative, wandering about with a look in his eyes like a lost dog, and wasting people's time with unnecessary questions. Things were really looking black for William Lewison. Quested could not banish from his mind a sneaking feeling of satisfaction. He told himself that his friend's misfortunes shocked and distressed him deeply. Yet he could not disguise from himself the shameful sensation —almost a sense of unholy glee—that he was so unwilling to acknowledge. The division in his mind made him thoroughly bad-tempered.

So when Tony appeared the old man was sarcastic and terse. He mentioned that William's sudden illness would entail a great deal of confusion, delay and extra work of various kinds, some of which must devolve upon Tony. Tony replied with short, careless answers that infuriated his father still more. The lawyer could not forget his secret illicit gratification, and this filled him with anger and dismay. When Tony remarked in his impertinent fashion that every dog has his day and that the long day of William Lewison seemed to be coming to an end, the father was roused to a condition of fury. His face looked more bloodless than usual, he became more laconic, and soon dismissed his son.

Tony drove back to Ethelbert Place whistling meditatively over the wheel. If he told Gwenda that her father was ill she would certainly think it her duty to go to him at once. He decided that he would prefer her to spend the night with him at Ethelbert Place, and that, therefore, he would not tell her until the morning.

The two of them spent the rest of the evening dancing together at a Kensington hotel where they were unlikely to meet anybody they knew.

4

An Episode sinks into the Past

ON the evening of the day on which they had visited the house of the Token, Martin Lewison had telegraphed his address to Starling Hill. He had two motives for doing this. Number one was a feeling of compunction towards his father which had been growing in strength for several days ; it was really unkind and unfair to leave the old man any longer in ignorance as to his whereabouts. Number two was less easily defined and included a sense of danger regarding his relationship to Anna Kavan. He felt unsafe with her and wished to re-establish contact with his home supports.

When, only a few hours later, a telegram had arrived informing him of William's illness and requesting his immediate return, he had experienced the most extraordinary blend of emotions. Anxiety on his father's account, the suddenly stirred force of a family loyalty that was really profound, mingled with a sensation of relief at the way of escape thus offered from his own dangerous and complicated position. At the same time as feeling relieved he was also filled with genuine distress at the prospect of leaving Anna. They had done more than share a casual love affair : they had done more than play and eat and sleep together. There was

something more in it than that, say what you like.
He had really felt agitated when he told her that he
would have to go home at once. He had been apprehensive, too, of a scene; but as to that he had been
mistaken. Anna had listened to him quietly and then
had said that of course he must go to his father. She
would go back to England too. But they would travel
by different routes. He would have to go via Bandol
to make arrangements about the car and about George
West.

As soon as Martin knew he was going away he looked
at the Italian landscape with new eyes. He had been
happier beside this lake than he had ever been in his
life. All lakes for him henceforward would mean Lake
Garda, all beauty was concentrated in the steep hillside
olive groves, all human intimacy was consummated in
the sleepy hotel with its vine-trellised arbours, and a
ring encircling Gardone enclosed his heart. He remembered that he had thought the place flashy and artificial,
a sideshow decorated up for tourists to gape at. But
the memory carried no conviction; it was in his head
and did not reach his heart. He made an effort to view
this lakeside episode in its true proportion as one of
many incidents in his emotional life: but the effort
was not a success.

While Anna was packing he wandered along the
paths where they had walked together. He lingered in
front of the house of the Token, the place where he had
told Anna that he would not marry her. The memory
of that occasion brought the three deep lines to his
forehead. He wished that he could have behaved
differently, that his principles had not obliged him to

reply to her as he did. He had made a sacrifice in order
to keep to his principles, and he did not feel proud or
happy about what he had done.

He remembered the dining-room of a certain inn
where they had lunched and where a calendar hung on
the wall. Anna had taken the calendar down. That
had impressed Martin; he understood the intensity of
unspoken feeling underlying the action. Now, although
he was about to leave her, he felt an overpowering affection for Anna, who had not protested against his departure or tried to detain him, but had dreaded separation
from him so much that she could not endure the sight
of a calendar. What a restrained emotion that must
have been which found no outlet but the taking down
of a calendar from the wall !

Take it all round, Martin Lewison's last afternoon at
Gardone was far from pleasant. Too many distressing
thoughts and regrets occupied his mind.

He had accustomed himself to the idea that Anna
was threatening his independence in some way. He
had looked upon her as dangerous. When she now
quietly renounced all claim upon him, it gave him a
sharp and unexpected pang. He had an uneasy mis-
giving that his attitude towards her had been wrong,
that he had made a mistake. Perhaps she had not meant
to interfere with his liberty. He went on to think of a
future bereft of Anna. He did not deceive himself,
he saw that it was going to be difficult for him to live
without her. But without his independence he could
not live at all. He could not afford to risk an infringe-
ment of his liberty. So that was that, and now the
affair must come to an end.

Martin Lewison threw a stone into the lake. There
was no help for it : an artist, even if he were in love,
must keep his integral isolation. The worst thing about
this parting was the doubt which had crept into his
mind as to whether it were really necessary. No, he
was not sure any longer that in order to keep his independence he must part from Anna. But he was sure
that he was not going to take any chances in so vital a
matter. He was doing the only safe thing in returning
to Starling Hill. There he would be perfectly safe.

Half an hour later he was back at the hotel. Anna
had finished packing and was standing on the terrace
beside the lake. The vine leaves on the trellis work
made a thick green shade overhead, the water looked
warm and opalescent, some white pigeons were flying
in large circles against the clear blue sky.

Anna's train went at five o'clock. There were some
minutes to spare before they need go to the station.
Martin was to leave later on in the evening. He felt
nervous and unhappy, standing beside her and looking
down at the water. He would be thankful, he thought,
when this leave-taking was over. Distress made him
feel resentful, and he determined, if the girl tried to make
a scene or started talking emotionally, to escape into
the hotel on some pretext or other. But Anna said
nothing at all emotional, and that distressed Martin too.

" I want you to remember one thing," said Anna,
" and that is that I will always come back to you if you
want me at any time."

Otherwise the conversation was stilted and quite
impersonal. While the girl was indoors putting on
her hat, Martin frowned at the lake, wishing that this

situation need not have arisen, and thinking of all the intimate things he would have liked to say had he not been so afraid of a scene.

When she came out again Anna brought him a parting present : a soft blue leather note-case which he had seen and admired in a window of a shop in Brescia. Martin was very much moved. He suddenly felt ashamed and cursed his own self-centred inadequacy. Why had he not thought of giving Anna a present? His self-condemnation was so strong that he wished not to accept the gift. But when she slipped the case into his pocket he kissed her hand.

On the way to the station they were almost completely silent. Martin escorted her to the train. He frowned more heavily than usual and spoke angrily to the porter about her luggage. She stood at the carriage window, high above him. He said that seeing people off depressed and embarrassed him, that he would wish her a comfortable journey and go away without waiting for the departure of the train. He reached up to the window and shook hands with her. But he did not go away : he felt in his pocket and gave her a piece of paper on which he had written down his address. He pressed her hand again as the train started to move, and only when it was out of sight did he slowly walk away from the dusty platform.

That same evening he too was in the train, the blue note-case in his pocket, travelling away from Italy, towards duty, trouble, loneliness, work, independence. Three figures appeared continually before his mind's eye. One of them lying on a narrow hospital bed, gazing at nothing with fixed, half-open eyes; the chauffeur George West. One reclining on a *chaise-longue*, wearing an emerald green dressing-gown, glancing at him with perspicacious, impenetrable eyes; his father. And one standing in an olive grove and looking at him steadily with eyes that changed from blue to a cloudy grey; the girl Anna Kavan.

5

"A Stranger Still"

ANNA took the train to Desanzano where she had to change. The night train from there had a through carriage which would take her all the way to Calais. She waited a long time at Desanzano on the dreary platform, exposed to the stares of other prospective travellers. She walked up and down absently, clasping her bag, so sunk in herself that people turned round and stared at her, wondering curiously what was in her mind. She was not thinking of anything in particular: only the necessity of getting through the business of the journey, of forcing herself to attend to one travel detail after another, occupied her attention. Her will seemed to be screwed into a hard knot of determination not to break down.

At the hotel she had packed her things in a trance of stony determination. She must remain calm, she must not show any emotion. Martin's attitude had helped her. He had been quiet and dejected, rather formal in courteous attention, unlike himself. She had been relieved because he had spared her the onslaught of his familiar charm. But all the time, under her relief,

had been a sharp and gnawing pain because he was parting from her so easily. She would not recognise the
pain, she would not acknowledge that it was there.

She had walked with him to the station in a strange
and dreamlike stupor, hardly realising that this was the
end and that in a few minutes she would be leaving him.
Was it possible that this was the end? But feeling the
cold determination to self-control like a stone frozen
into her breast, and seeing Martin's blank, frowning,
secret expression, she knew that something final and
irrevocable was happening to them. There seemed
to be an unbridgeable hiatus between them.

Then, just at the last, when she stood at the high
carriage window and Martin took hold of her hand,
she had a moment of agonised realisation. She looked
at the man standing below her, she looked at him clearly
and intently, so as to impress his image upon her mind,
and she knew well enough what losing him would mean
to her. She could not deaden herself any longer; she
realised that she was in despair, and her eyes ached with
the tears that she might not shed. Was it thinkable
that she would never see him again? That he would
be smiling and talkative while she was lost somewhere
in loneliness?

She would have to protest to him, make some appeal.
She could not lose him without a single struggle. She
must implore him to come back to her; she must start
pleading with him at once, at once, while there was still
time. When the train started to move it would be too
late. Here she was, looking on at the destruction of her
happiness. No one would save her unless she saved
herself. She saw it clearly and brutally: her life was

falling in ruins while she stood motionless at the carriage window.   She saw this like a revelation, framing and rejecting sentences of appeal in her mind.   Yet she could not conceive what to say to him.   She could not bring herself to speak any words.

Meanwhile Martin Lewison waited on the platform, looking up at her.   Anna gazed at his face, which a short time ago had been strange to her, but which now seemed part of the most intimate tissue of her life. She saw his mouth, which was sensuous and perfectly curved, his teeth, his broad forehead, now wrinkled above his green eyes.   He said : " Here is my address," and he put a piece of paper into her hand.   To Anna the train had suddenly seemed to leap forward away from the station.

And now she was in the other train, in the through carriage which would carry her on to Calais.   The porter had found her a corner seat.   Only the four corner seats of the carriage were occupied; two of them by a couple of large, florid business men.   In the corner opposite Anna was a thin old English lady, with a dogged, censorious face, alert and collected.

Anna sat back, looking out of the window, at the flat, dull landscape stretching on each side like the top of a table.   The effort of keeping her face smooth and impassive made the muscles round her temples feel strained.   She remembered that Martin had told her that she sometimes looked like a Botticelli.   When she was in repose, he said, with her eyes wide open and blue, and her nervous, flexible mouth at rest, she had the ethereal look of a Botticelli woman, quite self-possessed, and yet innocent, almost angelic.

229

Well, now she was sure there was nothing of the angel about her. She felt her face ugly and strained as she sat in the noisy train, motionless, with the difficult fixed composure of a victim going to execution. For a long time she sat absolutely rigid. Then at last she looked round the compartment, her eyes dark with weariness. Rapidly her glance ran over the people in the carriage. Then she opened her bag and looked in the mirror at her controlled, tense, unrevealing face. She was in despair. But she was quite determined : she would not give way ; she would remain in control of herself. She looked in the little glass for a minute and then closed it away in her bag. She put the bag on the seat and gazed out of the window again.

It had got dark outside. Anna looked at the black window square where the reflection of the carriage light burned unsteadily. She was exhausted by all her emotions, and despairing. But the will to control her life was set hard in her, she would never yield, she would never collapse, there was more obstinacy than pain in her heart. She thought of Martin with yearning and intense affection. She loved him immensely, but he had abandoned her, a great senseless barrier lay between him and her. His egoism had put it there. But she did not feel angry with him because he had done this. He had only acted according to his nature. Everyone had to act according to the pattern of his own temperament. Martin's pattern was evasive and egoistic and airy, just as hers was proud and egoistic and stubborn. The barrier was there. It was no use complaining or feeling angry.

She sat in the clattering, swaying train with her

despairing thoughts. With a violent protracted effort she kept her face smooth and gazed out of the window. She kept on staring at the black square in the window frame; her eyes closed involuntarily for a second; the darkness came at her, frightening, lonely, oppressive, like a nightmare she had had as a child long ago. She felt powerless, desolate; she was overcome by the sense of a terrible loss from which she would never be able to recover. Something seemed to have been torn violently out of the centre of her life. Never would she recover from the shock to her secret nerves, from the horrible, sickening wrench at the inmost fibres of her being. She was lost again now, irretrievably lost and homeless in the world.

" A stranger I came to your town, I left it a stranger still." She had come home to Martin, as she thought. And he had sent her away. There was no home for her now in life. Anna Kavan was condemned to remain a stranger until she died.

Dressed in green, her face pale and set, her eyes fixed in an unseeing stare, Anna sat on the dusty cushioned seat. People moved in and out of the carriage. Anna saw figures, darkness, figures, darkness again. She sat stiffly and woodenly, seeming not to notice if anyone pushed against her. The train stopped at a station, and after a brief halt crashed on its way. Anna saw the station, noticed the cessation and recommencement of motion. She sat all the time stiffly, without changing her position. When the other passengers looked at her young, immobile face they had an uneasy feeling.

It grew late, the lamps were shaded, and only the small night light burned with an eerie, uncomfortable bluish gleam, like some chemical experiment in progress. The two business men sprawled in loosely abandoned attitudes, their faces ghastly with mouths jolting open to the movement of the train. Like corpses or stuporous drunkards they looked in the unearthly light, their heavy heads rolling limply and inanely from side to side. The old lady slept too in her corner: but even in sleep she managed to keep her alert appearance, her air of being an experienced traveller. With her head neatly tied up in a scarf, and an air cushion behind her shoulders, she slept on doggedly, a bit blanched with fatigue, but decently arranged, and with an effect of drawing her skirts away from her companions.

And it was dreary, dreary; like the melancholy phantasm of some Schopenhauer-created world. The ghastly midnight dreariness of the great train travelling northward in the dark; pounding along in a blind, relentless, insensate rush, like an evil great monster at the heart of the night. Anna felt a grisly breath upon her, the deathly depression of the unwilling traveller wakeful and solitary in the chill midnight hours, disconsolate, drear, like a nausea of the soul. It was a nightmare to her, a thing hard to bear. The horror of the train rushing on in the dark trough of the night, carrying her away from all that was precious to her, and the little light burning solitary its infernal purplish-blue, like a light in the underworld, a little blue light of hell.

Through the long sleepless night she wrestled with her despair. She sat in the shaking carriage; the corpse-like figures sprawled round her; the devilish blue eye of the light never closed. She stared at the miserable light, she apostrophised it, she called upon it to witness her unwavering determination. Her will to control her life was intact and solid as ice. She struggled with despair like a nightmare in the dark, and would not give way. She had lost Martin, she had lost the love which had given a short significance to her life. Her justification was gone. She was back in the dreadful empty futility of her own aimlessness, without any centre, without any direction. It had to be so. She would accept it uncomplainingly in her stubborn pride.

It was not her fault, nor was it Martin's. For every action is predetermined by the nature of the doer and is in itself neither good nor bad but simply neutral, inevitable : and on the accidents of such neutral, unjudgeable actions the circumstances of life depend. The history of each individual is governed by such incalculable chances.

So the night passed somehow.

And morning came, the dismal, heavy, vitiated awakening from the long horror of the night, with the train gritty and overheated, crawling slowly now over a grey landscape, in a grey drizzle of rain. The passengers looked dirty and ill, surveying one another with hostile suspicion, the men with a stubble of beard on their yellowish faces, the women wan with a curious waxen smoothness, like wax dolls that have been left out in the sun. Their faces seemed to be starting to run.

People went off to wash themselves in the trickle of scalding water in the lavatory. A chain of dishevelled figures moved up and down the corridor. Steam came hissing in a white cloud from somewhere farther along the train, the windows were blurred with steam and

dirt, everything was black to the touch, grimy. There
began the procession of passengers going through to the
restaurant car, for coffee and rolls. The two business
men lurched away, rather subdued this morning, in the
evil grey light. The old lady also took herself off,
neatly and efficiently, in search of refreshment. Anna
was left alone in the carriage. She made up her face,
and sat looking out of the window. Her eyes were
wide open in the dark sightlessness of exhaustion as
she stared at the rainy sky. She was past feeling now.
Only the obstinate, unquenchable determination was in
her eyes as she gazed, the determination not to surrender,
not to be downed by circumstances. She did not want
to move. She was in that state of mental and physical
exhaustion when every movement of the body seems
maddening. She was hungry, it seemed a long time
since she had eaten anything. But her body could not
be moved. It didn't seem worth while making the
effort of going along to the restaurant car.

The train was off now on the last lap of the journey,
the last dash across northern France to the sea. The
flat, rain-smudged country passed by, and the time.
At midday the little bell went tinkling down the corridors
for lunch, the people started filing through again. This
time the old lady opposite Anna kept to her place. She
had got hold of a lunch-basket, it seemed. Out came
the packet of sandwiches, and the wing of chicken, and
the paper screw of salt, and the bread, all adequately
and discreetly arranged on a clean table napkin. Anna
watched the methodical arrangements with a half-
conscious wonder out of the tail of her eye, while the
Englishwoman steadily ate her way through everything,

genteelly self-possessed, and finally, at the fruit stage, offered the girl a banana.

"You really ought to eat something," she said, in a tone of reproof. It was evident that she disapproved of Anna and of the feckless way she ignored regular meal times. "It's very bad to make the crossing on an empty stomach."

At last came the end of the journey, the last of the train, and the grey, grim-looking sea, rolling drearily morose, and sea-gulls crying and swooping over a dead fish that floated and rocked on the waves. Anna walked on to the boat, her face white under her green hat. She went and stood at the rail, looking down at the ugly grey water. Then she said to herself quietly but quite distinctly : "My life is my own affair; I alone am responsible for myself."

The crowd of passengers pushed round her, talking and calling to porters. The sea-gulls were screaming over the water. "I must depend on myself alone," said Anna. And she said again clearly and distinctly above the shouts of the porters and the cries of the gulls and the noise of the water and the wind : "My life is my own affair."

6

Interview at the Clinique Miremont

MARTIN LEWISON was on his way to the Clinique Miremont to decide what was to be done about George West. As he walked along the familiar road by the sea his face was frowning and gloomy. Everything about Bandol reminded him of Anna: the houses, the hills in the distance, the blue curve of the bay: ahead of him he could see the little peninsula where he had first met her. Nevertheless, it was the approaching interview with George West which principally occupied his mind. He could not drive out of his head the idea that he had behaved very badly towards the chauffeur. When he considered how he had abandoned the young man, without even troubling to write and find out his condition, his guilty feeling urged him towards a gesture of reparation. He must atone to George West. It was important that he should compensate him for past neglect, that he should, as far as possible, put matters right. The importance which he attached to the coming interview made him nervous and apprehensive.

The steps leading up to the door of the clinic were steep and numerous. Martin felt out of breath as he rang the bell. His sense of urgency had made him walk fast, and he had arrived all too soon at his destination.

He was admitted to a darkened ante-room with shutters closed against the sunshine, and asked to wait. Instead of being confronted immediately by the man he had wronged, he was buttonholed by Dr. Henri Rimbaud, the dark little Provençal doctor, with his unshaven chin and his dirty white overall, his piercing black, bright, intelligent eyes. Dr. Rimbaud stood close up to him, told him a long story about subtle changes in the mental state, mentioned various schools of psychiatrists, the theory of the flight from reality and the possibility of George's symptoms arising from a psychological rather than a physical cause. He also spoke of Professor

Duclos of Montpellier, for whom he seemed to have a profound respect. Martin Lewison had no technical knowledge of such matters, though in the ordinary way his alert brain would have readily interested itself in what the doctor was saying. To-day, however, he was too perturbed to be interested. He had come here to see George West, the man he had injured and to whom he wished to make reparation. The doctor went on talking technically and enthusiastically. As he talked, he scraped away with his forefinger at the bluish bristles on his chin, making a small harsh rasping sound that set Martin's teeth on edge.

Dr. Rimbaud seemed to be saying that the chauffeur's mental condition was abnormal though his physical state had improved considerably. He first explained how various forms of paralysis might follow altera-tions in the brain tissue, and how there might also be noted a falling off in general mental efficiency, per-haps also a deterioration in morale. Definite mental degeneration had been known to follow such a crisis as George West had been through, though it was not easy to trace the relation of cause and effect, and the probability was that in these cases there had existed a predisposition to such abnormality. Then, he went on to say, there was always the possibility of dissociative schizophrenia to be considered. It was conceivable that all the symptoms were dependent, not upon physical causes at all, but upon a disintegration of the personality, a dissociation of a part of the patient's mentality which had gone beyond the control of the normal functioning of consciousness.

Martin listened to all this with a growing sense of

restless distress. Without taking in all that the doctor was saying, he followed the general drift of his words, and received a painful impression. His eagerness to be brought face to face with the chauffeur became tinged with panicky forebodings : what sort of a human wreck was he going to see ?

The doctor told how the curious mental symptoms had developed in the young man. He was obsessed, it appeared, by the idea that he had run over a child, that the child had died from its injuries, and that he, George, was confined in the clinic to await punishment. Apart from this delusion, his reactions were normal, as far as could be ascertained. He was at present, therefore, suffering from a single self-accusatory delusion which might well be the result of introversion, a state in which the sufferer withdrew from the external world and occupied himself with himself to the more or less complete exclusion of reality. Dr. Rimbaud had become excited and, as he talked, continually tapped Martin's arm with the earpieces of the stethoscope which dangled from his overall pocket.

At last he led the way to the chauffeur's room. Martin felt cold with apprehension, the palms of his hands were damp, he made each step towards the young man with a deliberate physical effort.

George West was lying on the narrow bed, staring straight before him. This time his eyes were wide open. When the visitors entered the room he slowly turned his head on the pillow towards them. His neck seemed unnaturally long and thin ; his face, too, was thin and of an unwholesome colour, his eyes seemed to have sunk back into his head ; but the most notice-

able change in his appearance was caused by the pronounced growth of his eyebrows which had become
peculiarly bushy and prominent. Martin Lewison did
not know what to say to him : he simply stood gazing
at the sunken-eyed, pallid face with the thick, bushy,
strangely accentuated eyebrows. It did not seem to
him that he was looking at the chauffeur whom he
knew quite well, who had often smiled at him in a
friendly fashion under the peaked uniform cap, but at
some unfortunate stranger, a victim whose sufferings
harrowed and embarrassed him and rendered him tongue-
tied with shrinking pity.

As slowly as he had turned his head George raised
his eyes, until they rested upon Martin's face. He
gazed at him eagerly, hopefully, wonderingly, from
where he was lying, with his unhappy, lost, homesick
eyes. Suddenly the lower part of his face started to
quiver, there began a slow, laborious working of the
facial muscles, his mouth opened, he was about to
speak. Martin watched, fascinated and horrified. He
dreaded very much the sound which was about to issue
from that travailing mouth. He would have given a
good deal to avoid hearing it. But he controlled himself and waited with a sympathetic expression.

"I wondered if they would allow you to visit me,"
said George in a blurred voice. It was clear now that
one side of his face was still partially paralysed. "It
was good of you to come," he added, and Martin noted
that he spoke with difficulty, as if in a foreign language,
hesitating before each word.

"I should have come before, but I've been away,"
said Martin. "I'm glad you're so much better."

239

The chauffeur continued to stare into Martin's face, so that he was troubled by the intensity of the deep-sunk eyes. Then finally George looked away from him and said almost normally:

"Yes, I'm much better now."

The doctor had gone out and left them alone together. Martin felt that he ought to sit down: but there was no chair in the tiny cell of a room, and the thought of sitting on the edge of the bed was repugnant to him. He went to the window and stood there looking out for a moment. A faded yellow sunblind blocked out the view, and all he could see below it was a section of the flight of steep steps by which he had ascended to the door of the clinic. He turned back reluctantly to the man on the bed, who suddenly asked in his thickened tones:

"How long are they going to keep me here, do you think?"

Martin had come to the interview full of sympathy, remorse and the desire to make amends: but the unfamiliar eyebrows and the strange muffled voice discomfited him and made him feel that he was addressing a stranger.

"I'm going to arrange for you to go home to England as soon as you're fit enough to be moved," he said.

"I can't go back to England," the patient replied: and the hoarse voice now sounded impatient, even cross. "Of course they won't let me out. I'm being kept here till the trial. Didn't you know?" He looked up, gazed at Martin with his distracted eyes, and his face worked painfully. "I've been worried to death

240

over it all. Though I must say they've treated me very decently since I've been here. But I shall be glad when it's all over and they've settled what's to be done with me." He swallowed loudly, regarded Martin with a somewhat suspicious expression, and said : " I suppose you think you can make things easy for me—perhaps get me off altogether—buy me off ? But I don't know that I want you to interfere. I'd rather take what's coming to me, really, and get the whole thing off my chest."

Martin felt helpless, his thoughts were confused and he could not marshal them into any sort of order. Was it possible that this was really the same man who had driven the big Sunbeam with so much impersonal, unshakable reliability ? The patient had changed his position slightly, and through some trick of light or posture the face lying on the pillow might now have been taken for the face of a man of sixty with its emacia-tion, its drawn pallor, its sunken eyes under the shaggy eyebrows.

Martin came up to the foot of the bed and laid his hand on the iron rail.

" Don't worry too much, old chap," he began rather awkwardly.

The chauffeur glanced at him darkly and suspiciously.

" I've got to take what's coming to me," he said at last, with stubbornness. " Otherwise I shall never have a moment's peace. I shall never get the thing out of my system."

" Everything will turn out all right," Martin said in an unusually diffident tone. He stood at the foot of the bed, as if cut off from reality, outside the normal sequence of cause and effect. He felt as though in entering the room he had come into a world of chaos where all his experience, as well as all his preconceived standards and values, were quite without meaning or application. He had never before been in a situation with which he felt completely incapable of dealing. It oppressed him that he could not think of the best way to comfort George West.

" Don't worry too much," he repeated, " everything's going to be all right."

He came round to the side of the bed and patted the bony hand which lay outside the coverings. Curiously enough, at that moment he sincerely felt that the chauffeur and he had become friends. A current of human warmth seemed to flow from him and envelop the man on the bed. George made no sign, but Martin felt sure that he had been aware of the warmth.

" I shan't let you down," he said, at last. He seemed to be speaking more to himself than to the sick man.

Martin went back to the ante-room again. While he was waiting for Dr. Rimbaud, he looked at himself in a gilt-framed mirror which hung on the wall. He saw a large brown face staring back at him with intense, lost, curiously bewildered eyes. A slight shudder ran over him. Yes, his eyes had just the same lost, urgent, confused expression that he had seen in the eyes of the patient upstairs.

He drove the Sunbeam all across France in the profound preoccupation of mind which is the accompaniment of severe nervous stress. He drove mechanically, mechanically stopped for petrol, mechanically followed the red-topped kilometre stones, kept to the right road by some unconscious instinct, and spent the night at a town of which he did not know the name. It took him twenty-six hours to travel the seven hundred miles from Bandol to Boulogne, twenty hours being spent at the wheel.

On the evening of the day of Martin's visit, the chauffeur, George West, astonished everyone in the clinic by raising himself unaided to a sitting position. He sat up in bed for a long time, looking out of the window. When the doctor came in to see him he talked quite rationally and cheerfully in his limited, badly pronounced French, and seemed perfectly normal. He asked for his clothes, and not without difficulty succeeded in extracting a promise from Dr. Rimbaud that he might get up for a short time next day. Then, after supper, he laboriously wrote a short letter to his wife telling her that he would soon be coming home.

7

William Lewison Half Remembers

LOOKING worried and pale, Gwenda Lewison accompanied Martin upstairs to the bedroom where their father was lying, complaining peevishly on the way, in a nervous undertone, that William had become incredibly difficult and unreasonable since his health had taken a turn for the better. He had developed a mania for economy, announced that they were as good as ruined, and had insisted upon dismissing one of the nurses on the pretext that there were plenty of people in the household who could look after him during the

243

day. It was only thirty-six hours since he had been
declared out of immediate danger, and already he was
burning to get up and begin attending to business.
Directly against the doctor's orders he had insisted on
making an appointment with the lawyer, Anthony
Quested, for that same evening, and Cedric, too, was
coming to talk business with him. It was quite impossible to manage him : perhaps Martin would be
able to make him behave more sensibly.

William Lewison sent Gwenda away after a few
minutes' talk. Martin studied his father's changed,
ravaged face with distressful concern. The impressive
dome of his skull was now painfully stark, the high,
fine curve of his nose seemed sharpened, the skin drawn
tight and brittle over the bones of forehead and temple.
The Adolphe Menjou moustache looked limp and be-
draggled ; there was a bluish tinge on his lips ; his
dark eyes were strangely opaque and weary. Gwenda
had hardly left the room before his hand was groping
under the pillow for the papers which he had hidden
there. He asked Martin to give him his glasses, and
when he had them on his face seemed less altered.

With somewhat unnatural casualness he replied to
his son's questions about his illness. He wasn't really
in such a bad way as the doctors tried to make out.
There seemed to be a conspiracy among the doctors
and nurses to frighten him and turn him into an old
crock before his time : his heart was good for another
ten years at least.

He had made up his mind, as soon as he had come
to himself and been able to think coherently, not to
treat his collapse seriously. It worried him that he

could not recall the details of his attack. All that he remembered was a feeling of breathlessness and dizziness combined with a powerful sense of apprehension as if some unimaginable blow were about to fall. When the world had gone black before him, he had realised for a short yet interminable moment that he was losing consciousness and that something serious was happening. But the true memory of that moment had gone from him. Nor could he remember how he had felt during the early days of his illness; his mind refused to recall the thoughts and sensations he had had at that time. The blank in his memory worried him and increased his determination to make light of the whole affair.

But there was one shadowy recollection which tormented him. When he was most gravely ill he had seen dimly that only one of his children was in the room with him. He had asked Cedric to send for the other two; but neither Martin nor Gwenda had appeared. The old man thought that he had asked several times where they were and why they did not come, and that Cedric had given unsatisfactory replies, had seemed to be evading the question, had seemed not to know, or perhaps had not wished to tell him the truth. Perhaps he had imagined all this, for the memory was very uncertain. But it was a memory which continued to haunt him, however hard he tried to drive it away. Now that he was himself again, it would be easy to find out the truth; all he had to do was to question his son and daughter; they would not lie to him. But if his memory were correct, it meant that Martin and Gwenda had failed him or deceived him in some way.

This was what he was afraid of finding out. He preferred to distrust his memory.

For the rest, he had no difficulty in treating his illness lightly. Anyone who arrived at his time of life must expect to be ill occasionally. Had it not been for that torturing half-memory, he would hardly have worried about his heart. But whenever the half-memory returned to him then his pulse beat painfully fast, he was transfixed by a sharp pain stabbing through his heart, the veins throbbed under the skin of his temples, and he lay back weakly, a broken old man on the edge of the grave.

Martin, sunburned and massive, sat beside the handsome four-poster bed from which the hangings had been removed. Illness always made him uncomfortable, and he was glad to accept William's own fictitiously indifferent attitude at its face value. He made a few cheerful and sympathetic remarks, and was relieved when his father began to talk about business matters.

Hubert Byrne was a knave and a swindler. William was fanatically determined upon revenge : " An eye for an eye, a tooth for a tooth." He would break the other man if he ruined himself in the process. He expected his children to be of the same mind and willing to sacrifice every penny if necessary in order that Byrne might be brought low. Martin perceived that the question of vengeance had assumed fantastic proportions in his father's mind : it had become a sort of crusade, a holy war to be waged without armistice.

William began to outline his plan of campaign. The first move was to get an injunction against Byrne to restrain him from using his ill-gotten majority holding. Then they would have plenty of time to prepare their case for breach of contract. It would need elaborate preparation and very careful handling because of that unfortunate slip in the wording of the agreement. It would be a long and difficult fight, and ruinously expensive. But there was no reasonable doubt that the jury would ultimately give a verdict in their favour, since the evidence could be made to show that Byrne's conduct was fraudulent and dastardly to the last degree. They would plan the evidence in such a way that Byrne's character would be hopelessly blackened, he would never be able to clear himself of the mud with which they would plaster him. The whole case hinged upon the partnership agreement.

"I've told Quested to bring the document here this evening so that we can go into the matter thoroughly," he finished up. "I mean to have the best company barrister in London to put the case. I don't care what it costs me as long as we win in the end."

"And supposing we don't win?" said Martin, turning his clear greenish eyes on his father and frowning deeply.

William Lewison took off his glasses, put the papers under the pillow, and lay back : he had overtired himself for no purpose, since with a feeling of intense disappointment it came to him that Martin and he were not altogether at one.

"We must and shall win," he said at last, without much conviction.

As he spoke the words he was assailed once more by the tormenting, dreamlike recollection of the early days of his illness. He seemed to hear his own voice, weak

247

and almost unrecognisable, asking questions about the absent Martin to which Cedric muttered unsatisfactory replies. He remembered certain suspicious incidents connected with his son's behaviour at Bandol. Should he question him and risk the certainty of what was now only an indefinite fear? As if he saw himself in a mirror, he was suddenly conscious of his body lying in the big bed, weak, weary, diseased and old, the ankles slightly swollen, the lips blue and parched : he certainly ought to rest now. But he said evenly :

" Tell me, Mart, did Cedric send for you to come home because I was ill ? "

" Yes, he sent me a telegram," said the son.

" How long ago was that ? " asked William.

" I came at once," said Martin, " but I had to bring the car, and that took a little longer."

" I had an idea that Cedric didn't know where to get hold of you," said William.

There was a knock on the door and Gwenda came in to warn Martin to go. He had already stayed too long in the room, she said, and William had talked far too much. She re-arranged the bedclothes and drew the curtains across the window. Then she went out with Martin. William Lewison had looked forward eagerly to his son's arrival, but now he felt more discouraged than before. He lay there with his dry, blue-tinged lips slightly parted and his black, glazed, exhausted eyes wide open in the darkened room. The half-memory was torturing him again : the talk with Martin had not banished it.

Presently the doctor arrived, the sober, respectable local practitioner who was attending him. The quiet, authoritative man examined his patient methodically. He repeated the specialist's instructions : absolute rest, silence, no mental excitement. When William impatiently said that it was essential for him to attend to urgent business, he answered politely that he would not accept responsibility for the consequences of such behaviour. When the doctor had gone, William lay wishing that he had not got the two interviews with Cedric and Quested in front of him. He did not feel up to talking business. It was not that the doctor's warning had frightened him, but that he suddenly found himself more tired than he had realised. All the same, he would not postpone the interviews and thus admit to himself the seriousness of his illness.

Cedric sat by the bed, gave him the week's figures for the turnover of the Hendon store and answered questions about other business affairs. As they talked William saw that the inefficiency of his elder son was even greater than he had feared. With unerring instinct Cedric seemed always to take the opposite course from that which he himself would have chosen. All his transactions showed a timid, half-hearted tendency quite at variance with the bold, direct and ruthless Lewisonian policy. William listened with growing impatience to the moderate, propitiatory words of his elder son. He knew he must not allow himself to become excited. Encouraged by his silence, Cedric talked on. The sick man followed him carefully, with restrained indignation. He saw now what Cedric was getting at : he was opposing the attack upon Hubert Byrne. Cedric did not believe that they had a case against the man, was frightened of the expense and the difficulty of fighting the action. He would prefer to knuckle under, to put up with defeat and the intolerable insult of Byrne's trickery, rather than undertake the task of smashing the the swindler.

William was furious; to think that his own son should turn out such a poor-spirited rabbit, a faint-heart, a pacifist. Cedric would let down the family honour if he were not very carefully watched. But now the father knew he must control himself, he must not become agitated. He listened expressionlessly to Cedric's mediatory proposals and replied coolly and non-committally. It was a quiet, almost formal interview between father and son.

He was worn out when Cedric left. What was wrong with his children? They were all disappointing him, failing him in his time of need. Just when he most wanted support he found them withdrawn from him. Even Gwenda, his darling, had not been beside him in his worst hours. He felt lonely, old and dejected. Now he must close his eyes and think of nothing more disturbing than the alpine plants which grew on his rock garden.

Anthony Quested sat down on the same chair upon which Cedric had sat. In his desiccated neatness, waxen-faced, he smiled bloodlessly at the invalid and enunciated phrases of conventional sympathy in his dry, legal tones. William felt at a disadvantage. He ought not to have fixed the interview at this time of day. As the evening drew on he felt wearier and wearier, and his head grew less clear.

The lawyer spoke of the injunction against Hubert Byrne. He would get the matter in hand without further

delay.   In the meanwhile they could begin to think out
the lines on which they were to conduct the case against
him.   That was, if William was really determined upon
the action.   Quested glanced sharply at his old friend
as he spoke.   He had brought the partnership agreement
with him and laid it upon the bed.   William unfolded it
slowly and then put it down again.   He felt too tired
now even to read through the document.   Yes, he said,
he was determined to fight Byrne to the bitter end.

Anthony Quested said he did not altogether agree
with William's attitude.   William did not stand to gain
any material advantage by the action.   On the other
hand, he was certain to lose a good deal.   Such a case
was bound to be long-drawn-out and excessively costly
and the outcome was very uncertain.   Was it worth
while spending money like water merely in the hope of
injuring an enemy?

" Yes," said the sick man, raising himself on the
pillows.   " I intend to bring the action against him if
it is the last thing I do in this world."

" Then I will set things in motion," said Anthony
Quested, putting the partnership agreement back into
his leather case.

As he drove back to town, the lawyer shook his head
several times and told himself that William was done for.
He was a very sick man ; his ideas were distorted by
illness ; he had no real case against Byrne, who had
been guilty of nothing worse than a piece of sharp
practice such as was constantly taking place among
business men.   The blow to William's pride had shattered his common sense ; this insane desire for revenge
would ruin him.

Many other business men, in the city and elsewhere, were also saying at that time that William Lewison was done for.

8

Anna sees her own Error

WHEN Anna got back to London she did not at first realise how difficult life was going to be for her. She had an unreal, nightmarish sense of disaster; but it was only after she had spent three days quite alone that she realised that Martin had actually abandoned her, even Martin, who had seemed the one person to be infinitely trusted. Even he had betrayed her and given her over to loneliness. The loneliness was more than she could bear.

She wrote a note to the address he had given her, telling him where she was living. Then she waited some days. No reply came. So he did not mean to see her again; he had finally cut himself off from her. If he had intended to renew their friendship he would have written; she felt certain of that. A letter was a small thing, it didn't cost much to write. He might have written her a few words. *She* wouldn't have abandoned anybody like that, without a solitary word.

She wandered restlessly about the room she had taken in Manresa Road, near the Chelsea Town Hall. It was a fairly large room, but dark—it faced east—and narrow, furnished with a gate-legged table, a bookcase, and some wicker chairs which creaked when anyone sat upon them. The window curtains had a design of

252

large brown and blue birds. How could one sit down peacefully in a room like that?

Sudden indignation against Martin welled up in her. It was unpardonable of him to leave her alone in such a room. It was unpardonable of him to have shown her felicity and then sent her back to this.

But the next moment she knew that she had no right to be indignant with him. He was not responsible for her. She must manage her own life; she was in control; it was absurd to try and shift the responsibility for her unhappiness on to Martin.

That evening she went out and looked up some of her old acquaintances. She felt out of touch with them. It seemed a very long time since she had even remembered their existence. She invited one of them back to her narrow sitting-room: he was a violinist named Vroom, a slender, quick little Dutchman of about forty, with intelligent, sympathetic, brown-yellow eyes. She studied his face as they talked. It was a wrinkled, uneven face; the soft, intuitive, very bright eyes gave it a look of comprehension and warmth. Yes, it was the face of a man who had both vitality and understanding. Perhaps he would be able to help her out of the gulf of depression into which she had fallen. She began to talk to him about the determination to control her life which was becoming a sort of obsession with her. The violinist listened with not unkind eyes and finally said:

" Of course, your mental attitude is simply fatal to happiness : it damns you irrevocably from the start."

" Why ? " she wanted to know.

" You cerebrate far too much," he answered.

" You're hopelessly intellectualised. You've thought all your emotions out of existence, and left nothing but a bleak mental consciousness of yourself. There you sit like a buddha, examining your intestines and gazing at your navel and seeing nothing of the real world."

" What must I do, then ? " she asked in a humble voice.

" Stop all this introspection," he said. " Stop willing yourself all the time. Let your emotions come through your will. Your conscious behaviour is too artificial—too intellectual. You're far, far too egocentric. It's no use concentrating on yourself all the time ; you must try to think outwards, towards other people. The old Christian doctrine of living for others is founded on a sound psychological basis, after all."

When the Dutchman had gone home she pondered over what he had said. There seemed to be a good deal of truth in it. How could a woman with a quite ordinary brain direct her life successfully according to a prearranged plan ? That could only be done by someone of exceptional intelligence and determination. She should never have set herself up on this pinnacle of isolation ; she should have forced herself to make contact with other people. Whether one had or had not got principles to which one adhered was unimportant ; the only thing that mattered was to make a place for oneself in the world ; to be needed in somebody else's life. She had not made a place for herself. No one needed her ; except, perhaps, Matthew Kavan, the man whom she had slighted and despised.

She had been on the wrong tack all along. Her behaviour had been fundamentally wrong from the beginning, capable only of bringing trouble upon herself and anyone associated with her. Martin had been clever enough to divine that when he decided to steer clear of her.

If she had thought of him instead of only thinking about herself everything might have been different. She saw herself now as he must have seen her. All he had seen had been an obviously self-centred woman snatching at her own chance of happiness.

She got up and walked about the room. The violinist had helped her to see things clearly. She saw her own error and wished to rectify it. It was night; the electric light burned with a hard brightness; the curtains with their pattern of blue and brown birds were drawn over the windows. For some minutes she walked up and down with a preoccupied face. Then she went to a suitcase that was in the corner of the room. She opened it and looked through the contents. Soon she found what she wanted, a Swiss woollen tie of many colours, a scrap of paper on which an address was written, an oil painting on a rolled-up canvas. These three things were all that was left of her association with Martin. She held them in her hands and examined them gravely and carefully, one by one. She looked at them for a long time; the painting, the tie, and the paper; she looked at them tenderly, with yearning, with sadness. These things were the relics of her happiness, the testimony of her past effectiveness; they proved that once, at least, in her life she had made a successful contact with another human being. But she had no right to live in the past. No, that was too easy an evasion. She must move forward to meet the future, and leave the past in its proper place. By what right did she sit alone, shut away from the world, living upon the luxury of a romantic memory? What justification had she for indulging herself like this?

Presently she carried the three things to the fireplace. Then in the lighted room, kneeling in front of the empty grate, she set about destroying them. The scrap of paper flared up easily at the touch of a lighted match. The thick woollen tie was slowly consumed. But the canvas refused to burn. She tried to tear it, but it was strong, and she did not succeed. She fetched a knife and laboriously sawed away at the canvas; that was hard work, too, but she managed it finally, and the picture lay before her in ragged pieces. Then she set fire to the pieces. They burned reluctantly, with sudden spurts and smoulderings of oily flame, filling the room with an unpleasant smell.

She went on kneeling in front of the charred fragments in the fireplace until she could bear the uncomfortable position no longer. Her eyes were a curious colour, neither blue nor quite grey. In the morning she sent a cable to Matthew Kavan.

9

A Fair-haired Scoundrel is behind it all

SOME days after Martin's arrival Gwenda Lewison received an invitation from Tony Quested to drive out to a roadhouse called " The Spider's Web " with him. She had not seen the young man since the morning at Ethelbert Place when she discovered that he had callously concealed from her the knowledge of her father's illness.   She had been so shocked and repelled by his behaviour on that occasion that she had fled from the flat in genuine horror, determined never to see him again.   But the passing of time had modified her feelings, she had begun to make excuses for his conduct, and now decided to give him the chance of showing up in a better light.

It was a hot afternoon, still and sultry, with huge clouds piling on the horizon and the sky dusky blue overhead.   Driving his fast car down the Great North Road, Tony was boyishly cheerful.   She sat beside him, feeling affectionately indulgent.   It now appeared to her that the callousness which he had displayed on the former occasion could not have been typical of his character.   Looking at him now, it seemed preposterous to accuse him of viciousness.   He was so happily absorbed in his driving, like a boy with his first bicycle. Would it not be best for her to forgive him ?   Wasn't there a chance of making something out of their relationship after all ?

While they were in the car he gave no sign of the empty, cynical, brutal behaviour which had distressed her so much in the past.   But when they were lounging in bathing suits beside the swimming pool of the roadhouse, which was not crowded at that time of day, he began suddenly, assuming an expression partly impudent, partly mock-regretful :

" I'm afraid this will be our last meeting for a considerable time."

She felt a swift sinking of the heart.

" Why ? " she asked with some difficulty.

"I'm going away for a holiday; abroad perhaps; perhaps on a cruise," he said with a rather mysterious air.

He began telling a fantastic-sounding story of how he had succeeded in bringing off a masterly stroke of business on his own account, thereby clearing a considerable sum of money. He could now afford to smile at the miserable pittance which he had been receiving from his father. It all sounded obscure, underhand, and improbable.

He told the story with enjoyment, in his usual racy, mocking style, lying on his back on a mattress of inflated orange rubber. Gwenda listened unhappily; she too lay back, gazing up at the diving-board where a scarlet clad swimmer posed decoratively against the smoke-blue sky. A warm air played over their bare bronzed limbs and stirred the young man's light hair. Disturbed and apprehensive, Gwenda clasped and unclasped her hands, the smooth, oval, highly polished nails gleamed in the sunshine. He went on talking. There seemed to be a deliberate undercurrent of malice in what he was saying. For some reason which she did not understand the malice was directed against her. Owing to the deliberately mysterious wording of the story, she could not quite make out what he was talking about. But if what he implied were true, he had obviously been involved in some very shady transaction about which he wanted to boast. He left her in uncertainty as to what it was exactly that he had done.

Gwenda looked at him with a sensation of angry despair. The exasperatingly casual, brazen superiority of his manner. The maliciously triumphant way in which he spoke, as if he had won a personal victory over her. He was really nothing but a bounder, a cad. She wished she had kept to her decision to have nothing more to do with him. She would wash her hands of him now for good and all.

But she did not make any move to leave him. Instead she turned her eyes with their long lashes towards him, opened her mouth, to which the waterproof paint had imparted a hard brilliance, and said slowly, a little unsteadily :

" I suppose I'm no longer of the least importance to you."

" Importance ? " Tony Quested repeated. " I must admit that people are only important to me as long as I find them useful or amusing. There are always new people coming along who are willing to help me or entertain me. Why shouldn't I make use of them ? When one of them ceases to function, I move on to the next."

" And the others can go to the devil for all you care," said Gwenda, still in the same tense, unsteady voice.

Tony Quested smiled in a sophisticated and scornful way.

" My dear girl, you can hardly expect me to concern myself with the fate of everybody who happens to amuse me or do me a good turn at some time or another. I'm an individualist, not a philanthropic institution. If people choose to become involved with me that's their affair and they can take the consequences. They wouldn't do things to please me unless they were pleasing themselves at the same time by doing so. And if I get bored with them in the end that's their affair, too, and they must put up with that."

He stood up, stretched his arms over his head, and dived negligently into the still green pool. Gwenda watched his sleek fair head reappear in the centre of a series of spreading glass-green rings which widened over the lighter surface of the water. His arm swung up, golden brown in the sun, cleaving the water with easy, indolent strokes. She went into " The Spider's Web " and started to dress.

During the drive home she was silent and antagonistic, and parted from him briefly and almost without regret.

At Starling Hill, attention to her father banished all reflections on Tony's conduct. She felt tender and loyal towards William. But at night, in her bedroom, the picture of young Quested rose relentlessly before her. His lazy, graceful movements, the careless, insulting arrogance of his words. It was as if the quiet room were filled with images of the fair-haired youth with his lithe, attractive body, his mocking, vindictive smile. What had he been up to? Where was he going? Why had he boasted to her of his half-admitted wrong-doing? Would she ever be able to drive him out of her mind? She was so distracted that night that she destroyed the manuscript of her novel.

Gwenda Lewison was not the only person to be haunted by the wayward spectre of the young man. Old Anthony Quested had got to work on the Lewison-Byrne case. He had always defended William Lewison's interests conscientiously, but now he seemed possessed by an almost feverish loyalty towards his one-time schoolfellow. Davis, the head clerk, was kept going from morning till night over the Lewison case. His face wore a sour expression as he thought of the cause of all this hustle ; it was all the fault of that young Tony, that tow-headed slacker, that bad lot. If he had been here to pull his weight in the office and help his father as he should have done, all this extra work would not have fallen upon the head clerk. Nor would the lawyer have behaved like a slave driver towards his staff, finding fault with them continually and complaining about everything that was done. Davis crouched over his desk in resentment, his face bitter and his eyes censorious.

Tony Quested had deserted the office. He had vanished completely and his father had no idea what had become of him. Something else had disappeared from the office at the same time as the young fellow ; the precious document, the partnership agreement, the last copy to which William had access. The document had lain in the safe, neatly sealed, in its strong linen envelope. Then, one morning it had not been there any longer. It had just simply gone. The lawyer hunted and hunted, the office was turned upside down. It was a serious thing that had happened, a calamity. It would be next door to impossible to fight the Lewison case without the document. Quested dreaded the moment when he would be obliged to disclose to William the loss of the agreement. Just now it was out of the question that he should be told ; the shock in his present state would probably kill him.

Meanwhile, the lawyer worked feverishly over the preparation of the case. Without any real hope of success, he pulled every string he could think of which might conceivably lead to the recovery of the document. He had heard that Tony and Hubert Byrne had been seen talking amicably together, and his heart had contracted when he heard it. In the course of a few days Quested had aged considerably. His always pallid face now seemed almost transparent, the bones of his prominent forehead seemed to be working through the brittle skin which was drawn tightly across them. He waited, with a hope that was no hope, for his son to reappear. Every time the door opened he looked up, hoping to see the boy enter in his casual, lounging, irritating, charming way. Anthony Quested waited. But there was no sign of Tony, who seemed to have vanished into the blue. Possibly—almost certainly—his disappearance was connected with the disappearance of the document. The whole business was horribly suggestive of some sort of dirty work : the lawyer could not find out anything definite. He decided to hush up the loss of the partnership agreement for the time being. Supposing that by any chance the other side did not know of it, there was no sense in giving information away.

Anthony Quested neglected his health, worked a great deal, slept very little and ate hardly anything. He felt ill, and appallingly worried. With scrupulous conscientiousness he dragged himself out to Starling Hill almost daily to discuss the progress of affairs, though it tormented him to be in William's presence, knowing the unsuspected blow that was soon to fall on his old friend.

The ordeal became less tolerable as William slowly recovered. In three days, two days, he would be well enough to be told the bad news. The lawyer held himself tense, and waited. Perhaps even now, at the eleventh hour, something might happen to lead to the recovery of the document: Tony might reappear on the scene. By circuitous methods Quested had discovered that there was some connexion between Gwenda Lewison and his son. William Lewison's fate was thus doubly involved with Tony. Tony's engaging, disreputable ghost seemed to haunt every occurrence.

William had now been ill for four weeks; he was much better but his heart was still uncertain, he felt feeble and exhausted. He had dismissed the night nurse soon after the day nurse had gone, and had refused to see the specialist again on the grounds that his fee was exorbitantly high. The local doctor monotonously repeated the same instructions: patience, rest, no worry, no exertion, no excitement. In the doctor's opinion and phraseology, William would never be able to go more than a hundred yards from his own doorstep with safety. The old man fretted and raged at his helpless condition. Lying there on the shelf, he felt suspicious of everyone. Infuriating it was, to have to lie there with throbbing temples and an erratic pulse while incompetent people bungled his affairs and disregarded his orders with a falsely placatory smile. There was not a single person whom he could trust. Old Quested knew well enough what he wanted done, but Quested was too cautious to push ahead as William wished him to do. Cedric was scared stiff of the case, the poor-spirited rabbit. And Martin had his own reasons, and Gwenda hers, too, for not supporting him.

William realised that unless he took charge of things

personally he would never succeed in revenging himself
upon Hubert Byrne. He was utterly determined upon
breaking his enemy. His heart was weak and might
fail him; his will was like iron.

When at last he heard of the loss of the partnership
agreement he went into a sort of delirium, lying there
on his four-poster bed. For a whole hour he raved
in such a paroxysm that it seemed impossible that his
heart should survive the strain. Then he suddenly
became quiet, turned his face to the wall, and refused to
eat or to speak to anybody. He remained in this
alarming condition for two days.

At the end of that time Anthony Quested called, and
to the astonishment of the household, William demanded
that he should be shown into his bedroom. It was
one of the lawyer's bad days and he looked so ill and
frail that William was stimulated into an assumption of
robustness. Speaking in a businesslike, matter-of-fact
way as though nothing unusual had happened, he
asked the solicitor what chances he considered they
had of winning the case in view of the loss of the
document.

Quested was so amazed at the other man's everyday
manner that he did not immediately reply.

" I suppose the prospects are bad," William said.

The lawyer removed his pince-nez, closed his eyes
for a moment and lightly pressed the thumb and forefinger of his left hand against the eyeballs which ached
and felt hot through the thin lids. Yes, he said at last,
he had to admit that the prospect was anything but
encouraging; it would really be advisable to drop proceedings altogether.

At that William smiled, smiled imperturbably, though he had never been angrier in his life. He went on smiling for several seconds quite in his old inscrutable manner.

Quested, who was really suffering, remarked acidly that he was glad to see William taking such a philosophic attitude. The accident which had occurred at his office and through his negligence made it quite impossible for him to go on with the case in any event. He strongly advised William to drop proceedings against Byrne, thus adopting an attitude that was at once more practical and more Christian than his present revengeful one: and he begged him to place his legal affairs in other hands at his earliest convenience. William let him go on talking for some time. But when Quested brought out the word " Christian " once more, and spoke of the undesirability of vengeance for its own sake, William said quietly but distinctly:

" I shall smash Hubert Byrne yet, and you are going to help me do it."

With that he turned back to the wall again, and the solicitor had perforce to depart, rubbing his prominent forehead, and bound as closely as ever to the Lewison interests.

At about the same time that these things were happening in England, Matthew Kavan was embarking in a P. & O. liner at Bombay. Shortly before his departure he had received a cable from Anna indicating that she would welcome a reconciliation. This threw him into a turmoil of indecision. There existed in his mind an old-fashioned, clear-cut conception of right and wrong. According to this conception virtue was good

and merited reward, sin was evil and deserving only
of punishment. Anna had sinned, therefore she must
be punished. It seemed simple and definite until one
took into consideration Christ's doctrine of the forgive-
ness of sins. Matthew's righteous indignation against
Anna had cooled somewhat of late. Ought he to forgive her? Certainly her sins were as scarlet, but had
not Christ himself forgiven the Magdalen?

Matthew Kavan re-read the cable which he had
received from Anna his wife. He had folded and unfolded it so often that the creases of the paper were
worn quite transparent. Once he had been filled with
bitter anger against her; it had seemed impossible that
he should ever wish to set eyes on her again. Now,
after reading her cable, he found his heart melting
towards her. On thinking the matter over he saw no
reason why he should not forgive her if she were really
and truly penitent; not immediately, of course, but
when she had given proof of repentance. She had
sinned most grievously. But she was his wife, it was
his duty to save her and bring her back to the fold; he
would deal leniently with her. He would save her
soul alive.

Self-analysis was against his nature. Yet, now that
he was going back to Anna, it seemed necessary that
he should justify his behaviour. He felt obliged to
bring his conscience to terms with his inclination. He
justified himself to his conscience, explained to it that
on moral grounds he must do what he could towards
Anna's salvation.

When he stepped off the gangway on to the boat
Matthew Kavan had already made up his mind. He

would forgive Anna. He felt noble, virtuous and full of complacency. He had come to a meritorious and magnanimous decision. He was elated by a sense of moral rectitude and the prospect of a luxurious reconciliation scene. He came back through the Indian Ocean, the Red Sea, the Suez Canal, the Mediterranean, and finally the Atlantic, building vaporous castles in the air, and filled with sentimental fantasies of his meeting with Anna.

10

" *Mine for Better or Worse* "

THROWN on her own resources once more, Germaine occupied herself with her old profession. An acquaintance from the past who owned a select hat shop in South Molton Street, remembering her business capabilities, gave her a position as *vendeuse*. Germaine, not without courage and a certain stoical fatalism, discarded the name Lewison, resumed the name Deligny, and settled down to earning her living. In her character there was a marked strain of tough, stubborn tenaciousness, derived from her peasant ancestry. She would not admit defeat, she would not relinquish a single iota of her claim upon Gerald Gill; through sheer inflexible perseverance she would wear down his resistance and capture him in the end. She came of a stock grown patiently obstinate through centuries of struggling against storms, droughts, pests, accidents, and the vagaries of a grudgingly reluctant soil. She knew how to bide her time. Meanwhile she would go on with

267

her work : she noted with grim satisfaction that she was still capable of earning good money.

Nevertheless, she was really unhappy at this time. A profound discontent consumed her inwardly. She was half tormented, half upheld by an endless resentment against the two men by whom she felt herself wronged. In the case of Martin the resentment was fixed and sterile : he had escaped her, and she was too practical to waste her energies on a retributive scheme which could never come to fruition. But upon Gerald her resentment battened as a parasite draws nourishment from its host. One day she would have her own back on Gerald Gill.

In the hat shop her sturdy, elegantly gowned figure moved about with quiet, rapid efficiency ; but as soon as the smile of professional politeness with which she greeted a customer disappeared from her face, there appeared in its place the bad-tempered, bored, dissatisfied look which had become its usual expression.

From time to time during her leisured existence with Martin she had felt a desire to be at work again, to wake up each morning to a day full of activity and responsibility. But now that she was back in the midst of the familiar workaday environment, the models, the showroom, the customers, the accounts, she found it all hateful drudgery, and she bitterly regretted the past. She remembered her exasperation when Martin used to go off all day to his studio, leaving her alone in the house at Worcester Road. She tried to recall the tedium, the irritating boredom of her life at that time and to contrast it unfavourably with her present existence. She could not by any means succeed in making the present seem anything but odious by comparison. "I was a fool to lose Martin," she said to herself many times, with the discontented frown on her face. "I did a damned stupid thing when I lost Martin," she said aloud to her reflection in the mirror, as she manipulated the brim of an Agnès model.

During the autumn days she became increasingly bad-tempered at the shop, and carried out her work in a trance of cheerless efficiency from which she was abruptly aroused by receiving a letter from Martin Lewison.

Martin wrote briefly to inform her that Number 7 Worcester Road was to be sold and that if she wished to retain possession of any of the things in the house she had better come and point them out to him so that they could be kept back from the sale.

Next Saturday afternoon she was at King's Cross, waiting for the familiar suburban train. It was a dull November day with fog threatening. In the dismal light her high-coloured face looked blanched and etherealised as she stood on the platform. With deliberate intention she had dressed herself in her oldest and plainest clothes and discarded her customary pronounced make-up in favour of a light coating of natural-coloured powder. She wished to look quiet, virtuous and, if possible, slightly pathetic. The grey day helped her to achieve her object.

Men with bowler hats, umbrellas and damp overcoats surrounded her; the late contingent of office workers returning to their suburban homes. Their faces were like those of the men she had been accustomed to see in the Hornchurch streets, of a standardised neatness,

with unobservant, somewhat anxious eyes under a
wrinkled forehead. She looked at them with contempt.

The train appeared, emitting a heavy smoke which
slowly unfurled itself and hung in a dingy cloud under
the roof of the station. She got in, sat down in a
corner seat, and began to think about Martin. Martin
Lewison, although he was lost to her, was still an
important man in her life. He was, after all, the man
whom she had dominated most successfully, with whom
she had lived in respectable matrimony for a number of
years. She remembered his large, pleasant face with
its easy-going smile. She remembered his good nature,
his shrinking dislike of any emotional disturbance.
Perhaps, even now, she might be able to work upon
his good nature, to exploit it in some way to her own
advantage. Perhaps he was not utterly lost to her,
after all.

Yes, the Lord certainly seemed to be on her side in
sending her this unexpected opportunity of an interview with Martin. Sitting in the corner of the dark,
smoky carriage, she felt her spirits rising. This
expedition to Worcester Road was like a kind of lucky
dip for her. She did not know yet what advantage
she might be able to extract from it. But if there were
any prizes to be won she could trust herself not to come
away empty handed.

Germaine took the mirror out of her bag and considered the reflection of her round, lightly powdered
face. She was not looking her best. The absence of
rouge, lipstick and mascara did not suit her. She
found her appearance washed out and insipid. All the
same, she had achieved the desired effect, she looked

harmless and appealing, perhaps also a little unwell. There was nothing about her appearance which could conceivably frighten Martin away; he might even be touched by it.

The train stopped at Hornchurch and she got out, walking quickly out of the station and past the row of taxis waiting at the entrance. She wondered if any of the drivers recognised her. In the old days she had always taken a taxi to Worcester Road: this afternoon she must walk, although the incipient London fog had here degenerated into a chilly drizzle. She opened her umbrella and hurried along, her footsteps tapping out a firm, fast, regular rhythm in the cheerless streets. Here was Worcester Road with its border of gardens, dismally dreary now, with empty flower-beds and bare-branched, dripping trees. Number 7 wore its old air of shabby aloofness behind the black, sodden boughs of the mountain ash. Germaine glanced at it critically: no, she could still feel nothing but a contemptuous dislike for the neglected little suburban house, in spite of the security and ease which she had known there. As she pushed open the garden gate the protesting squeal of the hinges recalled to her mind the doleful vacancy of a hundred wet winter afternoons.

Martin Lewison greeted her politely and amiably, but his handshake was brief, he seemed determined not to hold her hand a second longer than was necessary. He gave her one comprehensive glance from his penetrating, greenish eyes, and then did not look at her again. Leading the way into the drawing-room at the back of the house, he invited her to take off her coat before going through the rooms with him.

271

Germaine studied him while she unfastened her coat and laid it over a chair. It was only a few months since she had last seen his brown, agreeable face with the full, soft lips and the three frown lines ; but to her it seemed a long time and she realised that their relations were profoundly altered. He helped her with her coat and talked away in his rather drawling voice. He was not living here, he explained, but had come over from Starling Hill on purpose to meet her. The house had been shut up all the summer, she must excuse the dust everywhere. He had heard that she was doing well in business again. That was splendid, he was delighted to know that she was satisfactorily provided for. The Lewison business affairs, on the other hand, were in an extremely bad way. Owing to Hubert Byrne's trickery they were obliged to call in every penny ; all the property in their possession was being sold up immediately. In a smiling, faintly ridiculous manner he gave the impression that the family was on the brink of bankruptcy and the workhouse.

"You were quite right to leave the sinking ship when you did," he finished up humorously.

Germaine listened to all this uneasily and with some astonishment. It was the first she had heard of the fall of the Lewison fortunes. How much of what Martin said was she to believe ? In the quiet little unlived-in house he looked largely prosperous as ever. It seemed impossible to imagine him as anything but one of those carefree individuals who accept a sufficiency of wealth as their natural birthright. Yet it was clear that some change had taken place in him since she last saw him. He chatted to her affably and rather absurdly as though nothing particular had happened. But he had been granted a decree nisi against her, a number of unknown experiences had modified his character, his attitude towards her had subtly and inflexibly hardened. And Germaine knew that, in spite of her past domination over this man, in spite of his easy-going and kindly nature, she would never be able to influence him again.

He accompanied her from room to room, they visited the dining-room, the kitchen, the bedrooms, the scullery. Germaine saw nothing that she wanted to take away. During the few months that the house had been un-occupied everything seemed to have grown shabby and out-of-date. The furniture, of course, was solid and good, but she had no use for furniture in her present existence. The whole house was pervaded by a melan-choly and forsaken atmosphere : dust lay everywhere, scraps of paper and dead leaves had collected inexplicably in the corners of the rooms. In the front bedroom the depressing effect was so strong that Germaine wondered how she had ever been able to sleep there. Martin chattered away ; he smoked all the time, lighting one cigarette from the stub of the last ; he made facetious remarks that rang a little bit false. Germaine began to feel irritated and hostile. She could not be certain, but she suspected that Martin was secretly making fun of her. He urged her to take possession of ridicul-ously unsuitable objects, the electric water-heater in the bathroom, a huge mahogany compactom wardrobe. Her replies grew frigid and terse. She decided per-functorily upon a few small articles which she would like to keep, some ornaments, cushions, a reading-lamp, some of the house linen.

Eventually they went back to the drawing-room. Martin apologised for being unable to offer her tea. There was nothing to eat or drink in the place. She perceived with angry disappointment that there was absolutely nothing to be got out of him. He was absolutely impervious to her. He would not even take her out for a cup of tea. There was nothing left for her to do but to go away. Yet she could not bear to depart without having gained a single point; it went sorely against the grain for her to acknowledge defeat so tamely. She gazed round the room, frowning and nonplussed : the disconsolate air of the house made her uncomfortable, a baffled feeling crept over her. Martin Lewison went on talking, drew her attention to a wine-coloured Chinese vase nearly four feet high, and pointed out how charming it would look in her tiny one-roomed flat. He puffed at his cigarette and blew out a cloud of smoke. His face was impenetrably good-humoured ; William himself could not have presented a more inscrutable appearance.

Germaine saw definitely that she would have to admit defeat. She put on her coat in silence. She felt furious at being thwarted like this, by Martin particularly, the man she had dominated and despised. At the same time as feeling angry she felt helpless and dejected ; the despondent, chilling atmosphere of the empty house weighed on her spirits. Martin had come to the end of his chatter at last. He was now simply waiting for her to go. In the tone of one making polite conversation he asked :

" And how is Gerald these days ? "

She stiffened in violent hostility. It now seemed

obvious that he was mocking her. He must know perfectly well that she and Gerald Gill were not together, that Gerald had shamefully deserted her. The question was an insult. She wished very much to say something in her turn that would wound and insult him. So she said as offensively as possible :

"Gerald is very sorry for you. We are both sorry to have upset your life. You must try not to feel it too badly."

"Don't worry about me," said Martin amiably. "I know I can have you back at any time should I wish to restore my life to its previous conditions."

Still smiling imperturbably, he opened the door for her and let her out of the house. Germaine walked through the foggy dark to the station with rage in her heart. She had been insulted and mocked. She had accomplished nothing by the visit beyond the acquisition of a few trumpery oddments which she did not really want. She was trembling as she hurried along the suburban streets. In the train, too, she found that her hands were shaking. She could not escape from the cold, depressing influence of Number 7 Worcester Road. She was no longer sorry that Martin was lost to her : and this was not solely on account of the deterioration of his finances in which, in any case, she did not altogether believe. She no longer wanted him. Some of the distasteful atmosphere of the empty house seemed to have attached itself to him.

Trains and buses were all delayed by the fog ; it took her a long time to get home. When finally she reached her little flat she was delighted to find a message from Gerald Gill saying that he would be at his studio

all the evening and would like her to come and see
him. All her depression vanished in an instant. A
moment before she had felt nervy, tired, dejected and
bad-tempered : now her spirits rose again ; she had a
hot bath, dressed herself in different clothes, made up
her face, and went out through the fog to the Church
Street studio.

Gerald Gill was waiting for her.

" Hullo," he said as he let her in, just as if there had
never been an evening at the Café Royal when she had
left him in bitter enmity. The tall, bony, peculiar-
looking man appeared sullen and ungracious as usual,
but Germaine could tell that he was really pleased to
see her.

He did, indeed, feel a sensation of relief when he
saw her come into his studio. For a long time now
he had been living a completely inconsequent life, a
disconnected existence of spasmodic work, of quarrelling,
drink, sex, talk and confusion. But gradually the dis-
order of this life, the lack of balance, began to affect
his nerves. To be completely detached, without any
restraining influence to stabilise one, that wasn't the way
a man could live permanently and be at peace. He
began to feel the need for a woman in his life, a woman
who would be more to him than merely one of a suc-
cession of casual mistresses. He needed the heavier,
more practical, more material feminine ballast to act as
a check on his morose, wayward and ill-balanced temperament. Living as he did, among theories and
abstractions, he had real need of a woman to act as
interpreter and mediator between him and the everyday
world. He was constitutionally incapable of dealing

adequately with ordinary people and with the ordinary affairs of life. Left to himself, he found that he was continually losing touch with reality. His feet were not set firmly enough on the ground.

He entered into a liaison with an attractive model. But her character was not stable; she frittered away her energies upon parties, dress, intrigues, gossip, gold-digging. She had no real sympathy with Gerald; he suspected her of mercenary designs upon him.

One day they quarrelled violently and she unloosed upon him a flood of vindictive abuse, directed mainly against his appearance and bodily habits.

"You're both dirty and boring," she called back to him as a parting shot, when his door closed upon her.

That afternoon he was overwhelmed by a sense of restlessness, nervousness and disintegration. He had the feeling that his personality was splitting up into many pieces. The common expression " shot to bits " assumed a poignant personal meaning for him. In a hurry he sent off the message to Germaine. Her image rose before him, reassuringly positive, seductive, robust. Even the peasant suggestion about her appealed to him in his present mood, with its implication of stolid common sense. And she was his woman: she had definitely committed herself with him; unlike these light-and-airy Bohemians who flitted with butterfly promiscuity from one love affair to the next. Say what you like, there was a bond between him and Germaine. Why had he not sent for her before?

They sat down to supper together. Gerald had bought some provisions, a rich grey sausage from Appenrodt's and a bottle of good red wine with plenty of body. Germaine was hungry; she had had no tea and only a hurried and unsatisfactorily economical lunch. She settled down at the table and ate with a hearty appetite, with gusto, without undue refinement of table manners, enjoying the rich food and drink. A home-like feeling came over Gerald, the tension of his nerves slowly relaxed, he began to feel warm and comforted. With all his senses he appreciated the nearness of this plump, high-coloured, inviting woman. He could not understand why he had ever wished to get rid of her. He forgot his theories, his obsessions, his unsatisfactory love affairs, his quarrel with the model, the obscure cravings that hounded him and would not let him rest: all these vanished into thin air, exorcised by the warm physical presence of this woman whose painted lips grew greasy as she ate her sausage.

Germaine was astute enough not to reveal either her present pleasure or her resentment for his past conduct. She smiled at him, said very little, and tried to behave as though she had nothing against him. Her resentment could wait; there would be time for that later on. The immediate thing was to play her cards skilfully and bind him securely to her this time. It was all the easier to disguise her resentment because she was really delighted to be with him again. By contrast with Martin Lewison, Gerald seemed straightforward and easy to deal with. Martin, in spite of his superficial amiability, had that obscure, mocking, vindictive humour which she feared and distrusted and with which she felt herself unable to cope, not to mention the disagreeable atmosphere of the Hornchurch house which she now associated with him. She looked at Gerald's gaunt, haggard, sombre face, his fanatical blue eyes, his large, bony hands with their down of reddish hair. He was a strange, intractable, uncouth and brutal man, to be sure ; but his conduct was direct and comprehensible to her, he would not employ devious, evasive, subterranean methods, one knew where one was with such a man.

It was right that she should be sitting with him again ; she felt that they were well suited to one another.

After supper she told him about her visit to Horn-church and what Martin had said to her at the last. When Gerald heard Martin's words he laughed. He put his arm round Germaine's shoulders and felt superior and content. So Martin, the poor bastard, thought he could get Germaine back whenever he wanted her. He gave her a hearty squeeze and let out a harsh-sounding guffaw. "She's my woman, mine for better or worse," he said to himself; and the thought was satisfactory to him.

II

Migration of the West Family

WINNY, the wife of the chauffeur George West, was the daughter of country people. When she was eight years old her mother died, when she was twelve her father married again, when she was fourteen she left school and came to London to work. She was enterprising, good natured, sociable and self-reliant. At first she returned occasionally to spend her short holidays in the Oxfordshire village where her father and stepmother lived ; but as time went on the visits became less and less frequent, and after her marriage to George they ceased altogether, though she kept up a friendly correspondence with the old people and always sent her father a present at Christmas time. She had grown so accustomed to town life that the country made her uncomfortable and it was hard to believe that she had once been a village girl. Her stepmother, a childless, cheerful, elderly woman who had spent her youth as cook to a vicar's family, wrote from time to time suggesting that she and George should go down on a visit. Winny's father, it appeared, frequently spoke of her and wanted to see her again. Winny always refused the invitation. She told her friends that the country gave her the creeps and that nothing would induce her to go back to village life.

George West returned from France more or less of an invalid. When Winny first saw his face she had a moment of panic. It seemed to her that she was looking, not at her husband about whose mysterious illness she had been so worried all this long time, but at a sort of caricature of him. The face was the face of George, but with a difference, a curious woodenness about it : the vitality, youth and spontaneity had gone out of the face, leaving behind a wooden, ageless, spiritless mask with blank, anonymous eyes. A shudder ran over the young wife, the child in her womb stirred uneasily. Just for a moment she felt as though she were looking into the eyes of a lost person, an idiot, eyes from which the soul had withdrawn. She was a brave girl ; all the same she felt a great desire to run away from those eyes. But she pulled herself together and went up to the man ; she forced herself to embrace him. She saw now that she was really looking at the face of George, her husband, of whom she was very fond. Illness had altered his expression a little, his eyebrows had grown bushy : that was all. The strange, frightening moment was past. She laughed at herself and could not imagine why she had been afraid. She was overwhelmed with tenderness for George.

She nursed him devotedly, cooked nourishing food for him, scrupulously followed the directions of the doctor whom Martin Lewison sent once a week to see how the chauffeur was getting on. Martin was proving conscientiously true to the promise he had made in the Clinique Miremont; he was determined not to let George down. In spite of the difficult time through which the Lewison family was passing, he insisted that George's wages should be paid as before. Besides paying the doctor's fees, he also arranged for a masseur to give the sick man special manipulative treatment three times a week.

Take it all round, this was not a bad time for Winny. Thanks to Martin's conscientiousness she was not short of money. The pleasant-faced, slightly down-at-heel young woman went about her tasks with cheerful devotion, resolved to bring her husband back to health. He submitted impassively to her ministrations. He allowed her to do as she liked with him. She had complete power over him. With a smiling face she protected him from all disturbances. Most of the time she was satisfied. He was getting better each day. Soon he would be quite well again; her loving care could not fail to restore him. Only occasionally she felt a qualm of disquietude when she looked at his

impassive face from which something or other still
seemed to be lacking. The rest and good food were
having their effect on him, his skin was a healthier
colour, the contours of his face were filling out, he
looked almost plump. Yet there was that sort of
woodenness about his face, a heaviness that had not
been there before. And his manner had altered. He
now spoke little, and in short sentences, curiously
slowly. What he said was all right, he expressed normal
opinions, his words were not eccentric or out of keeping
with his character. But he spoke slowly, heavily, without any expression, almost as if the words were being
ground out of him automatically by some sort of
mechanical process. When he smiled it was the same
thing.

Seeing him sitting in his arm-chair, motionless, gazing
out of the window, Winny would feel obliged to hurry
to him, to draw his attention, to speak to him. Slowly,
with a peculiar reluctance, he would respond, his lips
would move, the blank look would leave his face and
he would make some quite normal remark; but in that
mechanical way which made it sound more like a feat
of memory than an expression of present feeling.

But most of the time Winny was too busy to feel
disturbed. All the time that she was looking after
George the children also needed constant attention.
There was all the shopping, the mending, the housework
to be done besides the endless duties connected with the
invalid and the young children. And then there was
the new baby on the way. It was too much for any
young woman to cope with alone, too much even for the
courageous Winny. When her stepmother wrote again

inviting the whole family for a long visit she felt a secret relief. She consulted the doctor who quite approved of the plan; the country air would be an excellent tonic for George. She wrote back accepting the invitation. She would not admit it, but she was relieved at the prospect of being in a house with other people again. The presence of her father and stepmother would act as a sort of buffer between her and her husband: being alone with him was starting to tell on her nerves. The idea of village life no longer seemed unendurable.

Winny's father had got on in the world, saved money, and now owned a public-house in the centre of his native village. It was a rambling old brick house facing directly on to the street. In front was the weather-beaten painted signboard, a black bull's head, which hung on an iron bracket from the tall post, and creaked in the blustery December winds. At the back was a garden with wooden benches and tables under the three cherry trees where teas were served in the summer. The house itself was roomy and old-fashioned, with large attics and dark, uneven passages that smelt of food, beer, mice, tobacco and age. There was plenty of room for Winny and George and their young family. The stepmother was glad to have them as company in the old house, glad of the children's voices, and glad of the money which Winny paid for their board and lodging.

In a shapeless, colourless wrapper, Winny sat in the kitchen rocking-chair after her baby was born. The kitchen was large, well-lighted and cosy with the warmth of the big range where an iron saucepan of stock was eternally simmering. Winny felt contented and pleasantly drowsy as she sat there rocking her baby. She had not wanted the child, but now that it was in her arms she felt a tranquil tenderness for the small, weakly creature which set up a plaintive mewing cry like a kitten if the rocking ceased for a moment. The young, good-natured-looking, rather untidy woman rocked back and forward, mechanically, hushing the infant to sleep. She felt pleased with life; she liked the big bright kitchen for its cosiness while the wind grumbled outside, she liked the sociable feeling of living in an inn where people were always coming and going. She felt she had made a good move in coming to live at the Black Bull.

She had been afraid at first that George would dislike the country, for he was a townsman in his blood. And indeed he had begun by seeming a little lost. Quite soon, though, he had settled down to a monotonous routine of apparent contentment. His appearance in the bar room had roused a good deal of interest, as a Londoner he found himself in demand, and on the whole his reception into village life was a favourable one.

His health continued to improve; he could now walk short distances quite easily with only the help of a stick; his hand shook rather badly to be sure, but he no longer fumbled and dropped things as he had done at the beginning. But he had never thrown off his strange lethargy, and now spoke less than ever. All through the wet winter days he would sit in the kitchen or in a corner of the bar room, doing nothing but stare at the pages of the newspaper which he never turned, or fiddle aimlessly with the coins on the shove-ha'penny board. Then, when the sun shone, he would walk slowly and heavily up the village street, leaning on his stick, and taking no notice of anything about him. At meal-times he would silently take his place at the table and eat steadily through the large helpings of food that were put on his plate. Winny no longer looked for any change in him : she accepted his present condition as permanent, her sensible, resilient nature accommodated itself to altered circumstances, the central interest of her life now shifted from George to her children.

Winny did not deplore the change. On the contrary, she felt that she had enlarged the scope of her life. It gratified her to think how much wider her interests had become since they now included not only her own family, her indulgent old father, her stepmother, her husband and children, but also the whole life of the village which, with all its complicated internal policy, revolved round and percolated through the Black Bull. She had quite forgotten that she had once thought village life dull.

All this time Martin Lewison stuck to his promise and remembered the chauffeur George West. He continued to see that money was regularly paid to him. But this was not enough. He felt that he ought to find out for himself how the chauffeur was getting on. He did not want to see him : he even dreaded the thought of the meeting. But his conscience would not let him alone. He felt obliged to go and see with his own eyes that things were as well as might be with George. He heard that the young family had migrated to Oxfordshire. He decided to visit the Black Bull.

He drove the cheap mass-production car which had

taken the place of the Sunbeam down through the thin, transparent sunshine of a December day.

The village where George was living was on the lower slope of a hill. Low, bare, grim looking hills ran all round the horizon. There were not many trees. It was a wheat-growing district and great sweeps of purplish plough-land striated the hills. Old brown brick houses lined the village street. One of these was the inn.

When Martin opened the door a black cat pushed past his legs and went out, arching its back, into the sun. The elderly landlord came from the bar to answer his questions and gazed at him with curiosity. George was out for a walk; he would be back any minute now; it was nearly dinner-time and he never went far away. Would Martin come in and wait? No, he preferred to look for him in the village. The cat went indoors again, the innkeeper stared inquisitively at Martin's departing form.

Martin walked up the street. The sunshine was pleasant, it was almost warm on the sheltered side of the street. He was pleased at the chance of encountering George outside. The meeting would be easier, less formal, in the open air.

Towards the end of the village, as he was starting to wonder if he had missed his man, he saw the chauffeur coming towards him. George West was walking slowly along, leaning on a thick stick; he looked heavy, bulky, and dispirited: that was Martin's first impression. As he drew nearer, he saw that the young man was muffled up in a woollen scarf as well as an overcoat and a thick blue fisherman's jersey. His face had filled out, it was no longer lean and brown, but puffy and rather pale. The face looked at Martin blankly, without recognition. Then slowly, reluctantly, recognition appeared; the face smiled stiffly, as if with remembered politeness, as one smiles at a person whom one just remembers.

Martin was disconcerted. He did not feel himself a stranger to George. He wanted to be his friend, to talk to him and help him if possible. But George put him in his place as a stranger with that mechanical smile.

However, Martin did his best with the man. He shook his hand and talked in his most friendly fashion, hoping for a response. But George did not respond, and Martin began to see that he was not able to do so. Heavy and muffled-up, he walked along leaning on his stick, in his thick, ill-fitting overcoat, and the scarf knotted about his neck; a strange, mechanical being beyond the reach of communication. Was this the young man whose eyes had shone with naïve and rather engaging candour under the peak of his chauffeur's cap? No, George West was lost, and his place had been taken by an automaton.

The automaton walked beside Martin and talked to him in slow, stilted, reasonable phrases. For decency's sake Martin went with the automaton to the inn and ate a meal there. But he felt unhappy and awkward and eager to be gone. He had not come to visit an automaton. As soon as the meal was over he got into his car and drove quickly away from the village.

On the evening of the same day Winny sat in her rocking-chair in the warm, comfortable kitchen. She felt that she had a right there, that she belonged there.

She did not think about Martin's visit. Instead, she listened to the subdued, companionable buzz of voices, the clink of glasses, that came with whiffs of beer and tobacco smoke from the bar room. Occasionally, above these friendly sounds, she could hear the creaking of the signboard outside. The kitchen was full of the savoury smell diffused by the stockpot on the range. She rocked herself backwards and forwards, hushing the baby to sleep, her eyes drowsy with the entranced physical contentment of maternity. She was at home; she felt warm and secure; it was good to be indoors, within sound of cheerful voices, on this wintry evening. Christmas would soon be here. They would have a tree for the children. She would give them a splendid Christmas, the best Christmas they had ever had. A slow, placid smile brightened her face as she rocked.

12

"*Nearer my God to Thee*"

THE Lewison store at Hendon, the largest store of the whole chain, was four stories high. The third storey was given over mainly to store-rooms and offices: on the fourth floor, at the very top of the building, were the staff-rooms, the dining-rooms, cloakrooms and so on used by the employees. In two of these fourth-floor rooms William Lewison took up his abode after the sale of the house at Starling Hill.

Accompanied by Cedric and an astonished secretary, the old man came up in the lift one raw winter's morning, wearing a thick overcoat with an astrakhan collar above which his face looked fragile and grey. Tapping his ebony walking-stick on the carpetless floors he made a tour of inspection, poking his fine, arched, delicate nose through the many doorways, traversing the dusty passages with a light, frail, determined step. When he came to a certain room in the front of the building he stopped. It was small and square and was being used as an additional office by some of the junior clerks, the floor was covered with piles of catalogues which had just arrived from the printers. The window was closed and there was a breath-taking odour of damp printers' ink.

"Have everything cleared out of this room," William ordered.

While this was being done he sat in a corner of the staff dining-room, wrapped in his heavy black coat, fingering his whitish moustache, and staring ahead with a strangely whimsical look in his unfathomable dark eyes. The first batch of assistants started to come in for lunch. The rumour that William Lewison was upstairs had quickly spread through the building. The workers came in quietly, subdued but excited, whispering together and glancing with covert curiosity at the old man in the elegant fur-collared coat. William roused himself to make a few good-humoured remarks. The girls liked him. They smiled at him, somewhat shyly at first, but soon emboldened by his politeness and his joking sentences. The men, on the other hand, seemed less friendly; their attitude towards their employer's overtures was almost one of suspicion.

Presently William was told that the little auxiliary office had been cleared according to his directions. Once

289

more his ebony-handled stick tapped its resolute way down the dark passage. The small square room was now perfectly bare. The charwomen had opened the window and scrubbed the shabby linoleum on the floor, so that instead of the odour of printers' ink there was now a strong smell of coarse household soap in the room. It was very cold with the window wide open. William Lewison did not appear to notice that. He stood in the middle of the room, on the dingy green linoleum which was still damp in patches from the scrubbing it had received. He looked slowly and carefully round the four walls: he then examined a hole which had been worn in the linoleum, and prodded it with his stick. Finally he announced his intention of using the room as a sitting-room; he would take over the room next door as a bedroom. In these two rooms he intended to live in future. As soon as possible he would move in with a few pieces of furniture salvaged from Starling Hill.

Cedric Lewison stared at his father in shocked, helpless amazement and with a sense of despair. For he knew he could do nothing. The ill, fragile old man was as obstinate as a mule; he would drop down dead rather than give way. Cedric begged him to alter his mind; almost tearfully he implored him to reconsider his decision. But of course it was no use. The father was quite immovable. He had made up his mind to live in two rooms over the business, and there he would live, and nowhere else in the world. Cedric was struck dumb when he heard this. He went to the doctor and besought him to bring the weight of his professional disapproval to bear against William's determination. He might have spared himself the trouble. The doctor told William that it was little short of suicide for a man of his age and with a heart in the state of his heart—a man, moreover, long accustomed to luxurious living—to change suddenly to conditions of such discomfort. In any case, it was madness for him to think of living on the fourth floor, even though there was a lift in the building.

William heard him out courteously and then remarked that at all events he would be nearer heaven in his new lodging and would not have so far to go when St. Peter summoned him, which was a consideration of some importance in view of the fact that they all seemed to consider the summons imminent.

Baffled by his patient's incorrigible flippancy, the doctor shrugged his shoulders, disclaimed all responsibility, and withdrew in a state of mingled annoyance and admiration.

Everything was arranged very quickly. A purchaser was found who was glad to buy the Starling Hill house as it stood, with most of the furniture in it. The rarer, more valuable period pieces, as well as the books and the carefully chosen pictures, were sold separately and fetched a good price. Bringing with him nothing but some unpretentious furniture from one of the smaller rooms, the Meninsky painting of Gwenda, a few books, and as many of the Alpine plants as could be transplanted with safety, William Lewison moved into the two rooms on the fourth floor of the Hendon store.

It was evening by the time the place was in order. He sat down at the small Sheraton table at which he was to eat his meals henceforward, and an untidy Lancashire maid-servant brought him his supper on a tray. If he was to live in poverty his artistic sense demanded that he should do the thing thoroughly. He was now a poor man and must stage a suitable environment. He derived a half-melancholy, half-humorous satisfaction from this stage management, and so he refused to bring a servant to wait on him or to have a special meal cooked for himself; he would eat the ordinary meals that were provided for the staff, and the staff servants should attend to him. No cloth was spread on the Sheraton table. Straight from the tray he ate the slices of cold meat, the bread, the pickled walnuts that had been brought in on cheap white china plates. He drank some water from a thick Woolworth tumbler. The Lancashire maid-servant came back for the tray and put a cup of coffee down on the table. William observed that she had the kind of hole in the heel of her stocking which in his childhood he used to call a " potato." He tasted the coffee and pushed it away with a wry grimace ; it was made from coffee extract to which boiling water had been added, and bore no resemblance to the coffee to which he was accustomed.

He got up and went across to the window. Far below him a heavy lorry thundered along the street. Opposite and also somewhat below him was an extensive vista of roofs, cowls, chimney-pots and attic windows. The overcast winter sky looked heavy as a black blanket hanging above. William Lewison smiled to himself sardonically as he thought of what he had said to the doctor about not having so far to go when he was called up to heaven. Just for a moment his tired, grey face wore an almost boyish expression, mischievous and sly, as he gently hummed in his throat the hymn tune, "Nearer my God to Thee." The changed circumstances of his life did not really afflict him. It was true that instead of a big, luxurious house he had now nothing but two poor rooms on the top floor of a business building, instead of his butler Flood a slatternly Lancashire girl with a hole in her stocking, instead of rich, high-quality mocha a cup of undrinkable coffee extract. But these things were as nothing compared with the satisfaction to be gained from the prospect of smashing Hubert Byrne : privations endured to that end were not only tolerable but inspiring. He felt strengthened and uplifted as by a sacred mission.

It was cold standing there by the window, and he turned back into the room. His face grew gloomy as his eyes fell on the big Meninsky portrait which had been hung over the fireplace and looked overpoweringly large in the small space. He missed his daughter badly. He saw now that it was hardly fair to Gwenda to expect her to live here with him, but surely she need not have treated him so cruelly when he had suggested it. He remembered how he had explained to her the need for the utmost economy in order to carry on the case against Byrne which would avenge the family honour. It had never occurred to him that she would not be altogether of one mind with him over this matter. But it appeared that she was not interested in vengeance. All she saw was that he would be ruining himself if he continued the case, whereas, if he dropped it and cut his losses he would still be a comparatively wealthy man. Cold and antagonistic, with her artificially bright face hard under her sleek hair, she accused him of putting his desire for personal revenge before the welfare of his children. The accusation was not unreasonable.

She was not prepared, she said, to spoil her whole life for the gratification of his revengeful spite against Byrne. There was no sense in such behaviour. She was young and attractive ; she meant to have her fling. Nothing would induce her to bury herself in a slum at Hendon. She had plenty of friends who appreciated her although her own father did not : she would go to them. She would soon be off his hands altogether. William was not quite sure what she meant by that. The one thing that was perfectly clear was that she was angry and unhappy and that she was leaving him in the lurch.

When she had started speaking he had been standing beside the library fire. As her harsh, unsympathetic sentences fell upon him he collapsed into an arm-chair where he sat motionless, his bald head with its fringe of curls tilted slightly backwards, his sombre black eyes fixed unhappily on the smooth face of his daughter. Gradually, as she went on talking, the loving trust which he had always felt in her was shaken. Unwillingly his brain recalled certain insinuations, rumours which had reached him as to her association with Tony Quested, the scoundrel who was in all probability connected with the disappearance of the partnership agreement. He had always resolutely refused to credit these rumours. Now he suddenly had to admit that there might be something in them, that Gwenda might possibly have come under the evil influence of that young twister, that rogue. The father's heart struggled and leaped like a live thing in his breast. Perhaps he had not been such a good father as he had thought himself to be, but he had always loved his daughter, he had kept her with him ever since she was born, and he could not understand how she could behave so cruelly and disloyally to him.

When she had finished speaking he talked to her again. He spoke quietly and gently, trying to explain to her that it was his duty to the family to punish Byrne and that it was her duty to aid and abet and encourage him to do it. Gwenda's bright eyes watched him steadily as he talked. She said nothing at all until he became silent at last. Then she repeated exactly what she had said before. William Lewison perceived that in revenging himself upon his enemy he was to lose his daughter. It was a bitter and heart-breaking alternative, but his resolution never wavered, though for the rest of the day he had felt shattered and very old.

And now he was alone in his two miserable rooms at the top of the building. It seemed very strange to be there in the winter night, lonely and inhospitable. He wished that he had accepted Cedric's offer to keep him company this first evening. As long as he could console himself with his little deceptions, staging the tableau of poverty, making clever, humorous remarks to shock Cedric and the doctor, things remained bearable. But when one was lonely and old and ill and the night came on, it was difficult to keep up one's spirits and to play an Adolphe Menjou rôle with no audience but oneself. He sat down and tried to read. But the sight of the coffee-cup which the maid had forgotten to remove was offensive to him. He got up and put it outside the door. The passage was full of flowerpots. His Alpine plants had been deposited there until such time as he could have a special staging constructed for them near his sitting-room window. He could not refrain from bending down to examine them in the dim light. One or two of them he touched with the tips of his fingers. As far as he could see they had stood the journey quite well. It occurred to him that they were not safe in the passage where some careless person might brush against them and damage them. Moving slowly and cautiously so as not to throw too great a strain on his heart, he carried them one by one to the Sheraton table where they would be out of harm's way.

13

A Debt is Paid

MARTIN LEWISON was working. Great changes had taken place in his life: Germaine was gone; Gerald was gone; the Starling Hill house had gone and so had Number 7 Worcester Road: but the dilapidated little shack of a studio near the Hornchurch railway embankment still remained. On the same day that William Lewison moved with his Sheraton table, his picture, and his Alpine plants into the two rooms over the Hendon store, Martin drove himself to the studio. In the back of the cheap mass-production car he had put a collapsible camp-bed, an oil-stove, a lamp, a kettle, and a suitcase containing night things and a change of underwear. Equipped with these articles, he prepared to take up residence in the studio. But first of all the place must be put to rights. Martin fetched a broom and swept the floor thoroughly, sweeping all the empty paint tubes, the cigarette ends and scraps of paper into a heap in one corner. Then he took the rubbish outside and set fire to it. When the fire had burnt itself out he went back into the studio, stacked all his canvases neatly against the walls, made up the camp-bed with some cushions and a couple of rugs, put the lighted lamp on the table, and set the kettle to boil on the oilstove. Having completed these preparations he felt himself well and truly installed.

While the kettle was boiling he sat down on the edge of the bed. Many images passed through his mind, but strangely enough they were not the images of his father, of Germaine, of Gerald Gill, or even of the chauffeur George West: they were images of the girl Anna Kavan. He had not seen Anna since he had parted from her at the dusty Italian station near the lake. Once she had written to him and he had carried her letter about in his pocket for many days, trying to decide whether he should answer it. He had not answered it. But he had thought about her a great deal.

Now, in the small, primitive, over-crowded studio which had never been meant as a place to live in, he was still thinking about her. The kettle suddenly boiled over, and he got up and made himself some tea. He ate the bread and cheese he had brought with him, eating in a preoccupied way, pushing large pieces of food into his mouth, letting the tea stand until it was nearly cold and then drinking it down in hasty gulps. The yellow lamplight cast his grotesque shadow upon the wall as he sat leaning forward with hunched shoulders, his hair pushed out at the back where his coat collar had disarranged it.

From time to time a train rumbled along the embankment above and shook the ramshackle building, but Martin did not hear it. The lamp wick burned unevenly and started to smoke, but he did not notice. There he sat, quite alone in the night, and thought about Anna Kavan. He thought for a long while about the time they had spent together beside the lake, and about their love for one another. He had really loved Anna; but it had not been possible for him to stay with her. He had been afraid of her egocentric temperament which threatened his own liberty as an egoist and an individualist. It was absolutely essential for his development as a creative artist that he should retain complete independence. And so he had had to leave her.

" The past is dead." He had read the phrase somewhere quite recently and now it appeared before him in fluid, illuminated letters like a Neon sign. He sat there and thought of the past; he remembered it and it lived again in its freshness. " The past is dead." Those words were wickedly untrue. It was wicked that a rare and beautiful thing should be allowed to die simply because it belonged to the past. It was a wrong to Anna which he must prevent. He owed Anna a debt. She had brought him a splendid and precious gift : she had given him love and happiness and added a new strength to his character. For all this he was indebted to her. He racked his brains to find a way of discharging the debt. Like a man sunk in contemplation of some abstruse problem he sat there beside the smoking lamp while the trains clattered and rumbled above, trying to think how he could pay his debt to Anna and make their past happiness live again.

The lamp went on smoking, the trains passed, the building shook and vibrated. He would paint her portrait, Martin decided; it would be a damned fine picture, the best work he had ever done. Smoke, noise, vibration. He could do it, he felt inspired to do it. This particular episode of the past should never die. He would immortalise it, he would paint such a picture that everyone who looked at it must recognise it as the symbol of a lovely thing which had never died. Anna would see it and understand, and know that he had paid his debt to her.

He started work the next day. To guide him he had some rough sketches which he had made of Anna at Bandol and in Italy. He chose a large oblong canvas. As he first touched it with the charcoal he felt tense in every nerve. He had no preconceived idea of how he was going to tackle the portrait. He had not made a single preliminary note.

Yet he worked on without hesitation, with force, with certainty, with a sure directness he had never known before. The stick of charcoal wore away and the form of Anna Kavan appeared on the canvas. He had drawn the girl standing up in a characteristic pose, graceful and negligent, the fine lines of her slender body accentuated by some formalised drapery. Her eyes looked out with a dreamy and yet penetrating expression; her hands, small and not specially well shaped, were folded in a touchingly childlike position; the legs, the sloping shoulders, the narrow waist, looked delicate, almost ethereal, and yet seemed strong. The whole figure had a suggestion of Ariel about it, poetical without any touch of sentimentality. Martin looked at his first day's work long and critically and saw that he had done well.

For ten days, all the time there was daylight, he worked at the picture. In the evening, as soon as it got dark, he usually went up to town, to Kleinfeld's or to the Café Royal. His friends were curious, teased him about his hermit's existence at Hornchurch, and wanted to know what he was doing. He told them that he was working; no more. They asked him why he preferred to live in the suburbs, thus giving himself the trouble of a tiresome journey each evening when he came up to see them. Martin looked round the crowded room, at the highly-decorated women with their hard, assured expressions that yet were at the same time strained and forlorn, at the young men who seemed not quite to have decided to which sex they belonged. His large, brown face lightened with its secretive smile.

"I'm a gregarious animal," he said, "so I come here to meet other members of my species. But that doesn't mean that I want to live altogether in the Bloomsbury mental bear garden."

Still smiling, he threw down the stub of his cigarette and trod on it to put it out. As he lighted another, he remarked by way of amplifying his previous statement :

"I've no objection to cigarette ends trodden into the carpet, but I don't like cigarette ends trodden into the brain."

Then he went back to the studio, lay down on

his uncomfortable camp-bed, and started work on the portrait as soon as daylight appeared.

On the eleventh day the picture was finished. With a feeling almost of terror Martin realised that there was no more to be done to it. He laid down his palette and brushes. Perhaps it was the heat of the oil-stove in the unventilated room that made sweat break out on his forehead and on the palms of his hands. He felt exhausted, he did not dare to look at the canvas. He sat down on the bed and lighted a cigarette with trembling fingers. At last, timidly, dreading what he might see, he looked up at the picture. It was the likeness of a young woman which confronted him, a young woman of no outstanding beauty. But this likeness of a woman had such a vividly arresting quality that his eyes could not leave it. Frowning deeply, Martin Lewison gazed at the picture which he had painted. He stared out of clear, critical, unbiassed eyes, the cigarette between his lips. He gazed at the woman upon the canvas, and from the canvas the woman gazed back at him with her blue-grey eyes, innocent, serious, remote, glamorous, strangely moving, as if watching him from a dream.

" I believe I've really succeeded this time," said Martin, under his breath.

He stood up and wiped his hands on a paint-rag. The lines on his forehead slowly smoothed themselves out. He turned the easel a little so that the light fell full on the canvas. His arms and wrists ached after many hours of holding the brushes and the heavy palette, and he stretched them over his head so violently that the seams of his jacket started to split at the back. He did not notice. All this time his eyes never left the picture. There it was completed, the materialisation of a past beauty which could never now be lost. He was suddenly filled with a strong emotion. He exulted in his achievement, he felt a great satisfaction because he had kept alive a good and lovely thing which otherwise would have perished. He felt that his debt was paid.

F
KAVAN

Kavan, Anna.

A stranger still.

74870

$30.00   7/96   51264
06/19/1996

DATE			